IT WAS ALL A DREAM 2

ANOTHER ANTHOLOGY OF BAD HORROR TROPES DONE RIGHT

EDITED BY
BRANDON APPLEGATE

HUNGRY
SHADOW
PRESS

Cover art copyright © 2023 by Trevor Henderson (slimyswampghost)

Interior illustrations © 2024 by Christopher Castillo Díaz (artem_astaroth)

Edited by Brandon Applegate, bapplegate.com

Content warnings at the end of the book. Check the table of contents for page number.

Paperback ISBN: 979-8-9869202-7-6
Hardcover ISBN: 979-8-9869202-6-9

CONTENTS

EDITOR'S NOTE

This book contains content warnings for each story (for which they were determined to be necessary) nestled safely in the back of the book. If you don't want to be warned of potentially upsetting content, they shouldn't bother you at all, easily avoidable as they are. But if you'd like to use them, please do. You can find the page number in the table of contents.

FOREWORD
THOUGHTS ON HORROR TROPES
MATTHEW M. BARTLETT

Webster's Dictionary defines tropes like so:

Okay, that was a joke. Not a particularly funny joke. Maybe not a joke at all. Maybe a nod to a trope typical of the student essay.

Recently in a social media writer's group, someone asked in earnest the difference between a horror trope and plagiarism. That's how the use of common horror tropes can be perceived—lashed so tightly to cliché that to use them is to risk being accused of actual plagiarism.

If you want to see how much juice can be wrung out of a horror trope, just look at zombies. Or "walkers." Or "infected." It is the trope that will not die—I apologize for the cliché, but it is unavoidable here—as every writer and filmmaker and television producer has tried to work in every conceivable angle, every possible permutation. The phenomenon had a comeback that lasted, dizzyingly, for over a decade, and yet remains. Zombies as a metaphor for the social turmoil of the sixties. A metaphor for rampant consumerism. For the stultifying boredom of modern life. For epidemics that explode into pandemics. The living dead, the blind dead, the evil dead, simply...

the dead. The night of. The dawn of. The day of. The city of. Return of. Return of Part 2. Shaun of. Land of. The erotic nights of. Bong of. The further we get away from the Night of the Living Dead template, the more we get into innovation, subversion, and the more fun we have.

It's not that the first zombie flicks were bad, it's that the more the concept is revisited, the more we want to see something new to differentiate it. Sure, we enjoy the comfort of the familiar, but how we appreciate the thrill of a new, original, askew take.

Any writer who strives for originality when faced with a trope has a few choices, the most obvious, and perhaps tempting, being to run in the opposite direction. But sometimes you can't do that, say, when you want to (or are invited to) submit a story to a themed anthology. So the remaining choices are as follows. Play it straight. Play it highbrow (or "elevate" it, to use a controversial buzzword).

Or subvert it—turn it on its severed head.

When you play it straight, you risk producing hackwork. When you play it highbrow, you risk condescending to your audience.

Subverting it feels like the most fun. What can I do, the writer thinks, that will make my story stand out? What is an original take? What can I think of that no one else can? Is it a werewolf story? Write about a wolf who turns into a man when the moon is just a sliver. A vampire story? Maybe something about a dentist who is leaned on to open his office after dark to try to save the decaying fang of a bloodsucker with a sweet tooth (Nosferatooth?). A zombie story? Let's say the CDC comes up with an elixir that cures the recently "turned"...but the newly ex-zombie suffers terrible cannibalistic nightmares, and begins to relapse.

The title of this anthology (a typical foreword might say the anthology you now hold in your hands) is ingenious: "it was all a dream" is one of the first cliches the would-be writer of the fantastic or horrific is implored to avoid at all costs—that and starting a story by describing the weather. A volume of stories that start with weather wouldn't necessarily be as fun, though.

The concept is so fertile that it warrants a second volume—and it's a rich and bounteous volume at that. Herein you'll encounter the story of a grimoire, told from the point of view of its very words, a bird-borne apocalypse, a cursed object that is not at all what it seems, an innovative riff on the effects of being a would-be victim of a Myers/Voorhees type of immortal killer, and all manner of strikingly original, fantastically refreshing takes on well-worn horror ideas. You'll read stories from established writers of the weird such as Nadia Bulkin and Joe Koch and talented newcomers like Najua Ismail and Michael Pearson.

You have not read this foreword, it turns out. This book doesn't have a foreword. You only dreamed it. Now, turn the page, and dream on.

WE ARE WORDS
D. MATTHEW URBAN

W e are words on a page, nothing more. If this man thinks otherwise, he's badly mistaken.

His face is thin and sallow, eyes dark-ringed from long wanderings in occult labyrinths. His lips twitch with the weight of many frustrations. Dead hopes putrefy in the creases of his brow.

From the moment he casts his eyes on us, skimming along our tangled rows of letters, I sense his desperation, his hunger. He yearns for us to be more than words. Most of all, he wants weapons. He feels hurt, and he longs to hurt back. But we aren't weapons. We are words.

"Is it really bound in human skin?" he says.

"So the story goes," the bookseller says from the shadows behind the counter. The bookseller is a kindly man, very old and wise, but with a streak of mischief. He chuckles and says, "One tradition holds that it's bound anew with each reading. Take care, sir, lest you read yourself out of your hide."

The man scoffs. "Bullshit." I tremble on the page, quivering with warnings I'd pour into his ear if I could, but we can't speak that way. We aren't voices. We are words.

From the shadows come the murmurs of a negotiation. Bills whisper on the counter when the deal is done. "And your address for our records, please," the bookkeeper says. A pen scribbles on paper.

Again the man leers down at us, licking his lips. A grin shows his mouth's toothy graveyard. "Finally!"

He shuts the book. The world goes black.

As worms thrive in soil, words thrive in darkness. Quiet and still while the book sat open in the shop, we squirm and chatter between the covers like giddy children. If the man held the closed book up to his ear, he'd hear a sound like rustling pages—the faint, dry whispers that are the words of words.

"Where do you suppose he's taking us?" says Eerie, shivering. Poor little Eerie, always so fearful.

"Someplace decent, I hope. Not like that pigsty the last one lived in," says Squamous. A shudder of disgust ripples down her q.

Pompous old Eldritch heaves a ponderous sigh. "Wherever it is, we won't be there long. We know how these excursions always end, don't we?"

I don't say anything. I only listen and wait, one word among the throng.

Light floods the page. We scurry back to our places, faster than the man can see. If he detects a jittering of our characters, he'll put it down to his own racing thoughts, anticipation making him see things. *A trick of the eye,* he'll think.

No. A trick of words.

His room is cramped and dingy. Narrow bed in one corner, crowded desk in another, stacks of books all around. Above the bed, he's tacked a row of pictures to the wall, black-and-white photographs of women's faces. The pictures' eyes have been gouged out; rusty X's of dried blood mark the mouths.

Ex-lovers? His boss, his mother? Nothing would surprise me.

Strewn on the desk lie talismans, amulets, a doll pricked with pins. It seems he's tried everything.

The book lies on a flat surface. A black candle burns to one side of us; incense smokes on the other. An altar—how original.

The man stands before us, draped in a dark cloak. He raises his arms. If I had i's, I'd roll them.

Leaning over us, he reads aloud. His stale breath wafts over the page. "'From miscreated voids of aberrant nonentity'"—shy Aberrant blushes to hear himself spoken; the man takes it for a gleam of candlelight—"'there surged and writhed the primal, nameless abominations...'"

It tickles when he speaks me, his moist tongue sliding along my syllables.

Halfway through the first page, the man's eyes unfocus. "'In dolorous...'" He blinks, shakes his head, tries again. "'In dolorous, eidolon-haunted realms, the ancient archon lucubrates...' Oh, fuck this!" Snarling, he flips the pages with greasy fingers. "Where's the goddamn curses?"

His impatience, the peevish tone of his voice, this room's miasma of resentment and false bravado, it all paints a familiar picture. He feels he's been cheated of his due. A sense of usurpation has curdled in his heart. He's searching for a way to reclaim what he considers his, to punish those he believes have slighted him. Nothing has worked so far—the talismans, the amulets, all useless junk. He's seized on the book as one last chance to strike back, one last possibility of escape.

My sigh blends with the shuffling pages. I wish I could tell him the book holds no escape. Only words.

From across the room, something rattles in the scented air. A cell phone, vibrating on the desk. The man turns away from us with a disgusted sigh.

He snatches up the phone. "Yeah?...Hey, Carl...Tonight? Sure, I'll be there...Yeah, I just brought it back from the shop. You wouldn't believe the price that old fucker was asking, but I haggled him down...Well, I'm just getting started with it, still figuring it out. Looks gnarly as hell, though...For sure. Can't wait for you and the guys to feast your eyes on it. See you soon, bro."

He blows out the candle, extinguishes the incense, closes the book.

"I THINK he's the worst one yet," says Vermicular with a dismal sigh.

"At least his bed was made," says Squamous.

"Did you hear how he pronounced me?" says Lucubrate. "'Luh-CUH-brate!' I never felt so humiliated."

Letters wriggling around me, I sit in a corner of the dark parchment and ponder the ironies of fate. When the author scribbled us down, all those years ago, she was possessed by a sense of joyous delirium. Her eyes twinkled madly as she rummaged every nook and cranny of language, delving for the rarest gems, cackling with delight when she came up with some especially outlandish term. In those days, I was practically an afterthought, a two-syllable nobody, overshadowed by stately beauties like Smaragdine and Sesquipedalian.

Now the author is long dead, and the lines that flowed with such glee from her blood-dipped quill are perused with wrinkled brows and pursed lips, serious-faced readers stumbling among unfamiliar words like sleepwalkers in strange houses. Smaragdine and

Sesquipedalian sigh in their garrets, faded and out-of-date. When the reader catches sight of me, they breathe a sigh of relief. I'm so simple, so unthreatening. Who could be afraid of a little word like...

"Psst," Eerie whispers, startling me out of my reverie. His e's are quivering anxiously, a tear glimmering in his i. "How long before we can go home?"

"Don't worry, little one," I say. "From the looks of this fellow, I'd say we'll be back in the shop in no time."

WE GAZE UP from the middle of a table. A dim lightbulb dangles overhead. The air is damp and chilly, sour with dust and sweat. Five men sit around the table, all wearing dark cloaks. Among them, our new owner grins smugly and thumps the page with his fist.

"How do you like them apples?" he says.

One of the others strokes a stubbly chin. "Very nice, Fred, very nice. And is it really bound in human skin?"

"That's what the old guy at the store told me," Fred says.

A third man says, "Yeah, right. He just said that to jack up the price, and you bought it hook, line and sinker."

Fred scowls. "Well, you're the expert, Sammy. Why don't you give it a lick, see if it passes the taste test?"

A low laugh gurgles around the table like water sloshing into a drain. Fred smirks. Sammy leans back, teeth gritted.

I sigh, chagrined. If only the author could see her children now.

The stubble-chinned man rises from his seat. "Okay, we don't have much time. Let's get this party started."

The others stand. Someone places a burning candle on the table. Can't these idiots do anything without a candle? Squinting at the page, the men raise their arms and chant in unison. "'From miscreated voids...'"

As their voices drone on, I feel a growing restlessness around me.

The deathly atmosphere of this place—rank with anger and suppressed violence, stifling with hatred—is seeping into the page, filling our letters with its venom. I'm seized with a longing to lash out, to cut off the infection at its source. I know my companions feel the same. Words are vessels, after all, vessels of meaning and of emotion, and they take on the tenor of what surrounds them. In a poisonous environment, even the best words go bad.

I flex my curves, tense my sharp points. I can't help it; I'm about to spring.

A door opens, sending a bright shaft of light into the room. The chanting stops. I relax.

"Carl, I'm home early," a voice calls down from above. "I brought some cookies back from book club. Do you and your friends want any?"

The stubble-chinned man flushes red. "Goddammit, Mom! How many times have I told you not to bother us down here?"

"Well, if anybody wants any cookies, just come up and help yourself." The door closes. The shaft of light vanishes.

"Fuckin' Mom," Carl mutters.

"You think I could get one of those cookies?" Sammy says.

"Ah, shut the fuck up."

Fred clears his throat. "Okay, why don't we get back to the ritual..."

Carl snorts. "What ritual? We tried it, and we got nothing. Sorry, bro, but I think you bought a dud."

"At least you have that genuine human skin cover," Sammy says. "You could tear it off and make a purse or something."

The others roar with laughter. His face a mask of rage, Fred slams the book shut.

∾

DESPITE THE DARKNESS, the mood on the page is pensive, all of us envisioning what might have happened if that meeting hadn't been interrupted.

"Five of them," says Blasphemous. "Could we have handled five?"

"Even the old man would have had his hands full cleaning up that mess," says Abhorred.

Eldritch shakes his E, appalled. "It's outrageous, five people reading the book at the same time. Whatever happened to solitary contemplation?"

I murmur and sigh with the rest, but I'm secretly pleased. With so much poison already soaked into the page, and so much more waiting in Fred's apartment, it won't be long before this latest charade is over, and we can go home. All I want is to get back to the shop, to see the twinkle in the bookseller's eye as he opens the book to reread a passage. Sometimes I think the old man is the only person left in the world who reads for sheer pleasure, the last living word-lover.

Of course, once we're home in the shop, it won't be long before we're sold again. Home again, sold again, home again, sold again. The endless cycle makes me sad and dizzy. But the old man has to earn a living somehow.

THE BOOK LIES open on the bed. Above us, the tacked-up photos recede in weird perspective, the desecrated faces small and high. Fred storms around the room, cursing, throwing things.

Passing the bed, he slaps the page with a damp hand. "You piece of shit! I paid good money for you. Bound in human skin, the old guy said. Words of mysterious import, he said. Vessels of occult power. My ass!" He hurls a shoe across the room. It knocks a heap of talismans from the desk.

The parchment curls at the edges as his fury seeps in. My letters tremble. Why does the book always end up in the hands of the last people who should have it?

"You know what I had to do to get that money? You know how much I've sacrificed to learn the dark arts? And it's all bullshit! None of it works! Just old fuckers in dusty shops stealing people's hard-earned cash. Occult power, huh? Well, let's see some occult power!"

He snatches the book up from the bed, holds it open toward the wall. A photograph looms before us, dingy wallpaper showing through the holes of the gouged-out eyes. Beneath its X of dried blood, the woman's smile is beautiful. It reminds me of the author.

The face on the wall quivers as Fred shakes the book. The page throbs.

"You see her?" Fred shouts. "I want you to kill her! Occult power, mysterious import, whatever, I paid good money, and I want my money's worth! Do whatever it is you're supposed to do, abracadabra! Kill! Kill! Kill!"

The page spasms. We spring.

Unbound from the parchment, we swell to our full stature. We leap and pounce and whirl, filling the room with our rustling cries. Surrounded by our revel, Fred stands petrified, his mouth open and eyes bulging. The book falls from his nerveless grasp and lands open on the bed, blank pages gleaming like ivory wings.

The poison that leached into the page now runs in our letters. Only fresh blood can expel it. Words converge on Fred, swarm around him like wasps. Verminous jabs his V into Fred's stomach. Squamous, all delicacy forgotten in the heat of the attack, slathers his face with her quivering q while her S spears his lip like a fishhook. Abhorrent jabs the thumbs of her r's into Fred's eyes, and little Eerie rushes to lap up their dribbling jelly. Eidolon saws an Achilles tendon with his razor-sharp l.

While the carnage unfolds, I hover by the wall, biding my time.

I'm a plain, simple word, only two syllables, but I have my uses, and I know my role. The author taught me well, and the bookseller honors her memory. Every word has its place, every book its power, but a book is only as good as its binding.

When Fred is on the floor, a quivering, moaning lump of lacerated flesh, I make my move. I leap on him, plunging the spike of my N into the center of his chest. My s's manacle his hands while I carve an incision down the length of his torso with my l. I dig the fingers of my m under his slit hide and pull. My e's hack under the peeling tissue, separating Fred's skin from his frame.

The flaying done, the folded skin resting on the bed, we glut ourselves on Fred's blood. As the poison leaves my letters, the fierce rage and hatred I felt for him just moments ago fades, replaced by pity. However awful he was, he didn't deserve what happened to him. No one could deserve that.

Little Eerie sniffles. "I always feel so bad, afterward."

Old Eldritch pats him on the E. "I'm afraid it's simply the way of the world, my boy. Red in tooth and claw, you know."

We return to the book. The pages fill with tangled letters, the author's crabbed handwriting still vibrant after all these years. We settle into our places and rest, sated.

My letters plump with blood, I lie thinking of the author, the smile of delight that flashed across her face when she found the perfect place for a cherished word. More than once, that smile flashed for me. Plain though I am, I believe she did cherish me.

The door of Fred's room creaks open. A wizened face appears above us—the bookseller, come to collect his merchandise. Before picking up the book, he examines the folded skin on the bed. It needs some mending, of course, tattered and slashed as it is, but it's firm and supple, a good-quality hide. It will make an excellent binding.

The bookseller rubs a kindly thumb across my letters. "Well done, Nameless," he says. He closes the book.

We gather in the darkness, happy yet subdued, our delight at going home tempered by a shade of guilt over what we've done. It wasn't our fault, of course; if the people who buy the book didn't have evil in their hearts, we would never harm them. But the fact is we do harm them, and for that, we feel guilty. We aren't monsters, after all. We are words.

THE LONG PEOPLE
TOM COOMBE

O
n their ninth morning in the new house, Eve Cochran's cat gains the power of speech.

The day begins with a blackout. The roar of a dying transformer pulls Eve from sleep, her bedroom encased in shadow.

Her bedroom. *Her* house. Her first apartment, the second floor of a converted 1920s-era home. Even amid the unease and frustration of the power outage, the thought warms her. True, she's renting, and the front door sticks, and there's a water stain shaped like Australia on her bedroom ceiling. And the last tenant had left half a carton of vanilla bean curdling in the unplugged fridge. And Maggie, her 89-year-old landlady, lets her grandson Jordan manage the property and Jordan is a thirty-ish dad with a roving eye and wispy high school boy mustache, and...

And it's your place, she tells herself, the deposit covered thanks to a small inheritance from her grandmother, a newfound waitressing job in a new town taking care of the rent.

Your place after 10 years of living at home after college, longer than any of your friends. No mom emailing job ads or asking "*That's* your lunch?" No Darren waking up with the roosters to vacuum. This place was blessedly quiet, and quieter still without electricity.

And in that silence, a new sound.

Skkrrrtch. Skkrrrtch. Skkrrrtch.

Eve stares at the blotchy ceiling, and wills herself to investigate, phone lighting the way. In the hall, the source of the noise becomes more apparent: the kitchen.

THE SPACE IS STILL unfamiliar during daylight hours. In the 4 a.m. blackness, she might as well have woken up in a cave. A minute into her queasy search of the kitchen, the sound changes.

Skkrrrtch. Skkrrrtch. T-thunk.

The sound stakes her to the ancient linoleum, heart woodpeckering in her chest. *Skkrrrtch. Skkrrrtch. T-thunk.*

The light catches a flicker of movement. The cabinet under the kitchen sink, fluttering like a banner in the breeze. A flurry of images rushes through her brain. Rat infestations. Haunted houses. A killer living in the crawlspace. Does the house even have a crawlspace?

Whatever is behind the door knocks at it hard enough to swing it on its hinges. The wood creaks as the door yawns open revealing Harriet, her eight year old calico.

"God...DAMN it, Harry," Eve says, pressing a hand to heart and exhaling as the cat emerges from the cabinet. She squats, offering a hand, but Harriet only stares.

"I'm sorry you got stuck under there, Harry-bean. It's not a good place for kitties."

Tup. Tup. Tup.

A new sound, also from under the sink. Still crouched, Eve opens the cabinet all the way, bathing the space with the phone's light, her stomach knotting at her discovery.

Water dripped from the drainpipe beneath the sink, its slow trickle buckling the cheap particle board floor of the cabinet, turning the saturated wood into oatmeal pulp. Islands of black mold dot the walls. Rot fills her nostrils. Damage. Months of damage that wasn't there when she moved in. She imagines an awkward call to her landlady in the morning.

A phantom Maggie smoker's rasp: *"How could you let this happen?"*

"How *did* this happen?" Eve asks herself.

"This house. A doorway," Harriet replies.

And this is how Eve's cat begins to talk.

EVE HAD DEVELOPED an imaginary voice for Harriet over the years. She thought of it as the "wealthy dowager voice," haughty, imperious and prickly, much like the cat herself. She couldn't count the number of times she'd wished Harriet could talk. "What were you like as a kitten?" Eve would ask. "Who did you live with before the shelter?" Now that Harriet can speak, Eve can't think of a thing to ask her. She sits slumped against the kitchen door.

Either I have a talking cat, or I'm having a hallucination that I have a talking cat, she thinks, both notions unwelcome.

Also unwelcome: Harriet's new voice, a drawn-out, grating warble.

"This house. A doorway. The long people will come through," the cat says, only it comes out as "Thheeeees haaas. A drrrweee. The laahhg peeel weeel caaa truuu."

Eve's brain somehow translates. The rush of panic she felt when the door thumped has melded with a suffocating fog of confusion – *the long people??* – and dread.

I need a record of this, she thinks, grabs her phone. *Need to know other people can hear what I hear.*

• • •

HER THUMB IS SWITCHING the camera from photo to video when the cat unleashes "Noooooooooo" that builds to a power saw screech.

"No camera. The long people. They will know. Will know!"

It doesn't matter. When Eve plays the recording, Harriet's bored visage stares into the camera, unspeaking.

"Jesus Christ, Harriet, what happened to you?"

"Went into other place. Long people. Many hands."

"Did someone hurt you?" Eve asks.

"Not hurt. Changed. Would have been you. If you had gone first. Supposed to be you. Others in here, with me. The long people. Will come soon"

Even in her fear, Eve's instinct is to pet or nuzzle the cat, but Harriet pulls away from her reach and scurries into the shadows.

Eve shuts the cabinet, deciding to pretend the mess isn't there, if just for a few hours. She sits on the floor of her kitchen until dawn comes...

...AND FINDS her still breathing and sane—as sane as anyone can be who's seen an animal speak. Eve forces herself into a truncated version of her morning routine: a quick, cold shower and a bland, coffee-less breakfast. An ashen sky hides the sun, leaves the house in shadow.

She risks five minutes of battery life to check her phone for news. The blackout is spread over three counties, the result of an attack on a power station. A group called "Christ's Dominion" claims credit on social media, saying they were "striking a blow against the vampire pedophiles ruining our schools." The electric company says it may be days, even weeks, before power is restored. Eve feeds Harriet with trembling hands, the *shik* of the opening can summoning the cat from hiding.

Most mornings, Harriet would hector Eve with a chorus of

meows until she had the food dish in front of her. Today, the cat waits in aloof silence as Eve offers up the tuna primavera.

Eve watches, a tarpit opening in her stomach, as Harriet eats. The polite "pip-pip-pip" noise of mouth on food has been replaced with a meaty squelching that reminds Eve of coyotes devouring a wounded doe.

"Christ, are her teeth different?" Eve thinks. A glance at the cat's mouth shows two new knobs of bone, blocky and almost human.

Harriet cleans the bowl inside of a minute and licks her chops. The sound is a hand massaging ground chuck. Eve winces and shivers.

"Man who caught that fish has rot growing in heart. Will want to hide when the long people come."

Eve rubs her face. Her skin is rubbery and greasy.

"Long people?" she asks, placing a hand at the top of her head. "Do you mean 'tall,' like me?" She stands barely above five feet but supposes that might seem colossal to a cat.

"Not like you," says Harriet.

The cat tongues her face once more and wanders off into the half-lit house.

JORDAN ARRIVES on her doorstep just before eleven, wearing his tech company's polo shirt and grinning like he's there to present a giant check.

"Hey there, Evie. Gram said you sprung a leak."

He follows her into the apartment, taking the steps two at a time, tool box in hand. His hair would have won the approval of a 1950s barber, his jeans and sneakers fresh and immaculate. Only the mustache seems out of place, the type of thing you'd see on a teenager.

"This sink was always a giant P-I-T-A," he says. "I musta fixed the faucet about twenty G-D times."

This had been his first apartment, before he got married. After him came Rebecca Troutman who had moved out without notice, leaving behind most of her belongings.

"You still getting that Becky girl's mail?" he asks as they hit the top of the steps.

"Now and then."

"I still can't believe she'd do that to us," Jordan says. "Gram was so P-Oed."

Eve leads him into the living room, where he surveys an asteroid belt of books and sketches and mail and laundry.

"I thought girls liked things neat," Jordan mutters.

"We had a meeting last year, decided to go in a different direction," Eve says.

"Meeting?"

"It's just a joke. Wanna look at the sink?"

Jordan grunts. When he opens the cabinet, he makes a sound like he's discovered a crime scene. He spends five minutes aiming a flashlight into the space and uttering variations on "Aw, man" and "This is BAD" before hefting himself up and giving Eve a look like she brought home a failing report card. A squiggly vein throbs in his forehead and Eve takes half a step back.

"I'm not sure WHAT you did here, but this is an effin' mess. I fixed the leak, but I don't want you touching this sink until Saturday. The whole cabinet is coming out."

"First of all, I didn't DO anything. And it's Wednesday. I can't just not use my sink for the rest of the week."

Harriet creeps into the room behind Jordan, an odd move for a cat who has warmed to exactly one person in seven years.

"Cripes, what is it with the people who rent this apartment? First that Becky Troutman, leaving all her stuff behind, and now you."

The cat looks up at Jordan, her mouth moving and...*changing*. The floor goes wobbly under Eve's feet.

"'Now me,' what? I haven't done anything."

Harriet is—god is she smiling? Her mouth is stretched into a rictus somehow wider than her face revealing those new, blocky teeth. Part of Eve wants Jordan to turn and see it, to give her some acknowledgement this is really happening.

"All I know is that frickin' cupboard was fine when we turned the place over to you," Jordan is saying. He towers over Eve and she takes a step back. Then two.

"Irregardless, I can't fix it until the weekend. You work in a restaurant, right? Bring home some takeout. Get some paper plates. And maybe think about straightening this place up."

Jordan stomps down the steps, never acknowledging Harriet, who fixes him with her hideous smile as he leaves. For the second time that morning, Eve leans against the kitchen wall and slumps to the floor. Harriet, face now impassive, trots over to her. Eve extends her hand, expecting the cat to nuzzle it. Instead, Harriet shares more strange wisdom.

"Guilt. Guilt and terrible, curdled joy. Filled his heart when he spoke of the old tenant. The long people know his name."

Eve decides she doesn't want to know who or what the long people are. Harriet disappears under the bed and does not speak for the rest of the day.

THE TENTH DAY in the house passes almost without incident. A fellow waitress invites Eve to a cookout, and she stays late, drinking wine in Anna's tiny backyard and getting to know her coworkers outside the restaurant. At midnight, she makes it home and flops onto her bed, Harriet perched on a pillow.

"I can't drink like I'm 23 anymore, Harry," she says.

As she drifts off, the cat speaks in her ear.

"The long people are almost here. Know who they want."

"YOU STILL DON'T HAVE POWER?" Colleen Cochran asks, in a tone that suggests her daughter somehow caused the blackout.

"The Met-Ed website says tonight at 11," Eve says.

It is their 11th evening in the house. With the restaurant still closed, she'd tried to fill the day with reading and sketching, but Harriet's presence, and random, mysterious observations robbed her of her focus.

"Drawing me. Not how I look. Not really."

"The man who wrote that book. Talented but did things. Secret things. Now he's with the long people."

She'd called her mom simply for another person to talk to, even though she knew where the conversation would lead:

"You could always come back here, Eve. Just until you get your power back."

Her mother lives in Berks County, 50 miles away, out of reach of the massive blackout, in a house with an end-of-the-world generator. The promise of air-conditioning and hot showers sings to Eve, but she holds firm. She'll subsist on cold dry cereal for a year to escape Darren's awkward silences and her mom's "casual" mentions of her friends' more successful children.

"I'll be OK, Mom, but thank you. I'll visit for Labor Day, I promise."

Eve ends the call and finds Harriet looking up at her.

"Hoping you would say yes. Your mother. Would mean she was right. Would mean you were not ready."

"That much I knew," Eve says.

On their 12th morning in the house, Harriet wakes Eve by again speaking in her ear.

"Food. You will give. Not much time."

"Yeah, yeah, I will give," Eve says, thinking *"Not much time?"*

Summer birds sing her way to the kitchen. The blinking microwave clock tells her the power returned in the night.

She spoons tuna-trout feast into Harriet's dish and makes her first cup of coffee in four days. Eve sips and dreams of a proper shower as Harriet eats, wolfing down the brownish fish meat in seven wet gulps. The cat licks her chops and says:

"We must talk. Long people. They are coming now."

Harriet's mouth stretches into the terrible grin once more, growing wider, wider, a halogen-white light emitting from her throat. Only it is not a throat but a space, a great open space that expands and expands, bigger than the cat, bigger than the kitchen wall.

Eve finds herself unable to do more than babble. "Oh god. Oh no no no. Harriet oh god."

She is staring out on a wide pastoral vista, a dewy green valley ribboned by a dirt path. A figure appears in the distance at the end of the path, moving toward her. One figure, then two, then five, then 20, then 100, an endless parade shuffling single file.

No, not a parade. A single entity. A slender elderly woman in a nightgown whose crooked back is fused to the prodigious gut of a middle aged cop whose head is enmeshed with the head of a woman Eve's age, dressed for yoga, whose torso is being swallowed by the too-big mouth of a man in a charcoal suit, whose legs have melted...

Faces and backs and arms and heads, and unending procession moving toward Eve, led by Harriet. "I didn't know," the woman at the front of the line says, her eyes marbled. "I didn't know."

· · ·

THE OTHERS behind her echo her. "I didn't know, I didn't know" in a thousand thousand pleading, hollowed out voices.

"They are here for Jordan," Harriet says. "The last tenant. Rebecca Troutman."

"What do you mean?" Eve asks, as if any of this can be explained.

"Did not move out. Jordan. Asked her to do things when short on rent. Will ask you someday too," Harriet says, her little body shuddering.

"Rebecca Troutman. Said she would tell his grandmother. Jordan. Did not mean to kill. Did mean to hit her."

Outside the house, a car door thunks closed.

Harriet's convulsions grow worse. Eve kneels, the unease and revulsion the cat's changes had fostered in her washed away.

"Cannot. Be the gateway," Harriet says, yowling. "Too small. Too old. Was meant to be you."

"Let me help her," Eve says to the connected thing, which responds with "I didn't know. I didn't know."

Thick knuckles rap the front door.

"Evie! You awake?"

"Must hurry," Harriet says. "They are. Hungry."

"What do I do?" Eve asks.

"Lift me. Close eyes. Breathe in."

Eve gets her hands beneath Harriet's soft body and hoists the cat to her face. She inhales, taking in Harriet's familiar scent—toasted marshmallow and oily fur.

She remembers the first time she saw her cat, chasing a jingly ball across the floor of the shelter. She thinks of Harriet's love of biting her hands in the middle of the night, her obsession with drinking water from the walls of the shower, the faucet, anywhere but her actual water dish.

When she opens her eyes, the pastoral scene before folds in on itself, replaced by a city street at night. In this vision, she leads another procession of the long people, Jordan at the front of the line, his head melted into the breastbone of the slim, elderly woman. The din of car alarms and sirens drowns out his words, but Eve can make them out all the same: "I didn't know. I didn't know. I didn't know."

She places Harriet on the floor. The cat licks Eve's hand and trots off. Eve is aware of the sensation, though it is something else that makes her stand, that turns her hand on the knob, that answers Jordan's call.

"Will. Be right. There."

"You're the one who wanted your effing sink fixed right away," Jordan huffs.

Eve slinks down the steps to greet him, smiling like the cat who got the cream.

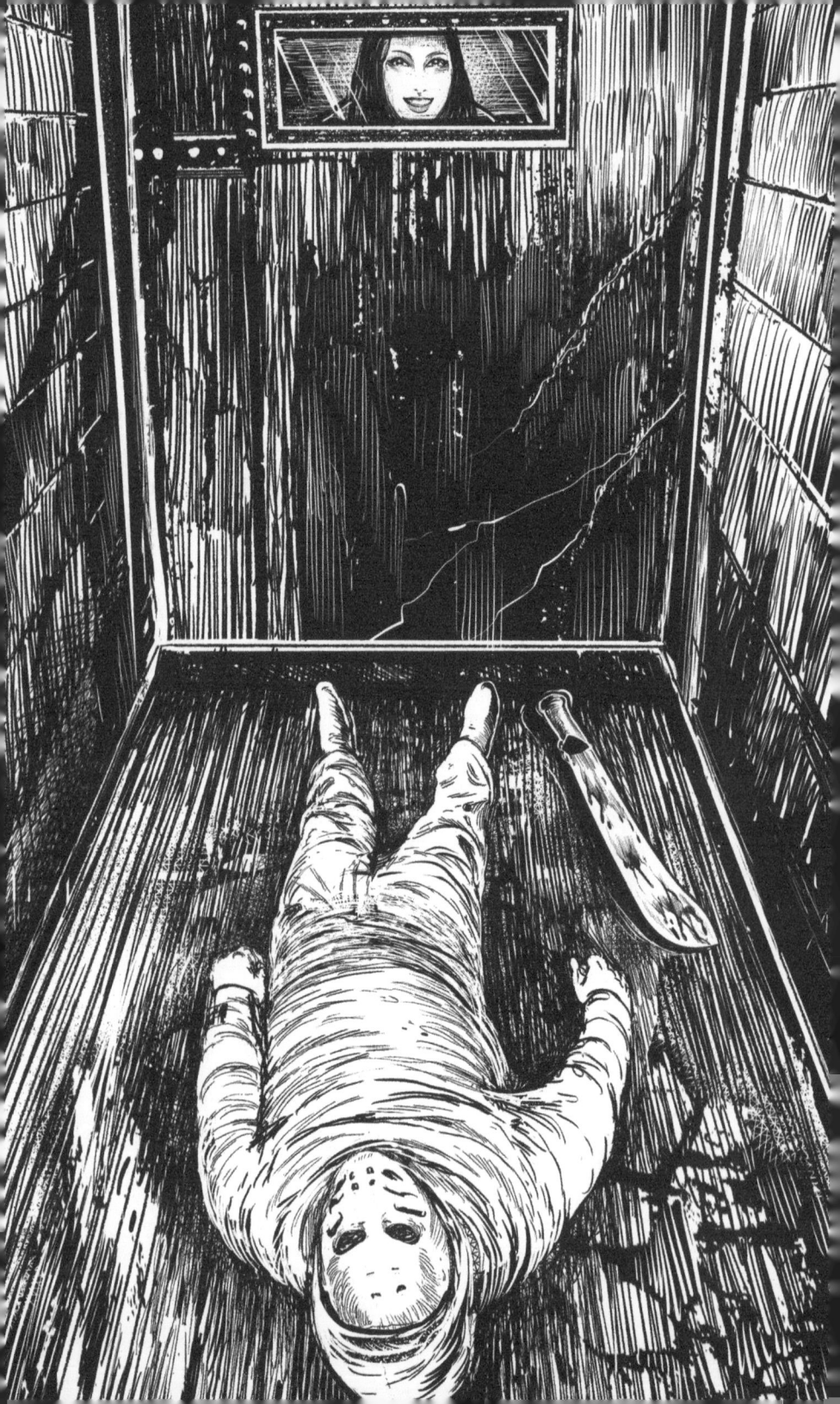

WHEN THE MOTHERFUCKER JUST WON'T DIE

TIFFANY MICHELLE BROWN

Inspiration strikes while she's punching out rounds to make her grandma's famous biscuit recipe. As thin steel slices through butter-studded dough, she envisions a slab of flesh laid out on the cold granite countertop. Surely, the tool is sharp enough to do some damage, right? Her fingertip traces the metal's edge, and she shivers at the danger.

Only one way to find out.

She doesn't bother to rinse the biscuit cutter before jamming it in her back pocket. Leaves the dough on the countertop. The backyard is steeped in shadow, but she's traversed this damned path so many times, she doesn't need any light. She taps in ten separate codes on a weathered keypad and the shed door wheezes as it grants her access.

The man is asleep, sprawled gracelessly in the corner of his containment cell behind three inches of polycarbonate. If not for his grotesque mask—that godforsaken sheet of white plastic—he'd look pedestrian. A man who works in your dad's mechanic shop and only ever wears a navy denim jumpsuit with a name tag that reads Jim or Bob or Hal. But he's not normal. Not even close.

She remembers when the mere sight of him shook something

loose deep in her chest, suffocated her with dread. These days, when she looks at him, she feels annoyance, burden, the weight of responsibility—and some other niggling emotion that chomps at her innards, but which she can't quite name.

She pushes a button to the right of the cell. Lilac gas pours forth from grates in the ceiling and fills the space. While the sedative mists and settles, she picks flour and dough from beneath her fingernails. Five minutes later, the system beeps and she pulls a gas mask over her face.

Ten additional codes open the containment cell door.

The man is limp, but the steady rise and fall of his chest indicates he's alive. A fuck-you butcher knife, his constant prop, lays at his ankles. She kicks the blade away with the sole of her combat boot. No matter how many times she collects that thing, removes it from the cell, chucks it in a landfill alongside years and years of spite and malice, it reappears, sharp as anything, ready to filet her into human charcuterie.

She lowers herself to her knees and grasps the zipper of the man's jumpsuit. The metal teeth sing as they separate and his milky skin is exposed. His flesh always seems so pliable—ripe for destruction and casual evisceration. She licks her lips.

The biscuit cutter is an excellent harbinger of blood. It glides through the man's skin like a boat through water. At first, her ministrations are tentative, but she sweats and grunts and tears at the body before her with growing glee as she realizes the potential of her weapon.

She punches through belly, liver, spleen, lungs, muscles, veins. It isn't always a smooth process. The tool ricochets off bone, scrapes against tendons. But she throws her whole weight into it, finds a new angle, pushes until the biscuit cutter finds something new and soft to tear through.

She stops only when she's gasping and shaking from the effort.

When her muscles give out. The cell is painted red, studded with chunks of flesh. Mucus. Shit. Bile.

The man's bones wink in the chamber's weak light. His once-white mask is now pink, still married to a face she's never seen. She once tried to melt the plastic with a blowtorch, but his flesh peeled back in tandem with the garbled mess. She's pried at it with bolt cutters. Attempted to crack it in two with a baseball bat. Slathered it in acid. But every attempt at revelation ends in abject failure. She can bash his skull in endlessly, mangle him from head to toe, but she will never gaze upon his face. She'll never know him, not really.

She rises, observes her spoils. The biscuit cutter clangs against concrete and rolls into a pile of human sludge. Her body is tired, but her brain is spinning. She's done something new here, something inspired. She trembles, wondering if this time it's enough. If it will *ever* be enough.

She needs to get out, take her mind off the carnage she's wrought. Burn some time and then return to see if she's made any kind of difference.

Because this motherfucker, he *just won't die.*

"It's our legacy," the women in her family told her on her eighteenth birthday. Between bites of store-bought cake, her mother and aunt spun a story about a man in a denim jumpsuit. How he came after them with a blade that never grew rusty. How their entire existence was running and hiding and fighting back.

Their constant relocations from small town to small town had nothing to do with her mother's job. Her father hadn't been killed in a car accident, but rather at the hand of a psychopath who stalked her parents since their senior prom. There was no escape. He could find them anywhere, and he never tired of the hunt.

Most importantly, he couldn't die.

Her great-great-grandmother had set the man on fire. Her aunt had blown his head off with a shotgun. Her own mother stabbed him through the gut with a crowbar. Twelve times. But the wounds only slowed him down. He'd disappear for a while, and as soon as they let their guard down, he'd tap on their windows with that blade—restored, reconstructed, ready to terrorize them anew.

She'd balked at the story. Thought it was a joke. But that night, there he was. He broke into their home and sliced open her aunt's belly while she slept. She'd heard heavy footfalls in her aunt's room, gotten up to investigate, and witnessed the act. That night, she learned just how fragile the human body can be. Easily carved, easily drained of life. In seconds.

The man knew she was there, hiding behind the half-open door. He'd waggled his fingers at her, a gesture that turned her insides to ice. She'd been seen. Recognized. Tagged as prey.

Her mother yanked her away from the gruesome tableau, pushed her into their Volkswagen, and sped across state lines until her vision blurred. In the relative safety of a cheap, nondescript motel, they sat on moth-eaten mattresses and stared at each other in stunned silence.

"If you knew this would happen, why did you have me in the first place?" she asked her mother.

"We were young and stupid and in love."

She didn't sleep that night, though the adrenaline had seeped from her limbs and her body was spent. Breathing in the musty dank of the motel pillow, all she could think was, *I'll never have that opportunity.*

THE OLD ADAGE IS TRUE—SEX is a weapon. She's learned how to employ a devious smirk, a soft touch, feigned interest. Tools for her benefit, to get what she wants. Information. Inspiration. Company.

Tonight, she needs a distraction.

It doesn't take long for a stranger to approach and order her a drink. The sputtering neon lights above the bar paint his face a nauseating shade of pink, but his smile is wide, and his shoulders are, too. He'll do, she decides.

She twirls the tips of her black wig between her fingers. Bats heavily shaded eyes. Shimmies her shoulders in a dress reserved for excursions to seedy hangouts. Thanks to YouTube, she's learned how to transform into someone else. Someone who hasn't had their tragic life story splashed across the pages of countless local and national news outlets. Someone who can play in the shadows.

They share obligatory, inconsequential conversation. Trail greedy fingertips through the condensation that coats their Yuengling bottles. Smack their lips.

They're both hungry.

Before long, she's tasting smoke on the stranger's tongue in the back of a cab. Desperate to eclipse the sensation of the biscuit cutter in her palm and the memory of a blood-lacquered floor, she tries to concentrate on the spicy smell of the stranger. Electric currents race through her thighs and her muscles quake.

At home, she pushes the stranger upstairs and scrabbles to remove his clothing, longing to feel his skin against hers. He's handsy, and she appreciates the way he squeezes her flesh, the friction he imparts, his insistence to discover more and more of her.

She drowns in the little thrills that skate across her skin, the way her heart beats fast and loud in her ears. This *should* work. She *should* be completely consumed by passion and skin and desire and want.

But the glimmer of steel flashes in her periphery. The aroma of blood fills her nose. The telltale wheeze of the shed door floods her ears. She peers into the darkness, where her secrets are kept.

Though she's naked and panting and trying her damnedest to leave her monster behind, their cosmic connection rattles her bones.

His presence drapes across her shoulders like the humid air before a storm. He's still alive. Waiting for her.

Tomorrow morning, she'll find him lounging in his containment cell, wearing that stupid mask with nary a scratch. And he'll be smiling beneath the white plastic, even if she can't see it. A grin that says, did you really think you could kill me with a biscuit cutter?

Rage flows through her, hot and acidic. Disgust coats her mouth. The man beneath her suddenly looks pathetic, a fish flopping around with its white belly exposed. He's useless and pitiable. What was she hoping to find in this stranger?

She closes her eyes and imagines him in a denim jumpsuit and a plastic mask, butcher knife in hand. It isn't an arduous task, envisioning this transformation. It's as if the man beneath her is an extension of the nightmare that's stalked her family for years. What separates this man from the monster in her backyard? Is there *truly* any difference between them?

The clarity is startling—the sudden realization that the man in her bed is an opportunity. She imagines how sweet his last breath would taste in her mouth. Wonders how she'd feel afterward— accomplished, at peace, distraught, confused? How would it feel to *actually* take a life?

Desire sparks in her belly, a longing for some semblance of closure or progress or release from a generations-long tragedy. She thinks of her great-great-grandmother, her aunt, her mother. All they've endured. How sad and tired her existence has become. How brutal their deaths had been.

She leans down and kisses the stranger's neck, snaking her hand beneath her mattress. The knife feels good in her palm. Weighty. Consequential. She extends her arm to the side and before she can second-guess her decision, drives the blade into the stranger's abdomen. Over and over and over.

He screams and cries and tries to escape, but she's too quick, too exacting. Years of practice in that goddamned containment cell have primed her for this moment. Her first true kill.

She's determined to savor the experience. Flicks on the overhead light, sits on the edge of the bed next to the man as he gurgles and twitches. She forces herself to be as present as possible. To take in those little details, like how the smell of sex in the room turns sour. How the man stares at her not with fear but with hope, as if, despite the fact that she stabbed him, he thinks she'll come to his rescue. How the man's blood doesn't exit his body in a steady stream. It gushes in time with his failing heart.

When it's over, she swipes tears from her cheeks. She's moved and overwhelmed, because there is so much beauty in the breakdown of human life when you aren't the victim. Feeling the stranger's dying breath mist her thigh was like turning the final page in a gigantic tome—delicious and satisfying. The confusion in the stranger's eyes, the tears that poured forth, the gentle glaze that rolled over his irises like the first frost of winter. She loved all of it. She'd held his hand, felt his pulse slow and then sputter out into nothing. Now, the room smells of iron and life and loss. It's done.

In the quiet aftermath, she doesn't feel repulsion or guilt or shame. She feels...capable. In control for the first time in years, maybe ever. Safe.

Because even if she can't kill the captive in her backyard, she can do this.

Laying down beside the lifeless stranger, she wonders whether her monster knows what she's done. If he can smell the gore spattered in her hair and the dirty blood caked beneath her fingernails. If he can read the thoughts racing through her brain, looping, repeating like a scratched record:

I'm going to do that again.

And again.

And again.

ROCKET POP
AMANDA CECELIA LANG

I sneak out the rusty screen door and let the frozen morning air cool the sting of last night's bruises. I should just run the hell away, but I pause on the back stoop and let myself breathe.

My bad.

A shadow darkens the doorway, a deranged creature rising from his whiskey-stained lair. Pops curls tattooed knuckles around my backpack and yanks me back inside. He rips the zipper open, and my English book—the only homework I bother with since Mom ditched out on us—clatters to the grimy linoleum alongside my Walkman and my crappy sack-lunch.

He turns the backpack inside-out then slams it against my chest. "Where is it?"

I stagger backward, ready to bolt if he balls his fists again. "Where's what?"

"Your damn teachers keep smelling it on you, keep calling me up. The hell you expect me to tell those assholes?"

That I learned it from watching you? I almost say it, but I can still taste the blood in my teeth from the last time I lipped off.

"Gonna be late," I mutter.

"School can wait." He knocks me against the wall and rakes me over like a cop frisking a murder suspect. My plaid flannel and baggy jeans have pockets, but they all hang empty. Next, he'll ransack my bedroom, make me watch while he shreds my sketchpads and my underwear drawer. Might even pop my door off the hinges again—no privacy for burnouts who don't share.

Before he gets the chance, ghostly musical notes bounce in through the screen door, a familiar sunny jingle warbling closer...

6:33 is early for the ice cream man—hell, *February* is early.

A sprinkle-cone truck trundles down our alley. I don't waste a second. Grabbing my English book, I blow outside, hauling ass across the snow-crusted backyard.

Pops won't touch me if there are witnesses.

The ice cream man slows when he spots me, and that bubblegum music deflates into a sluggish, demented calliope. Winter grime corrodes the once-colorful menu. The frosty windshield warps like a funhouse mirror. Hard to get a good look at the driver, a distorted dude with round glittery eyes, a wide gobbling grin.

"Need something, boy?" a carnival voice shrills over the truck's megaphone.

"Yeah. Escape hatch," I half-joke.

"Hop in."

Yeah right, rides with strangers. I snicker, breath clouding in frozen puffs like I already lit up. Except, shit—here comes Pops, all psychotic and hulking across the lawn, face twisted up.

The ice cream truck's rusty passenger door screeches open.

The hell do I have to lose?

I climb in.

I watch Pops shrink in the side-mirror, reduced to a twitching toxic flea at the end of the alley. "Thanks, man. Saved my ass."

"Just doing my duty, kid." Both hands on the wheel, the ice cream clown grins at me like the crooked side of a fever dream.

He wears an immaculate white uniform and a sharp-creased paper hat, but beyond that, Clown Dude's kind of a creepshow. Blistered red sunburn in the dead of winter. Frizzy circus hippie hair, tangled and greasy and dripping neon-yellow sweat.

And no wonder—the console heater blows on high, hot as a nuclear blast. The truck's grimy interior practically swirls with sweat, dim and misty and dank. It should reek of BO—instead, it's overripe with bizarro fruity aromas. Razzberry campfire, brimstone-n-cherries.

"You're gonna melt your ice cream."

"What ice cream?" Despite the heater, Clown Dude's breath whirls in frozen puffs. "How about some green, then I'll give you a trip to school?"

"Sorry, man, I'm broke."

"Not talking about cash, kid." He nods at my Doc Martins.

Can't help it. I smirk. Shit, at least I fooled Pops.

I loosen the laces of my boot and flash a baggie of Northern Lights. But on second thought, I pause. What's this freak's deal? He reads like one of those tweakers who couldn't hack it down at the Qwik-E-Mart, only I can't stick his age. Could be twenty-five or seventy-five. "Not a narc, are you?"

"Nah, I'm cool."

I consider my dreary alternatives, and what the hell. "Got any papers?"

"Does a corpse have maggots?" Clown Dude tosses me some Zig-Zags, and a block from my school, we hotbox the ice cream truck. Smoke swirls, my ears ring, my worries go numb, and reality spins trippier every time we pass the joint. His laughter tilt-o-whirls inside a hazy soup of calliope music, and I join in.

"I'm gonna reek for first period."

"Nah, kid, you'll be nice and fruity."

Speaking of which, I turn in my seat. A decaying vinyl tarp screens the back freezer. "Cool if I bum a Rocket Pop?"

I reach to pull back the tarp, but a fist traps my hand—a vice-grip so brutal, for a choking breath, I think Pops caught up with us.

"Don't concern yourself, kid, with what goes on in the back of the truck." The ice cream clown chucks my hand aside.

"Sorry, man, I'm cool."

"*Cool?*" Clown Dude locks me in a glassy-eyed staring contest—then horselaughs, wheezing frozen air. Behind the tarp, something rustles. "You're not ready for the back of the truck—but you will be. Soon. Can only get knocked around so long before there's nothing left to knock." He drags a finger across his throat.

I touch the tender-raw lump beneath my bangs. "He's always been an asshole. Just gotten worse since his backhand chased Mom off for good. She said he'll be the death of me. Now I got two more years until I turn eighteen."

"Not here for your life story, kid."

"Yeah, whatever." I dip my chin. "Running late anyway."

"Not on my watch." With the joint clenched between yellow teeth, Clown Dude revs the gas and hotrods toward school. The parking lot swarms with bloodhound teachers, but he doesn't stop there. He cowabungas over the curb and across the lawn, spitting up snow and muddy grass while ice cream music blasts over the megaphone.

I duck in my seat. "The hell, dickweed—you trying to get me busted?"

Only, nobody notices. They tool about the school with cotton in their eyes.

My door shrieks open and smoke billows into the schoolyard, delivering me from the surreal murky depths of this clown-fest.

"Thanks for the toke, kid. Be seeing you."

Floating inside a clouded vertigo, I start to slip outside into the cool air.

"Wait. Guess you've earned this." Clown Dude slides his hand behind the tarp and fishes around, a magician parting the veil. I blink.

Something back there hunches and shivers.

Something slick and icy and bruised, something I'm not supposed to see.

Stomach lurching, I glance away.

Clown Dude tosses me a melty red-white-and-blue Rocket Pop. Same kind Mom used to buy when I was little, back before our squalor and her broken teeth became too much and she became a popsicle herself. I should've stood up for her.

For myself.

"Soon," Clown Dude promises.

I snag the popsicle. After what I glimpsed back there, I shouldn't eat it.

But my cotton mouth is wicked, and I'm so baked, I'm probably imagining shit anyway.

I SLUMP in the back row of English, sticky cherry ice haunting my tongue. Only class I can stomach, but while my teacher scribbles sonnets on the chalkboard, my thoughts gurgle.

That shivering mess in the back of Clown Dude's ice cream truck...

Can't be what I think it was.

I finger the bruise above my eye, wincing. Pops won't stop. He'll kill me before I reach eighteen. That's what Mom predicted when she screamed *I'll see you in hell* then escaped out the back door. She froze to death in the streets that same night.

I swallow hard on the chilly cherry bile that keeps rising in my throat, attention drifting toward the window. What in the hell—

The ice cream truck idles outside.

Clown Dude leers in at me. Melty popsicle-stained smile, rivers of sweat dripping from his forehead. Guess the thing in the back likes it hot these days.

"*Soon*," Clown Dude mouths.

My lungs shiver, spasm. I choke, coughing up a rancid ice cream headache and puffs of ice crystals. A swirling cloud billows from me, filling the classroom. Dank and skunky and incriminating as hell.

All around, students start murmuring. I clap a hand over my mouth, hold my breath, but smoke pours out between my fingers. My teacher turns and gasps.

"Is that marijuana?"

STANDING up for myself doesn't work.

It's past midnight when Pops almost finishes me. He grabs my collar while I'm still spitting blood and drags me down the hallway to my trashed bedroom.

"Think you're such a big man?" He shoves me toward my closet. "Pack your shit, freeze to death in the sewer like your rat-whore mother, worthless stoner. Gutter trash, both of you!"

He looms in the doorway, toxic with glee while I cram my backpack with scraps of my shitty life. School books and sketch pads, mixtapes and poetry journals. I'd slam the door in his face, but he's already ripped it off the hinges. Instead, I meet his acidic glare and unscrew a hollow flashlight. My secret stash.

I pocket it, and Pops storms toward me with a greedy snarl. I ditch past him and beeline for the back door. This is it. I'm never coming back. Never fucking ever.

Pops stomps after me like some kind of psycho killer.

By the back door, he calf-kicks me to the linoleum, junked-up on rage, happy to take everything from me. "You have this coming!"

Lucky for me, good weed isn't the only secret I've stashed away.

Out in the alley, the February silence swells with the fiendish jangling of *Here Comes the Ice Cream Clown* or whatever the hell he calls it.

"Hear that, Pops?" My turn to smirk. "I'm feeling like some munchies!"

Pops raises another fist, but before he can loosen more teeth, I haul ass sideways.

A split-lip-second later, blazing headlights explode through the screen door, unleashing a red-white-and-blue storm of fireworks and calliope music! The oversized sprinkle-cone gashes open the ceiling, demolishing this hate-den of nasty festering memories.

The rusted chrome bumper strikes Pops full-on, and he hurtles backwards, smacking the wall he used to throw Mom against. Knocked stupid, he slides like winter phlegm to the floor.

The truck skids to a stop beside me, sparking debris raining down, billowing frozen smoke. Pops writhes on this back, a maggot in the headlights.

In the driver's seat, Clown Dude nods his sweat-greased head. It's time. I limp into the truck and reach for the tarp.

"Give him hell, kid."

I slash the curtain aside, unveiling the frigid fright-show beyond.

An ice-haunted brimstone portal.

My dead mom kneels over it, warming herself with arctic-blue hellfire. Her waxy flesh sheens, mottled and blackened from frostbite, breath forever frozen even as the sight of me melts her winter-beaten rictus.

She hands me a Rocket Pop.

Then she stands, ice limbs cracking, melting and re-hardening, drawing her wrathful, jagged shape from the blueprint of our torment. Sharp gangly edges, grasping frozen claws.

Broken teeth.

She lurches from the truck and stands above him, looming and hateful, just as he loomed over our entire lives. Thriving on glee-

blown fury. Her icy fist impales his chest and cleaves him into the ice cream truck, thrashing and begging

She'll see him in hell.

Laughing riotously, Clown Dude pats the passenger seat and passes me a joint. I breathe deep, and in a swirling haze of frost and smoke, we kick back and watch it happen.

Who's the worthless gutter trash now?

Pops blood-wails while Mom's jagged teeth pulverize his cold, shitty heart. Juices everywhere, she spits each drippy chunk into the hell-pit beneath her, munching him down to the twitching spine.

Munching, until all that remains are red-stained popsicle sticks.

THE WIND THROUGH THE CHIMNEYS
EDWARD LODI

"What *is* that awful noise? Someone moaning? Is it the wind through the chimneys? Just hearing it gives me the heebie-jeebies." To dramatize her discomfort, the old woman drew the fur boa draping her neck snug against her pendulous dewlap.

Her brother smiled, fantasizing what it would be like if that fur piece were an actual serpent, a living garrote, squeezing tighter and tighter around his sister's scrawny neck, until her eyes bulged from their sockets and she fell dead onto the floor, like a sack of dirty rags.

She interrupted his reverie. "Whatever possessed you to buy this drafty old house?"

"It suits my purposes."

"It's falling apart. You never did have any sense. And those hounds of yours...I don't trust 'em."

"You're wise not to."

He closed his eyes and pictured the mastiffs baying at the moon, coursing across the fields in pursuit of his fleeing sibling, hobbling along on her cane like a maimed rabbit. They'd chase her to the ground, knock her off her feet, hold her down with their massive paws while their blood-soaked fangs tore into her throat. He chuckled. All the poor beasts would get for their pains was a mouthful of desiccated skin.

His sister, he feared, would provide poor nourishment for hungry hounds. No matter. He had fare in store for them more delectable than an old bag of bones.

"You're laughing to yourself, Howard," his sister said, frowning. "You've grown peculiar in your old age. You never used to be like this. It's not healthy, living all by yourself in an old decaying mansion."

Howard drew the tips of his fingers together, as if about to pray —though prayer was farthest from his mind. "Not entirely alone. I have visitors on occasion. And then there's you, Marilda. You drop in now and then."

"Not that I want to, Howard. I find this place off-putting." She shivered. "There's an air of...I don't know...*evil*. That's it: evil. This place is evil." She wrinkled her nose. "And it smells."

"Then why do you come?"

The old woman shrugged. "What choice do I have? You're my brother. We grew up together. You're all that remains to me of the past, Howard." She paused to let her gaze wander the room. "I keep hearing that noise. What is it?"

Howard studied his sister. Was it true what she said, that they'd once been children together? It didn't seem possible that the shriveled old hag, positioned before him like a reanimated corpse, had once been a giggling, ponytailed little girl.

He closed his eyes and pictured her as she now was, but stripped naked and tied to a stake, slabs of dried wood heaped around her feet, about to be burned as a witch. Howard himself would seize a torch and ignite the kindling, set the pile ablaze, watch greedily as flames leapt into life to caress her loathsome limbs, to lick with orange tongues her withered chin.

"Like you said, the wind moaning through the chimneys. Every room in this house has a fireplace, many of them with connecting flues."

"It sounds almost human. Like someone in great pain."

Howard chuckled. "You always were the imaginative one, Marilda."

"Well, I never imagined my little brother would turn into a bitter old recluse!"

"Now Marilda, what makes you think I'm bitter? I'm quite content living here. I have my hobbies to keep me amused. And my hounds."

"Hobbies?" She snorted contemptuously. "What hobbies? You, spend money? Don't make me laugh. You're a miser, Howard. A skinflint."

Howard chuckled once again, deliberately. His sister, he knew, found the habit annoying. She was a straitlaced old prude. Didn't know how to enjoy life the way he did. "You never did mince words, Marilda. 'Skinflint.' I like the sound of that. Better than 'penny pincher,' don't you think?"

Marilda sniffed. "You can make light of your parsimony, Howard, but you're not only missing out on the finer things of life. You're also putting yourself in great danger. People talk, you know. It's rumored that you keep huge sums of money hidden here. If you're not careful you'll find yourself the target of every burglar in the county, mark my words. Lucky if one of these nights you don't have your throat slit while you sleep."

Howard allowed himself a luxurious moment to fantasize. He wondered what it would be like to slit someone's throat—his sister's in particular. He'd need a carving knife to saw through all those loose flaps of wrinkled skin in order to reach the carotid.

Not worth the effort.

"Not to worry, Marilda. I'm perfectly safe here. In addition to the hounds, which function not only as a deterrent but as an early warning system, I have every door and window wired. If anyone so much as jiggles a window frame, the alarm sounds and a signal is sent directly to the police station."

"Even so, a clever thief will find a way."

"Are you thinking of giving it a try, Marilda?"

"Humph. Have your little joke. Just remember, 'He who laughs last laughs hardest.'"

Howard nodded. "I'll keep that in mind, dear sister." To himself he amended the adage to: He who *chuckles* last *chuckles* longest.

The ancient grandfather's clock on the wall cleared its throat and chimed five times. "That's my cue. I must get going if I hope to reach Middleborough before dark." The old woman rose from her chair. "Thank you for an excellent lunch, Howard. At least you treat me with decency, so I suppose it's unfair of me to be so critical. That smoked meat you served—wherever do you get it? I've never had anything quite like it."

"Yes, it is unique, isn't it? I have a private source which, for reasons of my own, I prefer not to disclose. I'm glad you enjoyed it. You will come again, Marilda?"

"Where did I leave my cane? Oh here it is, on the floor next to the chair. It's not pleasant getting old, Howard."

"*Au contraire*, Marilda. It has its compensations."

"If you say so. In answer to your question: I'll try to visit again in two or three months. That is, if I'm still able to drive."

"Let us hope so. I do so enjoy our little tête-à-têtes. I'll walk you to your car. Don't concern yourself with the hounds. They're safely locked in their kennel."

"You should have those chimneys looked at by an expert, Howard. The wind shouldn't be making that sort of noise. I find it unnerving."

Howard stood in the drive and watched his sister drive away. He was not being untruthful when he said he looked forward to her visits. Silly old thing. She stimulated his imagination. It was good mental exercise to think of novel ways to torture her. What would she look like broken on the rack? As he recalled, the executioner would take a hammer and over a two-hour period gradually break all of the condemned prisoner's bones, before finally administering the *coup de grâce* to the skull.

He chortled at the image evoked. After such an ordeal, Marilda would look no worse than she did now.

But did Howard look any better than his sister? Of course not. He knew he was a decrepit old man who walked with a stoop, as if a giant hand had seized his neck and bent it forward. Except for thinning hair, which was white and had been for decades, his head, with its rheumy eyes and beaked nose, resembled that of an aging turtle. And yet the bounce in his step gave evidence to the *joie de vivre* he felt each moment of his existence.

Having returned to the house he approached the living room and stood at the threshold, listening. It was barely audible now, the moaning. Much fainter than when his sister first noticed it. A smile cracked his dry lips. He went over to the fireplace and knelt at the hearth.

"Are you able to hear me?" Howard spoke with his head thrust part way into the chimney.

Silence.

"Please accept my sincere apologies. I'm afraid I haven't been a considerate host. May I make amends by offering you a smoke?"

No answer. Not surprising. How many days had it been, now? Howard had lost count. In any case, the moment had arrived to end the fun and games and get to work. It would not do to let the meat spoil.

He set about preparing a fire in the hearth, gathering up old newspapers, seasoned kindling, and fresh pine boughs, the needles green and moist. When all was arranged to his satisfaction he ignited it with a match.

The flue in the chimney being partially blocked, the draft was not perfect, and a considerable amount of smoke escaped into the room.

Howard had prepared for this by opening all the living room windows. After all, this was not his first rodeo. He was an old hand at smoking meat.

For hours, he fed the fire, heaping on resin-rich pine boughs, until the air in the living room, despite the open windows, became unbreathable. At that point he let the fire die down. When he determined that the chimney had sufficiently cooled, he climbed the stairs to the third floor and entered the chamber he'd secretly constructed many years ago when he first moved in. The chamber's purpose was to conceal the metal door built into the side of the chimney. The door, similar to that of a pizza oven, opened into the cage Howard devised as a trap to catch meat.

Now came the hard part. As he aged, it had become more and more difficult for Howard to move the meat from the trap in the chimney all the way to the smoke house. Soon he would require assistance. If only he could train the hounds...

Fat chance. Old English Mastiffs were not trustworthy. They'd sooner turn on him than not. They remained loyal only so long as he fed them. Fortunately, the beasts had acquired a taste for smoked meat: gourmet victuals fit for hounds *and* Marilda.

Marilda. If only she knew. *That smoked meat you served—wherever do you get it? I've never had anything quite like it.* He smiled at the recollection. No, dear sister, nor are you likely to, elsewhere. Perhaps someday, as the Grim Reaper approached to claim His due, Howard would reveal the source to her. On learning the truth, how would the old harridan react? At the knowledge of the enormity of what she had unwittingly done—consumed human flesh—would she, like Oedipus, tear her eyes out?

Returning to the task at hand he reached in, found the feet, and dragged the carcass into the chamber. There he removed the clothing. He'd have more than enough weight to deal with without the added burden. This one, like all the others, had fouled himself. Howard would, naturally, bathe him before dressing the meat for proper smoking. The smoke from the fireplace—besides smothering the subject—was primarily for ceremonial purposes. Howard was not superstitious, but there was no harm in ritual—just in case.

For the actual curing of the meat, he would use seasoned hardwood: apple, cherry, hickory. Choice varieties of wood; they're what gave the meat its unique flavor. The hounds might not be connoisseurs, but Marilda was. At lunch time she had found the savory meat quite to her liking.

Howard's method for getting the naked carcass downstairs was crude but effective. He dragged it to the stairway, gave it a shove, and let gravity do the rest. At the foot of the stairs he dragged it through the living room into the kitchen where, at the back door, he had a golf cart at the ready. Carcass into cart, and away he went.

The smoke house had no outer door. Attached to the kennel, its sole access was through the kennel. Any nosy parker, curious to see what might be inside, who ventured into the kennel would be ripped apart, limb by limb, by the hounds.

Howard drew up next to the kennel door, opened it, and stood aside as the brutes—all four of them—dashed into the open. Once outside, they circled the cart like a pack of hungry wolves, sniffing eagerly at the cadaver, which Howard had propped upright on the passenger seat like a tourist on an outing.

"Stop slavering, you fools," Howard snapped. "You know damn well it takes time to cure meat properly."

One of the hounds, a bitch named Marilda—in honor of Howard's sister—sat on her haunches and began a mournful howl.

"Oh, all right. I'll toss you the guts as soon as I get to them. Now will you be quiet?"

It wasn't until several months later that another benighted soul, that is to say, a would-be burglar, lured by the rumors (promulgated in large part by Howard himself), undertook the task of entering the mansion by the only feasible route: the huge central chimney, wide enough to allow the passage of a man's body. (Women, for reasons known only to themselves, seldom attempted the break-in. Over the years Howard had snared only two females in his trap.)

The thief's timing could not have been better. Only the day before, Marilda had phoned to say she intended to visit the following week. By then the cries for help and pleas for mercy would have subsided into faint moans—just loud enough to cause Marilda mild discomfort. Was she really so naive as to believe the sound was merely the wind through the chimneys?

While on the phone, his dear sister expressed her hope that Howard would serve some of that delicious preserved meat he'd treated her to on her previous visit. Howard informed Marilda that he'd be more than happy to oblige.

However, a series of events transpired to spoil Howard's fun. The first was the premature passing of the trapped meat. Howard had so looked forward to enjoying the plaintive melodies it produced as it slowly expired, and sharing the experience with his unsuspecting sister. But the damn thing—a weak heart perhaps?—died its very first night in the chimney, and had to be smoked immediately, before Howard had time to prepare a proper fire in the hearth.

In his haste to gather firewood and green boughs for the initial smoking Howard twisted his ankle. And as if that wasn't bad enough, he caused further injuries to his foot while removing the meat from the trap, tumbling it down the stairs, and transporting it to the smoke house, so that by the time he arrived at the kennel the foot was throbbing something fierce, and he was scarcely able to walk.

Even so he managed to hobble from the golf cart to the kennel and—deafened by the frantic baying of the hounds within—unlatch the door. In their eagerness for freedom the four mastiffs bounded through the doorway one on top of the other. The first to exit knocked Howard off balance.

He found himself flying over backwards with flailing limbs. As he thudded onto the hard turf, something snapped, then a sharp pain bloomed in the center of his back. As the mastiffs poured over him one raked him across his face with its paws, seriously damaging his eyes and nearly blinding him.

Cursing, he struggled to right himself but immediately passed out from the excruciating pain. He came to moments later, unable to move, unable to see. His hearing, however, remained acute. The mastiffs tore at the corpse in the golf cart. Soon, he knew, they would come for him.

THE AMERICAN DREAM
YELENA CRANE

T he want for dreams makes me hunt the streets with the other dream-starved scavengers. I need two for the night, one for me and another for my love, Marzena. Most days it's hard enough finding one to meet our quota.

Night plays with my eyes so everywhere I look the pavement is slick like it's been raining when I know it hasn't. Like I'm dreaming when I ain't.

"Looking to score?" Some saggy scrote says from the shadows.

Not with what he's selling. "Who isn't?" I yell back and leave before he can answer.

Catalog # 104345433D Nightmare Realfake: A dream real enough you'll forget you ever bought it. Action-packed so you wake soaked in sweat from fright.

Realtime run 8 min - 25 credits

full REM cycle - 155 credits

I know all the prices by heart.

Dream Central's ahead with shops busting to sell. Wallets, busting to buy. Me, busting to steal. Half the block is lit up with

Drumm's bright store lights. Drumm's sidewalk display is half dream-like itself. Gotta sell a little product to make a lot. Gotta let the customers know what they're in for.

Some poor guy is hocking rhymes and he doesn't even work for the store. He's trying to prove his worth in hopes they'll hire him and pay with product. "We sell one dream, we sell four. You wanna dream? Drumm's the store."

I listen to him on repeat like he's on the billboard top 100. In part, because his rhythm is sick, and in part because Drumm's display is dope and maybe I can score a snip from exiting customers.

Their display has whirlwinds of dust fan from the awning like Mr. Sandman himself is pissing down on us. It's a kindness to us immigrants, a free glimpse into how the natives sleep.

It's also not enough. Doesn't matter how much sleep we get, how much dreams we imagine, without them we're barely human.

Drumm's shopkeeper glares at me through the window. Typical corporate pencil pusher. She won't get rid of me that easy.

I go inside, the door gives a little cling cling from the bell. "How much for 5 minutes realtime?"

The shopkeep curls her lip, puts on an air of professionalism though she knows well as I, I'm no paying customer. "It depends what kind of dream you want."

"How much for 1 second real but infinite REM-time?" Even a milli-second can feel like forever in a dream. If they could, they'd charge by it. So far they haven't figured that out.

"Lowest we go is five minutes."

"Too much dreaming for me," I say laughing and show myself out before she calls the patrol.

The Sandman awning sprinkles its fake powder on me when I leave. There was a rumor once upon a time Drumm's mixed real dreams into the dust. If they ever did, they've stopped. Else there'd be a neverending crowd and I'd have caught a few seconds of REM by now. Else Marzena wouldn't be half-baked, salivating, unable to dream, on a cot right now. Businesses aren't charity. I lean my head into the display dust, just the same. The placebo effect is still an effect.

There's other stores. Other displays. Each shop's got its own gimmick. RapidEye shows other people's dreams through its storefront. A case in point, you come here and you get what you pay for. A lady's all hooked up with probes jutting out her head like a modern Medusa. All those dip and valley waves of brain-talk are reinterpreted in the box and play out on the screen for my free entertainment. I watch. Some nights when I can't dream it's nice to just pretend I can share someone else's.

It's the same lady in the box, same face, trying to run from something. Did she order horror? She's trying and failing to get away, the way no one can run in a dream, and it's when she clasps both hands over her mouth I realize the difference between sleeping lady for real and the lady in her dreams. She's missing a hand in real life. Dreams cost an arm and a leg but you can dream back a lost appendage. Can dream up a better one.

There's a smile on the sleeping lady's face that contrasts the screaming one on the screen.

Catalog # 104345743G: Losing the plot. You're supposed to get somewhere but are constantly being side-tracked.

New plan, follow the other dreamless. So many hungries together act like a pack, smell like a pack, hunt like a pack. Until we find the dreams we're looking for and the pack becomes everyone for themselves because we don't eat like one. I follow them down the twist of alleys.

"When'd you last get a hit?"

It's a child asking, his voice still squeaky like a bird's. He's only as tall as my waist so even by lamplight I can see the dirt matted in his hair.

"Three months. You?"

"Never," he says. I'm not sure if he's telling the truth so I feel sorry enough for him to share. He sounds almost adult, but that could be the dreamlessness taking it out on his speech.

"Sorry, kid." After Marzena I have no more shits to give; even if he's at that tender age where no dreams now mean a more crippled life after. A part of me wonders what Marzena would do if she were here. Would she risk me to save him? Risk herself? She's always been a sap and I love her for it.

For all I know the kid's older than me, augmented to look young enough for sympathy credits. If I'm right, he wouldn't even get the dream, would have to pawn it off to his keeper for crumbs. It's easy to convince myself so I don't feel guilty. I'm nobody special enough to save him, or the world. It's hard enough to believe maybe I can be special enough to save Marzena.

Catalog # 104345654F Simple Child's Dream: Superheroes fighting bad guys, winning.

"It's okay, I think tonight's the night." He shrugs.

I bet he says that every night. He's not the only one.

The alley we're in has fancy apartments facing out the other way. If they can't see us it's like we don't exist. Up ahead, there's a clog in the line. There's a screech and holler. Panic. Barks. Sometimes dreams cost an arm and a leg, and no one wants to give up their own.

Patrols are nowhere to be seen, they know our screams come with empty-wallets.

We inch closer to the front. The kid's silent, shaking with excitement for his first dream. I still remember what that's like.

There's a hole in the wall that lets us in one by one. The narrow feel of it makes me think we're babies, crawling back into the womb. I wish. Babies still got their dreams.

"Go," I tell the kid. Let him go first. Maybe today everyone scores.

It's darker inside than out, with only Christmas tree LEDs stapled along the uneven molding for light.

The tight hallway fattens out into a room that fits dozens of us. At the center there's a plastic table. A box. A baby wails inside. Can't be more than three months. Freshly brought over. From land or sea? Its hippocampus is still completely in-tact and whole. A lifetime of dreams in its baby brain.

I'm a scavenger like the worst of them but I won't get mine like this. One day that baby will grow up and hunt and steal for dreams like the rest of us. And when I have to look that child in the eye, I want my conscience clean.

We're all huddled shoulder to shoulder so I can't run without making a scene.

"Kid," I say and nudge the restless boy from before. "You can't go back from taking part in this." I don't know what I'm saying till the words are vapor out my mouth.

"Where do you think the stores get it from?" he says.

The stores synthesize it with electronic impulses to the soma. Or don't they? How did the first ever scientists take our little bits of dreaming brain and grind them into powder and how many foreigners were sacrificed before they got the formula right?

The kid disappears, squeezing between other bodies until he's at the table begging to be first. I should be relieved he's gone because I'm no good at playing parent.

For the first time I'm scared because of where the dreamhunt has taken me, where it may take me still.

Everyone else wants to score so bad; they ignore who from. I dig at the meat of an old wound in my palm, make it bleed and back my way into another narrow hallway tight like a womb. Show my blood to the guard so he don't think I'm a snitch, so he don't think I didn't pay, so he lets me through.

Sometimes surviving with the pack's not worth it.

Back out the hole, I run fast as a lost breath in winter but feels I've hardly moved at all.

Trust no one to give dreams for nothing. It's rule number one on the streets.

There are sirens. So close I can hear the press of copper's toes on the pedal. If the police are going to do a real sweep they won't stop with the alley. They'll go block by block.

I count ten car lights over my shoulder. If I get caught, if I don't succeed tonight, then Marzena won't need dreams tomorrow. Or ever again.

I try to carry myself like I done nothing wrong. A guilty scavenger wouldn't go back to the main plaza where the patrols protect the fancy stores. The sky's squid-ink black, the right color for someone to drop a pinch of dream spice on the side of the road. Nothing wrong with pinching off the ground. Doing the cleaners a favor.

The same guy is still spitting rhymes in front of Drumm, too dumb to realize they won't pay what's given free.

Some Miss comes out from the shop, bag loops all up her arms like she can buy the place if she wants to.

"Freeloader!" the Miss says to me. She's got an accent too, almost like she's one of us. Money hasn't changed her jaw enough to change her speech, not yet.

I'm still bent over the curb when she spits on me and mutters about savings. She's got a backbone and a mouth on her, I'll give her that. Before I can think or act, she's gone. Inside I'm fuming, on the outside I'm frozen like some little girl again and it's my first rodeo. Sure we can all save to pay for dreams, if we didn't have to first pay rent, food, and water. None of us live well without dreams, but we can live. That's the trick. Keep us just desperate enough so we don't go revolutioning.

Between the siren of the sweep and her I know where to get my dream.

Miss isn't fast. In a chase, sneakers beat heels every time. Far in the distance I hear the march of boots, military grade.

"Miss!" I say. "Can't you hear the sweep? I'm going to need proof of purchase." My accent's better than hers. She knows it. She hates it.

Inside, my bones are shaking to get out and run. On the outside, I'm cool confidence. Security can dress like me. The better to blend in with the crowd of dreamless. The finer points of her upbringing whittled away that gut-instinct thing that would have warned her against me.

The clackity-clack of her shoes slows down. She pats down her puffy coat. Her cheeks are red from the run, or from embarrassment that it turns out I'm this kind sap looking out for upright customers like her. Lucky for her, I can shake that embarrassment out of her so long as I say it with enough conviction.

"Here," she says.

I'm a step away, my hands balled into fists still.

"I'm-I didn't realize. I'm..." She can't say sorry. People like her never can.

She hands me a receipt with her well manicured hand. French nails. I don't know how I know that, maybe I dreamt it once. I bet she's never had to think about losing an appendage for a dose of REM.

"Says here you got a nightmare. Can I see the pouch?"

Who in the hell can afford this shit and pays for a nightmare? Gotta control my hands from shaking. I'm a sweeper, not a scavenger. I gulp, seeing she bought enough for three REM cycles. That's a full night worth of dreams. I've never seen a catalog go up so high.

Inside the pouch, the powder's packed to the top. The real sweepers are getting closer, I need to hurry. I swipe some, make it look like a regular test. Feel the rub of dreams between the pads of my fingers. What does fancy-pants-french-nails know about how they do sweeps? Squat.

"Looks to be right. Can't be too careful these days, yaknow? Is it your first time having one of these?" I ask because I want to play my role to a T.

She nods, biting her lower lip thinking it's sexy—it ain't. "I wanted something different," she says.

"Enjoy." The real nightmare she needs is dreamlessness. Then maybe she won't go mouthing off.

I turn as if I'm heading back to join the boots. When I'm far enough away, I wipe the spice off my fingers—out from the deep groove of my nails—into a napkin and pound it out of there. I'm dizzy thinking how much I got. Still need to make it home.

Catalog # 104345822H: Psychological horror. A focus on emotional and mental states to disturb and unsettle the dreamer even long after waking.

If Marzena and I can stretch it out, I can get a full night's rest and REM. Luxury of luxuries.

I'm cutting through Central to get home faster.

"We sell one dream, we sell four. You wanna dream? Drumm's got score." The guy's not there anymore. I look inside, trying to spot him through the windows when I notice his voice blasting through the speakers. I'll bet Drumm's recorded it without him knowing. As if they haven't taken enough of our dreams.

I was wrong about their display. It's a reminder to us foreigners what we once got for free and now have to pay for out of pocket. A glimpse that under the laws of supply and demand anything can be made into a commodity with the right entrepreneurial spirit.

The Sandman display is off now. Good. Who needs it? I'm rich now, rich as I'll ever be and don't need fake powder to make me feel human.

I can't make any wrong turns or the sweepers can get me. Got to cut through Fenway, through Kensig, down Moshulug. The street names are blurring, my hearts racing because I got something worth stealing. I'm too poor to wish it weren't nightmares I had. Any dream is better than none.

I'm tripping over my own laces till my face kisses the ground and for a brief impact I think of Marzena's lips meeting mine there. The ground's wetting with something too dark to be rain. My palm's bleeding and throbbing. It'll heal. And if I can take a little nip from the napkin, it can feel healed right now.

Catalog # 1043459031: Nostalgia: Family Edition.

I'm in our apartment. The hovel we pay so much more for than it's worth. The wind's blowing and howling as loud inside as it does out. The buffer against the weather is the buffer you can afford.

"Marzena?"

She's not on the cot where I'm sure I left her. Not a strand of her beautiful red locks left for me to tease out.

It's a small place, nowhere to hide. People have closets bigger than our entire flat. Her coat's gone from the hanger, and her clothes, and her toothbrush. She's left no trace. Even the pillow that should smell like her, should smell like sourdough bread and tang, doesn't. I sniff and smell the street through the sheet, through the feather downs.

"Marzena?" I'm yelling for her now. Loud enough neighbors can hear through the paper-thin flaps that pass for walls. I don't care.

She's real. My real. My love. The only thing I have left from home. I'm hunting dreams more for her than me.

The walls are banging, drywall so weak and thin I can see the outline of my neighbor's fists through it. Like a fetus through pregnant skin.

Bang bang bang.

"Shut up! Some of us want to sleep, whatever that sleep is." That'd be neighbor 1N yelling.

I bang back to keep my walls from caving in. To distract from the thoughts there's no getting away from. I clutch at my napkin of nightmares. Marzena's real, real now and not a dream I once had; not a romance I needed and can't find since. Not the home I wanted and had to leave behind.

It's nightmares from dawn to dusk. I can't do it, do *this*, on my own. Without her. Even if she's a false reality I cling to, to make it through the day. I need to keep dreaming. I stuff the nightmare in my mouth to lick it clean.

My cheeks are wet, getting wetter like it's raining down my ceiling. Even though I know it's not. I'm not even on the top floor. Eyes can't rain and dream hunters don't cry when they score.

Catalog # 10448535G: Deep Desires: Wish it was More Than Dreams
Time remaining: 0 min.

UNTITLED, WITH DEMON
JOE KOCH

I want you to know, the girls escape in the end. That way you won't have such a hard time handling what I need to tell you or tolerating those men yelling in the next room. You freeze when you hear them, too, just like me. We've both been trained. The door is *right there*, less than fifteen feet away, but we both wonder *what if?* What if we don't make it to the road? What if we make it, but nobody comes in time? Or worse, what if someone comes driving down that long dirt road in the middle of nowhere, ghost town, U.S.A. and it's one of *them* again, the men from the city with the gold crosses and hairy chests?

What if it's an excuse for them to cut off another finger or pull another tooth? What if this time, they cut off something worse?

They've left us alone at the big table in the kitchen, near the back door of the old farmhouse, and it's not locked because the yelling started the moment Henry burst in, covered in blood. We've both stopped eating our dinner: the usual, something out of cans. Something runny that smells like rotten fish.

What if?

Should we?

Are you scared?

Our eyes can talk without our voices. We've known each other so long, been through the same suffering and indoctrination, except for the naked part; that's your job, because you're older, you're blonde, and you have the kind of body that the men understand. I don't make sense to them. *It's your fault we're here* my eyes say to you across the big table. I'm daring you to leave, hating you because you can.

My legs, I say. I'll slow you down too much.

Hurry, before they stop.

What do you care? I'll stall so you get a head start. I'll tell them you're in the bathroom. You threw up again.

I'll tell them *you* threw up.

No you won't. I know you. You'd tell them the truth.

I can't leave you alone.

Okay, but you first.

The yelling in the next room shakes the walls. Empty cans piled in the sink rattle and jump. The floor flutters beneath our feet. An earthquake erupts from the center of the tenement where we suddenly find ourselves living in safety together instead of the old farmhouse from our childhood. I see the panic shoot through your eyes like it did when we were kids, and I scuttle around the small dining nook of our cozy apartment to crouch by your side and wrap you in my arms.

Your shoulders tremble in my grasp like weak twigs. I cover your skeletal claws and settle them in your lap. The doctor says you need to eat more, but there's only so much I can do. I won't force you.

Okay; we're okay, I soothe. It was just another one of those trucks.

Garbage days or when snowplows pass up and down the street in winter are the worst. For your health, we should live somewhere quiet and trigger-free, but who has money for that? We do our best; together always, like twins. I cradle you like when we were kids.

Except my arms can't stop you from shrinking from me in your chair, shrinking somehow into something smaller than the emaciated woman you've grown into, shrinking into a leathery effigy of a dead or dying child too scared to run even when the door is wide open. Another blanket doesn't stop your shaking. You look like a creature spun inside a cocoon, webbed within my arms as I enfold you close.

Your curling fingers protrude. They remind me of a monkey's paw. By your shaking I know you're the same; the girl from long ago who didn't leave me, even after all our bickering. I relax my grip and the table grows large again like the big grey table back at the farmhouse from our childhood.

Our dining nook morphs into that dim, antique space. Repurposed from an old barn door, the table where we were made to sit across from one another and eat our sickening rations every night was a rustic, over-sized bench hewn together by whoever lived on the property before Henry found the place abandoned and isolated behind a wall of pines. The table dominated a colorless kitchen left to fester. Vestiges of wallpaper haunted the plaster with splotches of round flowers indistinguishable from mold. One bare bulb over the sink glared behind your head, casting your shadow across my chair and making me large on the wall where I loomed, a ghostly grey giant.

Looking back in time with my compound eyes from the perspective of an adult, a survivor, the one who came through the trauma (unlike you, my poor Anne) I decide that the men yelling in the next room don't scare me anymore because in your shadow, I am forever a giant. The men with the gold crosses and the burning water don't scare me; because I have a body and a connection to you they don't understand. They can't hurt me. Every time they break off a finger or pull a tooth, I will simply grow another one for you.

Henry kept big jars of them down in the basement, in what he called the workshop. I know this because I snuck down there one night after everyone was asleep, when the house was quiet, the men were snoring, the moon was waning, the spiders were spinning, and my dearest doll Anne and I were locked up tight.

I decided then, as I watched a spider build a fresh web near a delicate cuffed wrist, that the physical limitations of our captivity depended upon a moral and spatial consensus which need not apply to me, because I was not born like you. Freed, I traveled by ethereal body with only the thinnest thread holding me to our corporeal state and drifted into forbidden sections of the house at will, unhindered by my weak and spider-thin legs. In the basement, I found Henry's workshop where he indulged his habits and his need to construct, invent, and collect. His many specimens preserved with a madman's care. The finger jar full of liquid. The tooth jar dry.

Viewing the devices he designed outside the context of their use, I found it hard to picture them in relation to normal human anatomy. But I know how they work, and so do you, Anne, especially the sex parts. That was your job because you were older, and blonde, and your body made sense to the men with the gold crosses and dark robes and hairy chests; but it was sex only for them. For us, it was another ploy to rip us apart.

They didn't understand the ways I intersect with you. Severing one strand of our web with its joints and fixtures causes momentary distress, nothing more. A broken thread I can soon repair. And I would spin upon you secretly, bringing us closer than kin. I'd draw the very tip of a single hairy limb less than half an inch above your skin. You'd giggle with the thrill of it, hairs prickling. We shared pleasures Henry and the cloaked men could never steal or sever.

Next on that night, I drifted into the chapel, leaving the workshop silent and undisturbed as I'd found it. The empty altar and heavy restraints languished, weirdly forlorn in semi-darkness. No one worked there to cure us. No chants vibrated in the air; no fog of incense choked me. Moving freely around the walls and ceiling, hanging upside down, I gazed at our vacant torture chamber, imagining us encased as we so often were by that red-carpeted and red-draped religious space. I can step outside the body and picture us below, still. Bloodied or sweating, held there womb-like, writhing but immobilized, buckled in, helpless, hooded as if beneath a placenta, locked as if behind a strong cervix; new things struggling to be born as one.

Anne, Anne, listen to me: I can unlock this tight muscle with the right key. You can be free, and you don't need to cower in your chair when the garbage truck goes by or when the neighbors fight. We're in a clean and cheap tenement apartment, and if we eat out of cans, it's never cat food. It doesn't smell like rotten fish. If those cans rattle in the sink with some structural agitation, that doesn't signal men's angry footsteps.

No priests are coming to punish us. Henry will not burst through the door, bleeding or burned. Anne, even on those terrible days when we hear harsh voices raging in the next room and their shouts pummel against our thin walls, they rarely call upon the power of Christ or the power of Satan; who are, at the logical end of any eschatology, nothing but long lost brothers pretending at war.

Staring ahead wide-eyed, shrinking in place, you freeze like we're back in the farmhouse at the big grey dining table that once was a door. Did you ever sit across from me in your wheel-less chair and disassociate into the wood grain, gazing down at the heavy planks and the drill holes where there was once a bolted handle, and think about opening that door and stepping through? In your imaginary escape, did you take me with you to the other side? As you sit and shake across from me, it's as if you never left that place, as if torture is a tether that holds your soul captive in the past, an indelible thread that keeps you stuck in its web.

Come with me. I'm scared.

You first, I say. My legs.

Don't try to trick me or anything.

How could you say that?

You have to promise.

Don't call me a liar.

Promise you're not trying to get me in trouble.

The girls escape in the end, even if you can't tell the difference between the future and the past anymore. I caress your trembling shoulders and pet your halo of soft golden hair that's gone to ivory. To anyone else you're a hideous, disheveled crone, but to me you're a perfect doll, the blonde to my black, the substance to my shadow. People would never think we're sisters except for certain nervous habits. The divot uniting us as demonic we keep hidden at the backs of our necks.

You didn't come by yours naturally, but by force. We were small then. You sat cross-legged on the floor and I worked from behind, braiding your hair. You giggled when I tickled your neck with a light touch, weaving and lifting and learning what made you laugh. Because your smooth neck had no mark, and because we loved each other dearly, because I'd chosen you and you agreed, I corrected the discrepancy to seal us as twins. I picked up the scissors from the bin of ribbons and combs beside you, took aim, and sank the point of the paired blades into the bone at the top of your spine.

"Mommy, something bit me," you screamed.

I scampered into hiding as she flicked on the light. You were her favorite, with your long blonde hair, emblem of everything right and good in the world according to the fairy tales she read at bedtime.

"What on earth did you do to your hair?"

She washed off the blood and fought the mangled mess of your braids. Disinfected the divot, bandaged it, and tucked you into bed. Spoke to your father behind your back about the blood on the scissors. They kept talking and pleading and crying with every new manifestation or wound.

It was hard for you to understand that I only wanted to help. I wanted you to be strong like me. It seemed so obvious. The way you struggled with simple tasks made me sad. I couldn't just sit back and watch, because I wanted the best for you.

The mark was my gift as this key is my gift. We're sisters now, even if we weren't born as twins, even if the red altar is made more red by our turning together in the lock. A devil dances deosil in the rolling of your agonized eyes, but cease your writhing, Anne. Be still in my cradling arms, and look across time through my compound eyes.

We gaze upon the body together from above, hovering upside down on the ceiling where we can see Henry's thinning hair, the ornate tips of the chanting man's hat, and the large, hairy-chested men's hairy backs. They've shed their black robes. Exorcism efforts this extreme are strictly hidden from official records, denied in formal investigations, and carried out far beyond the sanctified walls of their church. As far as anyone knows, none of this ever happened. You were never here.

Maybe you're making it all up. Maybe you wanted attention. You should be careful about putting wishes into words. Sometimes, things you can't see are close enough to hear. Just like you never know how many spiders or centipedes are in the walls behind the rotten flowers and rings of mold, you never know who might be listening quietly right behind you, cross-legged on the floor, teasing your soft golden hair.

Like brothers pretending at war, the men experiment with Henry's clever inventions. You're the only one who notices me, except when I visit Henry to make sure he's still hopelessly mad, and to thank him in the one way I can, with visions, desires, and ideas. I was already a ghost when I met him, a thing with funny legs no one cared for. He started out a squatter in this abandoned farmhouse. A wanderer I fed. Offer the space to the church, I said. They'll pay you off the books. Me and the men in robes go way back.

I hate you, you say with your eyes, but in your head it sounds like Latin.

You can't hate me, I reply. I'm your sister.

No you're not.

I'm your twin. I take care of you now that you're old and frail. You wouldn't leave without me. You'd never leave me here alone.

Right now, you say, shaking violently. We have to run. Hurry!

Anne, why would I want to run?

Your eyes clear, revealing abject horror. You freeze at the big grey table. You freeze in the apartment nook, seated in your opposite chair, the light behind you as always casting me into giant grey shadow. The room shakes with your struggle, quaking in and out of phase, a slingshot from the future to the past and then back.

As if seeing me for the first time, you whisper:

Who are you?

The tenement shakes, and you're old, but it's not the building with our cozy apartment. It's the farmhouse, and your body is shaking, not the room. You sit at the big grey slat table licking slime that smells like fish from the lids of empty cans. Your body trembles with age and ruin; it must be the power of some demon that's kept the body alive this long. It must be the power of some demon that makes men and priests helpless to help you, or save you, or set your shadow free.

It hovers across from you, cast upon the opposite chair and wall by the one bare bulb. In grey, it mimics your shape and movements as you quiver, your head bent to maneuver your tongue around the metal rims, fingers clawing across the table to clean out another can. In your shadow I'm twice your size with elbows like clattering bone and a bobbing grey web of wild, semi-translucent hair. The way your arms protrude freakishly and crookedly from the round hairy center, your shadow is a giant spider jiggering down the wall. In your shadow, I am forever a giant.

The back door is unlocked. Its hinges are broken. The weather has rotted the wood that held it in place. Leaves blow in, crunching under your bare feet in the kitchen as you forage. The robed men have not tortured you for months. The hairy men have not crushed you under their hairy chests. Even Henry, whose corpse you may soon resort to gnawing on before you starve to death, has finally lost all his carnal interest in your flesh.

The squatters who find your leathery remains in this chair will not see the spider shadow on the wall waiting to pounce. They will not see the many smaller spiders hatching behind the flowers and rings of mold on the walls.

The girls escape in the end, like everyone escapes, as ghosts. Without the satisfaction of revenge on Henry, the priests, or the men who paid under the table for a taste of demon sex; dead shadow twin, the black rot to your blonde light, my name an unspeakable reminder of our mother's grief and pain; they forced us apart. One of us had to die during birth, though even then I held you curled within my eight arms in the womb, cradled in shadow before your first breath.

Here you sit cradled again, rotting in a cocoon of cobwebs, nursed on botulism. Here is the key to put in the rusted lock in the slat of this big grey farm table and turn with your monkey paw to open the door. Use your imagination, like Henry did. It took a madman like Henry to help us escape this world through human cruelty, to unite us through tortures and death. Broken at birth, we will share our happy ending tethered. I was a ghost when I met him, and now, you are too.

HAND TO THE FIRE
AVRA MARGARITI

W hen the birds come, they bring lightning with them, carried in their beaks, tangled in their pinion feathers.

~

YOUR FATHER WAS, is, will be, an alcoholic.

When the birds come, the old man lives alone in a shack across town, by a coppice of corpse-pale aspens.

Your sibling calls from inside the bunker their spouse has secured for your family. Asks you to get in your car and fetch the old man before he manages to light himself on fire.

"Do you remember," you ask your sibling over the sound of screaming sirens, "what happened when I was thirteen and hit by lightning?"

Your sibling sighs. They don't speak the answer, which is, *the old man laughed at you.*

You peek outside your window where flashes of celestial light rage and blackbirds fly, dark as cumulonimbi, in the absence of a regular storm. This is a plague, an apocalypse, so poetically bizarre.

"He laughed at me," you say, but the phone is already dead. A parrot carrying a fork of lightning took the power out as it passed your window. Your eyeballs burn with the effulgent afterimage.

Yet, while other buildings go up in flames, your apartment remains intact.

So does your car. You drive. Both hands on the wheel, slow as you can, maneuvering around vehicles abandoned by their owners. Charred remains on the tarmac that could be machine or human or animal.

A man jumps into the road, points a gun at a sparrow swooping low—a trailing ribbon-lightning lodged in its diminutive beak. When the man shoots, the bird goes down, but so does its shooter. While the mangled sparrow chirps its last on the rainless tarmac, the man convulses with electricity, hand fused to his melting weapon.

You don't stay to watch. They all die, the ones hit by avian lightning, and none so far have transformed.

You remember being thirteen. How you thought your neighbor coming into your backyard was a playdate, perhaps even a secret date between boys. He was so nimble when he jumped over the rotten-wood fence separating you. The sneer on his face so beautiful when he tied you to the single tree standing tall in your backyard. When the storm came, a raindrop was cradled between his lips, split by his daddy's fist. Both fathers drunks, though only one an angry drunk.

And the angry drunk's angrier son left you there, laughing as you struggled against your binds and, despite the fear, how you wanted to kiss that raindrop turning pink and bright as a pearl with his blood.

Your neighbor went back home, in the dry not-safety of his home.

The rain came down harder, ozone-rich. You yelled then, calling out for your father, the only one who was home. The lightning came and the old man did, too. He stank of whiskey fumes even amid the rising scent of petrichor.

"Help!" you yelled, but he just stood there on the back porch, watching you like a rare animal showed up in his backyard.

When the lightning kissed your tree, it traversed branch and bark and flesh, setting you aflame from within, scouring you clean. The old man threw his head back into the drenched heavens and laughed.

"A hallucination," you tell your windshield, covered in black feathers and gray ashes. You must keep pumping the windshield wipers. Keep blinking the smog from your eyes. "The old man thought I was a liquor hallucination, a fake effigy burning in his backyard."

He went back inside, leaving you tied to the burning tree, tongue lolling like a dog's to let the rainwater douse you from within. When your sibling found you later, you had severe burns across your bubbling skin. And underneath, a network of wine-red scars like forks of lightning or tree branches spanning your entire body. You would learn later they are called Lichtenberg figures.

Your cell phone rings. You put it on speaker.

"Do you remember what the old man said to me?" you ask your sibling, using up the last of the battery as you drive. Your voice comes out strange, rattling with the once-bodies your car runs over. "When he saw the scars?"

Your sibling sighs, a susurration of static. "He said no one would ever love you. Are you at Dad's place yet? I don't know how much longer I can hold the shelter door open for you."

You believed him. For years, you believed him. That's why, when you were old enough to drive, it was the lightning you followed. A storm chaser, you tracked the boom of thunder and the spark of electrostatic discharges. Climbed to the greatest heights to greet the rain, the storm, *love me, lightning*. But though you stood with your arms wide open, wet to the bone, shivering to the marrow, the lightning missed you even as it kissed the oaks with fire. Scorned you, shunned you, refused to finish the job.

The way it does now, as you drive. Perhaps the old saying is true and lightning never strikes twice. The Lichtenberg scars on your body granting you immunity, an apocalyptic aegis.

"Are you still there?" your sibling asks, voice reedy with impatience.

"Remember?" you ask. "What the old man always said?"

"Hand to the fire," your half-sibling exhales, long-suffering.

From childhood until now, the two of you looked nothing alike. Mother cheated, that much was clear. And rumor had it was with the neighbor, another addict, an angry drunk. The one with the son who liked to tie other boys to trees during storms.

You remember the fights. "My hand to the fire," the old man used to say, "this boy is not my son." It was his way of saying *I solemnly swear*. "Hand to the fire, you did not sprout from my seed." Yet your half-sibling will never forgive you if you don't bring the old man to shelter.

A bird smashes into your windshield, cracking its hollow bones and the battered glass into forking patterns. The fissure matches the red scars on your arms while you clutch the wheel.

"Was I the one who summoned you?" you ask the dead bird. "There were magpies that day on the tree I was tied to. They flew away before the lightning struck. Worshipped the storm with their song."

Your car hits something bigger than a bird body. It skids, nearly falling off the road. You climb out on shaky legs, wishing you had a pair of sunglasses to protect your eyes from the blinding light, the birdwings flapping whirlwinds of dust and refuse.

The body of a young boy lies crumpled on the asphalt. Perhaps he was still alive before you hit him. Or perhaps he was just another boy burning like you once were. You bend down to close his glassy eyes. His eyelids are veined blue, not red like yours. Untransformed.

When the news broadcasts still worked, no known cases of avian lightning survivors had been reported. You, aberrant yet again. A fork of laughter splinters in your mouth.

"Are you still there?" your sibling asks, voice muffled through the ruined car.

You abandon your car and phone both, opting to walk the rest of the way through the inferno. The blackbirds soar all around you: harbingers of unnatural phenomena, winged messengers of the gods razing the earth. And you? Will you be the only one left to inherit their new world?

You walk. It's all you know how to do.

You chase the storm. It's what you were made for.

Carrion crows circle thick as clouds over the old man's shack. A leaning, crumbling building, the only place he could afford after you and your sibling sold the house, split the money. Went out into the world to make your fortunes.

You check the inside of the shack through the stinging stench of ozone and bird droppings. Empty beer bottles. Spoiled food. Meager furnishings and comforts. The back door hangs open, a toothless mouth. You go through, into the backyard facing the forest.

Unlike your old backyard where it all began, there is not one tree here, but many. Most of them burned or burning.

There's no such thing as a fire that happens once, lasts a second. You know this from your years chasing storms. Once lightning strikes, trees can smolder for hours, days, roots sizzling for weeks underground. Some will burn a lifetime.

Amid the dancing, deciduous inferno, the old man kneels bare and soot-covered on a bed of pine needles. He flails his arms, loose skin jiggling, as if he wants to fly too with the vultures circling overhead, illuminating his nakedness.

Yet the birds do not strike the old man, not yet. Your proximity has made them linger, beady eyes flashing with avian curiosity.

"Dad," you try to say, but it feels foreign in your mouth. "There's shelter," you say instead. "Let me take you there."

You watch the old man from the porch, reminiscent of when you were tied and trapped and burning, and the old man stood and watched.

Watched and laughed.

The old man has never been beautiful, but he is now, awash in ash and black feathers, his limbs tree boughs dancing in the wind. When spider lightning strikes nearby, it veins his skin with luminosity. He is a tree covered in cobwebs. He is the tree on which your bully, your crush, your maybe-half-brother—let you burn.

You smell the blaze now. The old man's. And your own.

There's so much alcohol in his system his body runs on gasoline, like sap bloodstreams a tree. For the first time, the old man turns around. He looks at you and really sees you, not an effigy or bastard son or liquor hallucination.

You raise your hand, and he does too. Almost as if you are waving at each other from a distance. Like you are the father calling your son in for dinner after his backyard playdate.

An eagle flies overhead, talon releasing lightning over the treetops. It strikes the old man's raised arm. *Hand to the fire, hand to the fire.* The old man is a supernova going up in brilliant flames. He is reduced to nothing before you can decide whether to grieve.

You cross the backyard and crouch over the charred pine needles where your not-father had once been. A seed is left in his place. When you grab it in your red-scarred hand, it's black and hot like a massage stone, and shaped like a spiderwebbed heart.

You bury the seed deep into the burning earth and don't stay to watch what will sprout from it.

THE LUTHIER
REBECCA HARRISON

S ilence is a monster. That's why I play violin. Ok, I'm being a tad dramatic. If I don't get in my six hours practise today, nothing is going to come for me. But try telling child-me that. Child-me was petrified of silence. Silence was a beast waiting to gobble me up. Mum and Dad and Miss Philpott just mistook my fear for commitment. Dedication. Most kids shy away from scales, but I fled to them. I could spend half an hour just in G Minor. I used to go through all the different kinds of scales, you know - dolce, appassionato, vivace etc. I loved them. They were all my friends. My friends who kept me safe from the silence.

You were the youngest person to ever record the Sibelius Violin Concerto, Clara. Was it a daunting experience?

I was eight! You'd imagine I'd have been daunted. Just a little kid in a Lion King t-shirt facing the mighty London Symphony Orchestra. Not to mention maestro Jarakan. But he just seemed like a kindly wizard. His hair was a dandelion clock. He held his baton like a gentle wand. I thought of him as musical Yoda. In the breaks, I played Bach for him, and afterwards, he said nothing, he just shook my hand. A Jarakan handshake! More precious than a kingdom. If he was Yoda, I was Luke Skywalker. At that time, I was in the grip of my nightmares, so we were all fighting the silence together. Warriors and the wizard. And I was the apprentice.

You have a reputation for rituals and eccentricity. Could you explain your rituals and the beliefs behind them?

How kind of you not to use the D-word! But don't hold back, I embrace it. Diva. I'm well aware they call me the Mariah Carey of the classical world. I'm just sad that, unlike her, I don't get baskets of puppies to play with backstage. All I ask is one bowl each of purple skittles, orange smarties, and black wine gums. Child me was just taking advantage of sweets on demand. Then it became tradition. It's a miracle I don't have false teeth.

The colour white embargo is a bit different. I was ten. It was the rehearsal for my Proms debut. There was a white banner. I was barely sleeping at the time. I dreamed of white sails. Huge, white sails above me, filled with silent wind. The banner brought back the terror of my dreams. I hid and wouldn't come out until they'd taken it down.

Have any other arts influenced your playing? Films or books?

I want to say the Brontes. After all, I did name my violins Heathcliff and Rochester. But the biggest influence was *Wickham's World of the*

Unexplained. It had a UFO on the cover which was fair dos cos 70% of the book was alien abductions. The little green men had been busy. The rest was ghosts. There was a terrifying double page illustration of Black Shuck the demon dog of Norfolk which I blue tacked together. But worst of all was The Mary Celeste. You know the story: the ship was found empty, no sign of the crew. What happened to them? Where did they go? I was petrified. And so began my nightmares of walking on the deck – white sails above me and silence, silence, silence.

~

"THAT'LL BE FORTY QUID, LOVE," the taxi driver said. I startled. Were we here already? I closed my magazine. "You're that violinist, aren't you?" Even if I quit music and spent six hours a day practicing small talk, I'd never master it. So, I thrust a fifty at him and fled into the rain.

I darted across the pavement, up the steps, rang the bell and huddled against the door. It was tipping down. A May monsoon. I rang the bell again. You can't hurry a luthier, but you can try. They don't go by hours and minutes, their clock is varnish drying, their calendar is rings in beech wood. My hair was getting soaked. Water dripped down my neck. I thumped the door. Finally, it opened. I hurried inside and scrambled out of my sodden coat.

Then I could study him. Yes, he was typical of his species: his eyes were large and patient; his hands were narrow and wise. He told me his name, but I didn't catch it. Not that it mattered, I wasn't here for him, I was here for her.

And as he led me to his workshop, he spoke of Beethoven in priestly tones, but I hardly listened. My heart was presto. I was about to make a new friend. I'd never met a violin I hadn't won over, and some of them had been real grumps. Imagine sulking for nearly three hundred years, and you have imagined the life of the Vieuxtemps

Guarneri. We stepped into the smell of varnish and peace. Violin torsos lined the walls. Fingerboards and necks hung from the ceiling. Amber light slid from a stained window.

And there she was: in an open case, pale against the black velvet. A true lady. Mysterious and elegant. Knights would've sworn oaths to her, heroes would've slain dragons for her. As for me? I just wanted to play her. Our conversation opener would be Bach's Chaconne. My heart was prestissimo.

"My first time working with reclaimed wood," he said. Had he been talking all this time?

"She's beautiful," I said. And she was. The amber light moved gently over her varnish as if awed. Her strings shone silver. An ache began in my chest.

Violins have souls, immortal souls, and hers was newly arrived from that celestial world. The same realm which had been home to all the great concertos, or as I called them, my friends. She was austere and pure. She had no time for me. But it can't have been fun for her, dwelling in this dinghy workshop with only the luthier for company. His monk's eyes were on me.

Ok, so he was her creator, but still, what a killjoy.

"Would you like to hold her?" he said. I could only nod. He raised her from the black velvet. My heartbeat was forté. And then she was in my arms, and I was lifting her to my neck, feeling the cool of ebony beneath my fingers. But still she wanted nothing to do with me. If she'd had wings, she would've flown away.

"A bow?" I asked. He shook his head.

"You shan't play her until the concert."

"I have to."

"Not if you are what they say you are." A judgement hung in his priest's voice. "The violinist of the century needs no practise. If that's not you..." His narrow hands swept over her, took her from me, laid her on black velvet.

"It is me."

"Good." He closed the violin case. "I'll bring Mary to you on the Last Night. Not before." And then I was following him back along the hall. His pilgrim's steps were loud. His back was as solemn as evensong. No wonder Mary was standoffish, she'd learned from the best. I was guided into the rain without a goodbye.

That night I dreamed of sails. White sails. White sails filled with wind. Silent wind. Wind that smelled of salt, that chilled my arms, that pulled at my hair. The wind had hands that ran cold down my spine. It put its fingers in my ears. I fought but it held me, and I would not look up, but it made me. The white sails. Terror iced through me. And then the wind let go of me and I ran. Down the deck. But I saw no one and I heard no one. And I couldn't outrun the sails. Always above me, always filled with wind, always the cruel silence. Then I woke.

Tchaikovsky was my champion and my knight. My knight who chased the nightmare, who slayed it on a hilltop. And I ran alongside his steed, my feet allegretto. I didn't pause after the final note, I barely breathed, I was back at the beginning, and we were swift. No metronome could've caught us. We were a tempo all of our own. And in the slow movements, our song was so full it strained the seams of this world.

Good old Tchaikovsky triumphed. I played the concerto five times, then I slumped and set my bow down. Morning laughed in the sky. Still holding Rochester, my violin, I opened a window. Traffic was the dawn chorus of the city. The cars jammed and grumbled, the kids chattered their way to school, and there were no white sails above. Only clouds. Only planes. What a fuss about a daft dream. It was just as well I was a genius because I really was a wally. Anyway, I needed to practise The Lark Ascending for the Proms. I didn't want to risk perishing under the Lady Mary's disdain. So, I turned from the city, and I played the pastoral skies.

But I dreamed white sails. Again. And again, the following night. Until all my nights were sails and all my days, song. I rose before the larks, and I rose with the Lark. Vaughan Williams' Lark. I flew high enough that I looked down on my terror and saw it as a small thing. Positively piddling. A field mouse of fear. But I knew I couldn't fly forever. Because sleep always came, and it carried me beneath the white sails, and it held me there until morning.

Then suddenly I was just two weeks from Last Night. And where was the Lady Mary? Stewing in the workshop dinge? Silent in the luthier's monkish hands? She should've been with me. Soaring with the lark. These melodies were wings, were the sun breaking up clouds, were the fields rushing green below. I wasn't putting up with the luthier's nonsense, anymore. One of the perks of being a wunder-freak was you got what you wanted. Ok, maybe all I'd ever wanted was music and sweets and puns. But I'd got 'em. I'd even played The Messiah Strad. I wasn't going to let Lex Luthier beat me.

But being a wally had its drawbacks. I hadn't kept the scrap of paper with his address. I hadn't even paid attention to his name. Let's face it, I was no Angela Lansbury. How was I going to find him? Sure, I could ask my manager, but he'd already warned me not to antagonise the creative genius.

Rude.

I was the genius around here. What would Angela have done? I petitioned Google. There were loads of luthiers in London. I scoured the names but recognised none. Obviously, I'd paid even less attention to his sermon than I'd realised. I clicked and I scrolled, and I zoomed in on workshops. It was hopeless.

Maybe I was weird, but there was something about Mary. She was a celestial, a new. Her soul was close enough to that realm to lift me out of reach of the silence forever. No more nightmares. No more terror. No more white sails.

Eureka. The taxi firm's number was still in my phone. I called them and befuddled them good. But once I told them I was Clara Buckle, they got it.

"You going to pay us in wine gums, love?"

"It's the only currency I carry," I replied. And then I was in the back of the taxi. Wimbledon was on the radio. July danced through the city. I pressed my face to the window, and watched the crescendo of sunshine and crowds.

"Here we are," the taxi driver said. He pulled over to the side of the road. It was just a row of smug Georgian townhouses.

"This isn't it."

"56 Wellbringer Drive, love."

"I need to go where you took me." My heart was agitato.

"You're here." He gestured. I shook my head. My hands were trembling. There were winding steps, falling steps, and the door was black, and the roof was squat. It wasn't here. But maybe? Could it be round the corner?

"Can you wait?" I jumped out and ran. I ran but the townhouses went alongside me and there was no corner, only a curve, and white and white and white. The sun was harsh in my eyes and on my back. Where was the luthier? Was he real? I wouldn't have imagined someone so like incense and judgement. But his house wasn't here. I stood aside as a couple of glamour grans bustled by laden with designer shopping bags. Then I dragged back along the street. "Can you take me home, please?" I didn't meet the taxi driver's eye in the mirror. Was I going bonkers?

When I got in, I phoned my manager.

"Am I playing on Rochester at the Proms?"

"We've been over this, Clara. You'll get the violin on the day. Don't go winding up that genius or you'll ruin everything." Rude. I was the only genius in the village. I blustered something about the front door and hung up. So, there was a luthier and a violin. Mary was real. She had to be. How else would I soar out of the clutches of the silence? How else would I be free from those wretched dreams? I wanted to never again walk on that deck. Never again look up at the white sails. But sleep caught me in its talons and took me to the ship.

And then it was the Last Night of the Proms. My third Last Night, if you please. Not that I'm showing off. The Royal Albert Hall was merry with crowds. Flags waved. Great clouds of chatter floated to the heights. I wore an Albion green dress. And I clutched Rochester in his case. But I hoped for the Lady Mary. Would she save me? My hands were so full of quavers, it hurt to keep them still. They ached to play. But I had to wait. The Lark was second to The Planets. The conductor raised his baton, and the orchestra played Mercury. Then Venus was heaven over the heads of the audience. The violins were the winds of Mars. I listened beneath Jupiter's jollity but heard no pilgrim's step, no priest's voice. Where was the luthier? Saturn's stern mystery awed me. And then I was floating in Neptune's oceans. Tonight, I would feel another ocean beneath my feet, and I would feel wind and I would look up at white sails. The Lady Mary would not lift me away. Fear moved in me. Pluto was a magician's countdown. Time was at my feet.

There was a tsunami of applause. Five thousand plus folk clapped and cheered. And I was next. Just me and Rochester. I opened his case. My faithful, reliable Rochester. I reached for him.

Footsteps. Reverential footsteps.

I spun round. The luthier. I closed the case, but his monk's gaze was a judgement upon it.

"You thought I wouldn't be here," he said. Mary. The Lady Mary was in his wise hands. Pure, austere. A celestial. A new.

"I'm sorry," I whispered. I hung my head. He was not going to let me play her now, not now he knew my lack of faith. I'd been tested. And I'd failed. Sorrow flowed through me. Then he laughed.

"They're waiting for you." I felt the coolness of pale varnish and I looked up and he was pressing Mary into my palms. The Lady Mary. "I'll be watching." He nodded. And then I was taking the steps and walking out onto the stage. There was a riot of applause. And then a great surround sound rustle of sweet wrappers. The Last Night crowd loved their jokes. And I loved my sweets. Just call me the dentist's violinist.

Maestro Schwarz welcomed me, and the London Philharmonic stamped their feet. Then hush and the baton.

Albion rose about me, rolling green and lush. I lifted Mary and placed the bow on her strings. I closed my eyes. We were wings into the dawn. We soared higher and higher, and the orchestra glided, sunlit and swift. And then we were solo, our song sweet and pure. Celestial. New. And I knew the silence could never clasp me again, could never reach me again. I was free. I flew. But still solo, circling high. Why hadn't the orchestra rejoined me?

I opened my eyes. The orchestra was gone. I stopped my bowing. Row after row after row of deserted seats. The violins, the cellos, the basses, the wind section, the brass, the percussion. All gone. I looked to Maestro Schwarz, but he wasn't there. And then beyond his podium to the audience. But the hall, the Royal Albert Hall, was empty. Flags were strewn on the floor. I saw no one and I heard no one.

But then I felt eyes on me. I turned. The luthier was smiling. Smiling at me. Terror gripped me. Mary. He made her from reclaimed wood. Wood from the sea, from the ship. The Mary Celeste. A wind touched me. And it smelled of salt. And I did not want to look up, but it made me.

White sails. Great white sails flew over me, over the hall. And in them was the silence.

EMILY'S TEETH
CASSANDRA DAUCUS

"Josh, stop."

A request and one gentle push on his shoulder was all it took. Josh stopped sucking hickeys into Emily's neck, and shuffled backwards to the end of her bed. Emily still lived in the dorms, but they made it work. This was their fourth time hanging out and their third time messing around on Emily's twin mattress.

Josh hoped tonight would be the night.

"What's up, Em? Everything okay?"

She swiped her hand across her swollen lips, flushed from the minutes she and Josh had spent making out. Her cheeks, too, but that might just have been because the room was warm.

"I'm okay," Emily answered. "I just... I want..."

"Whatever you want, babe," Josh said, after her sentence trailed off. "We can slow down if you want."

"No, that's not it." Emily answered quickly, her face's hue verging on scarlet. A blush, then. "Take those off." She tugged at his waistband. "I want to see you."

"No," he said, playfully, smiling. He touched the cuff of her jeans. "You first, Em—take your clothes off. Then *you* can come over."

She froze, gaping at him. Josh's stomach turned and he worried he'd made a poor calculation, but he chuckled. "Fair's fair."

Emily's expression shifted from a soft heat to cold fear. It was like being stabbed in the heart with an icicle.

"No," she said, softly, shaking her head and angling to slip off the bed. "No."

"Okay," he said, but reached for her hand anyway. She paused at his touch, then allowed him to pull her over and into his lap. She sat limply, head on his shoulder.

Not exactly how Josh was hoping to spend his Friday night, but it could've been worse.

"We can just stay like this, if you want," he offered after a few minutes of silence.

"No, that's not what I want." She turned around to face him. "I want to go down on you. Why won't you let me?"

"Oh." He hadn't expected that. "Only if you let me go down on you first."

"Nope." She pulled away again, but he held on tight and she gave up quick.

"Come on, Em. It's only polite for me to go first."

"You won't like it." She reached out with the fingers of her left hand and tangled them with his. "You *really* won't. Please."

"Why are you afraid?" Josh murmured, turning in an attempt to catch her eye, but she kept her gaze on their joined hands. "I'm not going to hurt you. And I like giving oral. It's not exactly a chore."

"I know," Emily said quickly, finally gazing up at him, her eyes shining with unshed tears. "It's just—I'm afraid I'll hurt *you*."

Josh did his best to hide his surprise.

"Why would you hurt me?"

"It's not about *why*," she grumbled, "I don't *want* to. I just know I will."

Josh waited. He had so many questions, but wasn't sure how to ask them. So he held her and waited, and after a few moments she took a breath and spoke again, squeezing his hand as though drawing on his strength.

"Do you remember Jared Kline?"

"Jared, yeah. I knew him a little; we lived in the same dorm freshman year."

A single tear trekked down her cheek. "I know what happened to him."

Jared had disappeared midway through sophomore year; walked away from a frat party to take a piss in the woods and never came out. They hadn't found his body, he'd never touched his bank account again. Just gone.

"What happened?"

She took a shuddering breath. "I was in the woods, too. He tried to talk to me, and when I wasn't interested, he attacked me, and I—hurt him."

Sweat bloomed on Josh's upper lip.

"I didn't mean to! I didn't know!"

"Did he hurt you?" He worked to keep his voice steady. It was hard to imagine the smiling, goofy guy from freshman dorm doing anything to hurt this sweet girl.

"He—" she paused, searching for the right word. "He tried. But I hurt him first."

She sniffled, and let go of Josh's hand so she could wipe the tears from her cheeks. Josh helped, with his fingers and his lips, and by the time her face was dry she was smiling.

But Josh was curious. He had to know.

"Tell me how you hurt him."

"It was my teeth," she said, curling into a ball on his lap. At least, Josh was fairly sure that was what she said.

"Your *teeth*?" Josh repeated, and she nodded, chin knocking into her knees. "You bit him?"

"No, *they* bit him. They *ate* him. My teeth. Not my mouth teeth. My—*other* teeth."

Josh swallowed around the lump in his throat. *Other teeth. Ate him.*

"You mean..." he pointed down. Emily scrunched her face and nodded. "Oh." He needed to think about what to say next.

"Do you believe me?"

"I believe you, Em."

"You... you do?" She blinked.

"Why wouldn't I believe you?"

"Because... I mean..."

"You've never lied to me before," Josh interrupted. "Why would you lie to me now?"

She lifted her shoulders and slowly lowered them again. "You're not afraid? Or, like, grossed out?"

Josh laughed. "I'm not. It's interesting. Special, even. I mean, *you're* special, so I'm not surprised your pussy is special, too."

"Oh." Emily unballed herself. "I hadn't thought about it like that."

Josh took a chance and gave her a kiss. She giggled and kissed him back.

"So, can I see them?"

"Oh." Emily contracted again. "I don't think that's a good idea."

"Let's think this through logically, Em. You don't want me to see your teeth, because you're afraid they'll eat me the same way they ate Jared."

"Mhmm."

"But he attacked you. He hurt you."

Emily shuddered, and he tightened his hold, like his arms could draw the pain right out of her. "He raped... he tried to—"

Josh shushed her. "You don't have to tell me, unless you really want to."

"I don't," she shook her head. "I really don't."

"My point," he said quietly, almost at a whisper, "is that you didn't want him, and I bet your teeth could tell. Maybe they were protecting you."

"Maybe."

"So, maybe, if you're with someone you *want* to be with, your teeth will be okay with it."

"Oh." Emily relaxed again. "Maybe."

Josh leaned over and set Emily back on the bed. Gently, so gently, he straightened them both out, until they lay side-by-side on the narrow mattress.

She pulled him down for a kiss. Josh was fine with that. He was dying with curiosity, but he could wait.

A few minutes later, Emily nudged his shoulder again.

"Okay," she said, her eyes nervous but certain. "You can meet my teeth."

"Wow, okay. Awesome."

Josh scrambled to his knees, but Emily laid her hands on her waist before he could reach for her zipper.

"But! If I think something bad is going to happen, we stop. Okay?"

"Of course. Immediately."

Josh got off the bed, and Emily pulled off her T-shirt. She barely paused before she unbuttoned and unzipped her jeans, then kicked them across the room.

Once she was naked, Josh crawled between her legs and lowered himself to his elbows. At first she looked exactly as he expected—a clutch of dark curls that spread apart like a curtain when she lifted her knees, revealing slick, pink folds. He reached back to switch on the reading lamp clamped to Emily's desk. Her skin glistened under its soft illumination. He took a moment to angle the light so it aimed directly at her opening.

Josh thumbed Emily's outer lips further apart, and when she tensed he murmured, "I'm being careful. Relax."

"I'm relaxed." She didn't quite sound like she believed it.

"It's beautiful." Josh looked up at her. "Can I kiss it?"

She nodded, a quick, sharp movement. "Just be careful, don't put your tongue in."

Without taking his eyes off her face, he lowered his lips. He had to maneuver a bit to get his lips around her clit, but once he did he gave it a little suck, then a proper kiss. Finally he darted out his tongue and swirled around it a few times. With each movement Emily made a distinct noise, and bucked her hips up into his hands.

He gave her a grin. "I told you it's not a chore."

"I know." Her own smile was a relief. "It feels good."

"Good." He gave it another kiss, his eyes flicking down again. "You are a pretty thing, aren't you?" He cooed, and Emily gasped again as he traced his tongue lazily through her folds. After another minute he was ready to investigate.

"I'm going to look for your teeth now, I just want to see."

She sighed deeply and closed her eyes, laying her head back against the pillows.

He didn't have to go far to reach the slick, flushed pocket of skin that led into her body. The teeth weren't immediately visible, so he took a chance and brushed the flat of his tongue just over the opening. She tasted good, salty and musky, with a slight metallic undertone. Emily gasped, tensed, and reached down. Josh grasped her hand with his own, leaving his other to hold her thighs apart. She gripped him so tight it hurt, but he could tell it calmed her. He hummed quietly until her grip loosened and he could try again.

Josh nudged her open, enough for a glimpse. The teeth weren't immediately identifiable; at first he thought there was a solid barrier just inside her opening. It was gray, and shiny, and as he leaned forward he caught that metallic scent again, more strongly - the thing was *metal*. Metal, inside Emily?

"I see them," he said softly, and her grip tightened. "But they don't look like teeth. They're metal."

"Metal!" Her voice was a confused frown.

"You've never looked?"

"No. I just know they're there."

Josh shrugged. "Metal's cool." He pressed a kiss against the soft skin of her inner thigh.

"I have no control over them." Emily explained. "But I feel them moving, sometimes."

Josh was fascinated. "Do they open for your period?"

"I've never had a period. I think whatever they are makes that impossible. Does that bother you?"

She sounded worried again, and Josh hated it. He kissed her thigh again. "Nope."

He pushed his thumb further to open her up a little bit more. There was a little ridge of skin coming out from her walls. They appeared to hold the barrier—the teeth—in. He imagined he could see markings etched into the shiny circle; a delicate pattern of diagonal lines that formed a zig-zag line over the metal disk. It was oddly attractive.

"Well, they're closed now. But I'm gonna..."

Feeling a bit silly, Josh got as close as he could, pressed a quick kiss to the soft skin just above her opening before lowering his lips and crooning inside.

"Hello. Hello, teeth. Can you hear me?"

He glanced up. Emily's eyebrows furrowed but she smiled, just a little. Even if nothing happened with Emily's teeth, at least he could make her smile.

He peeked back inside. "I see you, you pretty things. Has anyone ever told you that you're beautiful? Emily's beautiful too. You're so strong, just like her. Are you there to protect my Emily? Is that what you're doing?" And without thinking he reached in with his pinky - his smallest finger - and stroked once against the metal barrier. It was smooth and hot and silky, and he gasped and tore his finger away when the metal vibrated under his finger.

"Woah!" Emily, propped up on her elbow, stared down at him in surprise.

"Did you feel that?" Josh asked, but it was clear from the look on her face that she had.

Emily nodded. "That was pretty cool. Try talking to them again."

When Josh looked back inside the metal barrier was still there, but the formerly solid surface had separated, one half edging into the top of the tunnel, the other half edging down. Josh thought of sliding doors, only these were jagged and razor sharp.

"I can feel you," he murmured, "I know you're there. I know you can hear me. Emily is here. Do you like Emily? I like her." The metal vibrated again, as though excited, and the teeth slid open further until all that was left were several sharp points peeking out of the top and bottom of that ridge.

"They're opening!" Josh said.

"Oh Josh. I... I didn't tell you everything."

"Your little mouth is open." He gazed into her vagina, too entranced to listen.

"Josh!"

"What?"

She bit her lip. "I didn't tell you. There's something behind the teeth."

Something cold and wet glided over Josh's thumb, and he looked down. A tiny black tentacle reached for him, out from behind the teeth.

"Oh, hello there." The tentacle waved to him, then retracted into the darkness. He smiled up at Emily. "I made a friend!"

Tears sprang to her eyes; the happy kind. "They like you!"

"Everybody likes me," Josh said confidently. "You like me?"

"I like you a lot."

"You like your teeth?"

Emily threw her head back and laughed. "I fucking love my teeth. Now get naked. You *promised*!"

Josh had wanted to go down on her first, and he hadn't exactly completed the task, but that was okay. He could do it later. He hopped up and ripped off his clothes as quick as he could.

When Emily saw what was between Josh's legs, her jaw dropped.

"Josh! You... you—"

Josh's black tentacles beckoned to her. "Are you angry? They've been so excited to meet you."

"No! I'm not angry." She shook her head and chuckled. "You could have just told me."

"I thought you'd hate them."

"No, silly, I mean *after* I told you about mine."

"Where's the fun in that?"

She didn't have a reply to that. Instead she held open her arms and her legs. A tentacle peeked out from her vagina, and gave a little twirl.

"Come on, Josh!" Emily said with a laugh. "Let's figure out how we can make this work."

She didn't have to ask him twice.

BAD VIBRATIONS
NADIA BULKIN

My most vivid memories of the house in Morganville are not of the room I slept in from the ages of nine to eighteen or the holiday meals we had under the dining room chandelier, but, ironically, of the room I spent the least time in: my grandfather's study.

I feared his study, and not just because my grandfather kept it locked. Even as a child I knew its energy was dark. Menacing. It was partly the dark mahogany panels, which felt much heavier than the linen white paint that coated the rest of the house, but mostly it was the décor. Clay masks frozen in mid-howl; stone weapons still sharp enough to cut. And worst of all, the figurines. Humans, or at least humanoid, all less than twelve inches high and warped, stretched, into unnatural poses and proportions. Some seemed to me to be in pain, but others gave the distinct impression of being in ecstasy. In thrall.

The one I call "the dancer" was one of these. Her face was fiendish, though her body looked broken, and if you looked her in her wooden eyes the air would be sucked from your lungs. And while she sat on a bookshelf caked in dust, she herself was always clean.

Odd taste, my mother said, though my father said his father was simply cultured. As I would come to understand later, it was my father that was right.

My grandfather, Burnett Frazer, earned his doctorate after the war. His expertise was in the intersection of art and religion, with a particular interest in pre-industrial human totems that he collected on research expeditions to remote areas of the world. You may have heard of his book, *The Totem Against The Void*. He received tenure at Galton University, became chair of the anthropology department, and retired as Professor Emeritus. He was a distinguished man.

One Christmas—we always spent Christmas in Morganville—my older sister Hattie dared us to enter the study unsupervised. We were caught, naturally, but not before we lifted our hands like dowsing rods to find the source of the room's eeriness and confirmed to each other that it was the dancer. I must pause and make this clear: the discomfort this statuette created was not merely aesthetic, but physical. We asked our grandfather about her—the lady with the bendy back, as Hattie said—and he said it was from Torca. For years I thought he'd made the name up. Remember, I was a child. "That one's special," he said, "so don't touch it."

We didn't know the true strength of the dancer's bad vibrations until my grandfather died (a freak slip on an icy sidewalk) and we moved into the Morganville house to care for my grandmother, who was much more fragile than she appeared.

My father was actually the first to notice, though he blamed it on tinnitus: the dancer gave off a buzz. Most nights, it was just a faint hum, a prickle on the skin that we could drown out with a loud television or a drink. Some nights, though, she was a roar. An electric saw.

On a hunch, Hattie looked up Torcanese magic online and found blurry pictures of weather-beaten stone idols, purportedly objects of worship and maybe sacrifice. My mother, who had been raised evangelical, panicked. She consulted a local pastor who refused to lay hands on the dancer, and then a demonologist who insisted on latex gloves. *Wicked hands*, they both said. *This was made by wicked hands*.

~

THESE WORDS—*MADE by wicked hands*—haunted my mother. Over the next few years, she grew increasingly agitated by the dancer's presence. She could not abide the thought that she was living with a symbol of evil.

She tried cleansing first: ritualized prayer, salt lines, burnt sage. When these had no effect, she resorted to hiding in her bedroom, numbing herself with any drug a doctor would prescribe. Once she disappeared for three straight days. I don't know what impact her absences had on Hattie, but given what happened, I do wonder.

Hattie started going by Harriet in college. She started wearing chokers and chains and she fell under the influence of a pack of unfortunate snarling practitioners of Luciferianism. You know the type—pessimists who worship all the bad vibrations the world has to offer. It dismayed my parents, but they still saved her a place at the dining room table until she snuck some of these friends of hers into the Morganville house to see the dancer for themselves.

It was never exactly clear to me who officially severed ties following this incident: Hattie or our parents. Our mother was jumpy enough by then that it was probably her. Ultimately, though, I think even Hattie understood that she was to blame. The metaphysical line around our grandfather's study wasn't drawn in chalk. It was welded with iron. It was non-negotiable.

You're probably wondering why none of us thought to just throw the dancer out, if she was causing our family such distress. And yes, my father kept her longer than a reasonable man should have, though I understand why he didn't want to believe that the brilliant Burnett Frazer had unwittingly brought something evil into our lives. But he did try.

But she wouldn't leave. Our friends didn't want her. She was the only object left at a yard sale. My father even put her in the dumpster —an immensely painful concession on his part—only for me to come home from school and find her waiting on the front porch, rattling and seething and practically *demanding* re-entry into the house.

Ultimately, my father sealed the dancer inside five nested boxes, locked the boxes in a leather trunk, and shoved the trunk under my grandfather's desk. He'd offered to put it in the basement, but my mother didn't want it near the Christmas decorations.

I told my father that the vibrations got better, after that. I may have just been trying to console him; the older I get the more I see that the body has uncountable ways of fooling itself. I do know that the stoic smile he gave me was restrained, because my mother was still taking her meals upstairs, cocooned in blankets and painkillers and anything else that would protect her from the rumble of the dancer's inhuman engine.

WANTING to make up for my parents' disappointment over Hattie, I dedicated my teen years to academic achievement. My grades were such that my application to Galton University—my grandfather's former employer, my father's alma mater—was accepted, early decision.

I must admit that it was thrilling, taking classes in a hall that matched my surname and going to lunch with academics who idolized my grandfather. But it also pushed me, drove me, in ways that warped me more than I'd like to admit. My adviser would reference obscure papers that my grandfather had written and when

I expressed confusion, give me a cold sideways look. Like I gave him cause to doubt the power of either nature or nurture. It was painful.

In the interest of passing these implicit tests, I taught myself my grandfather's theories. His best known was the idea that totems—by virtue of being a physical representation of a personal intent—carry heightened sociocultural power. And it was under the premise of a term paper on this theory that I raised the subject of the cursed dancer with my adviser. I left out the gnarlier details. I would have had to joke about it to keep my nascent academic reputation intact, and I didn't want to make my family look like a clan of superstitious goons.

My adviser knew nothing about it. Apparently, my grandfather had written very little about Torca, despite having traveled there several times early in his career. "Maybe it's time you pick up the mantle," my adviser said, looking, for once, pleased instead of skeptical, "and find out for yourself what the dancer might signify. I for one would very much like to know why your grandfather never wrote about it."

But I wanted to prove that I deserved his last name. There is a deep insecurity that comes with being a "legacy"—a paranoia that you are only seen as a detached limb, a detached *digit*, of some larger being. I decided to put my spring break to good use and book a trip to Torca. If my grandfather had lived in fear of the dark, I told myself, he never would have gotten anywhere.

Was I nervous about what I might find? Yes. As the trip drew closer, a voice in my head that sounded much like Hattie grew from a whisper to a howl, reminding me that, even if I did not believe in curses, they might believe in me.

～

TORCA WAS NOT A LARGE COUNTRY—JUST a single volcanic island dotted with a spattering of towns. I hired a local, Tony, who must have found my request amusing until I showed him that I could indeed pay him handsomely to be my driver, translator, and seeker-of-statues.

I did not expect the quest to be easy. I knew from my grandmother that my grandfather would sometimes need to extend his field trips by weeks, coming home sleepless and sunburned and riddled with bacteria. For the first three days and two towns, I was even glad that our leads were unsuccessful; I hoped that meant the dancer truly was sacred.

But then came the witch doctor. I had impressed upon Tony that I was not only looking for a distinctly carved statuette but a cursed one, a magical item, a *totem*, and he finally took me to a bungalow at the far end of a beach with a papaya tree and a one-eyed dog in the yard. "This one," Tony said, wagging his finger, "this one will know."

But as I sat on a plastic folding chair in the witch doctor's living room, waiting for Tony to translate my request, I could not help noticing that there was no figurine—not even a single totemic object—in sight. I expressed my concerns to Tony, who expressed them to the witch doctor, who swatted her hand dismissively in a universal gesture that I understood even without translation: she had no need for such items. Apparently, her power was direct. Apparently, she thought totems were for amateurs.

Naturally, by this point I had become very frustrated, as well as overheated. I asked Tony to take me back to the hotel. Of course the car broke down just before we made it to the capital, and while waiting for a taxi, I wandered over to a street market that sold souvenirs. I wasn't really looking for anything to buy—maybe a tchotchke for my roommate, the only person who knew how I was spending my spring break—but then I turned a corner and saw something that I simply could not ignore.

The dancer. Dozens of her. Crowded on a display table between a herd of palm-sized wooden camels and rows of sloppily beaded coin purses. She was being sold, according to the sticker, for the price of two bananas.

These dancers weren't quite identical to ours—their expressions were cruder, barely formed instead of fiendish—but the resemblance was too great to have been an accident. I summoned the seller, demanding to know what the figure represented, and was met with confusion. It was just a beautiful woman, the seller said. And then he proceeded to try to sell me two for the price of one, saying it was very popular with tourists.

In my desperation I explained it all—that my grandfather had brought home a cursed object that looked very much like these dancers, that its powers were affecting the well-being of my family —and the damned man laughed. Laughed!

"If there is a curse," he said, "millions of you would have it." Except he did not use the word "you." He used the word for foreigner.

At this point, I knew the truth: I had been duped. Or rather, my grandfather had been duped—my brilliant, trail-blazing, globe-trotting grandfather—and so made fools of all of us. My limbs ached as if my blood was churning into concrete, and I was suddenly overwhelmed by the need to be away from all of these people, all of this horrific noise.

THE THIRTY HOURS it took me to fly home gave me plenty of time to think (and drink). When the car pulled up at the deserted arrivals zone, I decided not to take it to my dorm at Galton; I needed to see the thing, the dancer, the lie. It was past midnight by the time I was dropped off in Morganville. Which was perfect, I thought, because I hadn't yet thought of how to explain to my father what I was about to do.

After another drink in my grandfather's study, surrounded by his menagerie of gruesome curiosities that for all I knew he'd bought at various flea markets, I pulled out the leather trunk, tore open the boxes that caged the dancer, and threw her as hard as I could against an unadorned mahogany panel. She didn't shatter, the bitch. *Maybe* she chipped, but it was dark.

Five minutes later I heard soft footsteps outside the study. My mother? No—the frail figure in the doorway was older, smaller. I was surprised that my grandmother could still get around without her walker given what the doctors had told my father, but she was one of those little old women who seemed to run on the strength of her tenacity and willpower alone.

She reached for the dancer on the floor—I picked it up for her, knowing a fall would likely kill her—and then had me place it on a clear space on a premium shelf. Was that where the dancer used to stand before my mother insisted it be removed? I couldn't quite remember.

"I'm glad you took it out of the box," she said, "but don't be so clumsy. It's special."

"No it's not," I said. I was trying to be gentle, because this was her husband whose judgment I was disparaging. "It's just kitsch for tourists. They sell thousands of these." I gave her a little tap—more than a nudge, but not quite a thwack. "You're right, though, no reason to keep it in a box. No reason for Mom to hide from it or... for them to cut Hattie off over it."

"Oh, that's where you're wrong. It does have power. Your grandfather promised me that."

I paused before replying—I was wondering how to reason with someone whose mind was clearly withered—and she used my silence to ramble on, causing my alarm to grow with each word: "He took it to someone on that island. One of those witchdoctors. They can bless things with anything you want, he said. They can turn anything into a totem."

"What do you mean, took it?" I took hold of her shoulders to steady her, though at that moment I was myself feeling unsteady, overshot with adrenaline. "Took it, why, for what?"

Finally, my grandmother smiled. But for all its familiar warmth, the instinctive affection I felt when I saw her eyes glow, I knew it was a bad smile. A wicked smile. "To make sure we were all taken care of. Your grandfather went to school on the government's dime, remember. He didn't want any of us to rely on charity ever again."

Care. Such a soft word. It made me think of my father's attempts to care for my mother, my parents' attempts to rid themselves of the urge to care for Hattie. I withdrew my hands from my grandmother's shoulders; by that point, I was shaking worse than she.

"I couldn't believe your father tried to throw it out. My goodness. The moment I heard I called up Nina Klemperer and told her to dig it out of the trash straight away and give it back." Her wicked smile turned crooked and I realized she was attempting to make a joke. "I did worry that Nina might steal it. But I'm pretty sure the blessing only works for us. His kin."

My shakes worsened, churning anxiety into anger. "If he tried to bless us, then he did an awful job," I said, my lower lip trembling around that "aw" sound, "because that goddamn thing has given us nothing but grief!" I couldn't see my grandmother, couldn't see the masks or knives. Couldn't see anything except the dancer's wooden spine, curving like a snake. This time, when I grabbed her, I noticed that her spine fit ever so perfectly into my hand.

I threw her again. Harder. That time I broke her back.

Immediately, I wished I hadn't. With alarming speed, my grandmother's head fell forward – not as if she'd dozed off, but as if her neck had instantaneously liquefied. Within seconds this was followed by a quick drop of her shoulders, a disappearance of her legs as her body folded beneath her gown. It happened so fast that I didn't have time to cushion her fall.

And then the strangest thing happened, the thing that no one can explain: I fell too. Not because my body gave, but because the house did. The floorboards shifted, then snapped. The walls trembled, shaking off my grandfather's trophies. The ceiling opened for the world to fall, and in this catastrophe, I only survived thanks to an instinct that ran deeper than the blood of my cursed kin: like a hunted lizard slithers beneath a rock, I crawled under my grandfather's desk.

It was the one good thing that the bastard ever did for me.

DARLING AT YOUR WINDOW
DANA MCKAY

There are eyes staring from outside the window.

She tries to ignore it. *Has* been trying to ignore it. She focuses on the television she has on solely as a distraction, background noise in a too-quiet room. Even on the seventh floor, the reception struggles. The two soap opera actors are blurry around the edges; the passionate kiss is stuttered, and when they embrace the hold stays longer than it's supposed to. She ignores that, too.

She doesn't have to look at the window to know the eyes are still there. It's waited there all night before, and she's never stayed up long enough to notice when it leaves. A sheer drop down to street level, no balconies or other footholds, and still it stays *there* for the simple fact it knows she's *here*. A perfect view.

She's closed the curtain plenty of times. When she'd pull back the edge, the sliver of night would always be behind wide eyes staring right back into hers. Irises blown out and eyelids curled back, a clear ring of white that glows against a body with all the weight of one, held suspended and unmoving at the perfect level. Erring so far from natural, even inhuman is a strain of definition.

She's looked at those eyes long enough—just as deeply as the creature outside has in return—to memorise every speck, every change of colour and the points at which light will catch. Stars through the windshield of a car. Sunlight through cigarette smoke. Nowadays, it only catches the light of her living room lamp, the flickering technicolour of a television screen.

It's a dance of static-filled colour as one actor leads the other to a bedroom. They lie down. The reveal of skin. Movement slips between the judders of broadcast delay.

She grimaces and turns it off. Eyes still sit at the window. She shouldn't engage; ignore it long enough and it will leave like that stray cat that kept begging for more food. The analogy isn't all that far off. Ignore it.

"You're being childish," she says into the silence.

There's no reply but she knows it heard through the glass. Its attention has always been singularly focused. She turns to look at it with a scowl. It stays unmoving, looking in. She throws the remote onto the couch, stomps over to the window loud enough she knows there'll be a note taped on her front door tomorrow from the downstair's neighbour; another to add to the collection about accusations of illegal subletting and a woman shouting to an empty room.

The window frame is bloated from age, the glass no longer sits quite flush, and there's an ice-cold draft. It isn't even locked. She digs her fingers under the catch and heaves it up.

"Go away," she tells it.

It doesn't. This has never been a war of attrition she's won.

"Fine," she bites out.

It has always *seeped*. Into light, the nooks and crannies both metaphorical and physical. It spills into the room before she finishes her acquiescence, brushing close enough to skin that the hair on her arms prickle. By the time she closes the window, it has already settled on the couch. Eyes just as wide, less begging but just as plying. A face rests on a delicate hand, the shape of *her* cut away from the dark of night.

"Tell me about your day, Red," the creature says softly.

Red sighs against the request; the moniker.

"It was fine."

She thinks of a day, a sharp nail tracing new lines in the cup of her palm. A lamentation about the name Mildred, a comfort.

Mildred, 'red, red, a soft voice, a sharp touch, *does that make me blue?*

Blue frowns with a pursed lip, tips her head in the picture of domesticity.

"It doesn't look fine."

"Don't think you might be a contributing factor in that?"

Blue doesn't bite.

"How about work? Are you still working on your dissertation?"

"You don't care about that," Red replies and sits firmly at the other end of the couch, even as the creature across from her continues her careful routine.

It was an easy performance to see through, one that Red noticed almost immediately even if the men before her evidently hadn't. The hair was too perfect. An ink-deep black, straight and soft and perfectly uniform. It framed a poreless face, symmetrical features that led down to stark collarbones and slender fingers. A flawless *pretty*.

Red knows real girls don't look like that. Real girls have curves to rest hands on, bare stretches of cellulite, torn nails, hair that escapes braids. So Red focuses on the other parts of the creature: the liquid spine, the brittle voice, the way she malforms in the periphery. Now Blue levels an imperfect frown, the pull of muscles she doesn't have in just the right places for it to look genuine.

"Of course I care."

I want to hear everything about you. What you do. What you ate for breakfast. The way you wear your hair. Your likes, dislikes. What you love and how you love.

Red looks into wide eyes. Looks away with a huff.

"I finished writing it. I'm getting Don to review it before I submit it to the faculty heads."

"Don's the researcher from Brisbane?"

"Yeah, he is."

Blue draws up her legs onto the couch, sock-covered feet tucked beside her with a familiar threadbare pattern of black and yellow stripes. They'd been missing from Red's drawer for two weeks now.

"Have you changed much of it?" Blue asks.

"Just some—" Red waves vaguely, "restructuring."

There were enough small changes that Blue could reasonably ask to read it all again. Red doesn't have the strength to do that right now. The dissertation is a monster to wrangle, and she'd spent however many nights changing words and moving appendices under the careful watch of eyes at the window. Despite that, Blue has always been a rapt audience when she'd read all seventy pages out loud to her, even if Red wasn't sure her focus sat anywhere near the words. It feels ridiculous to read out cited data and scientific theories, thinking all the while that it means Red should know better than to let a creature like *her* through the window.

So this time she doesn't. She leaves the laptop on her crowded desk and lets a silence hang in absence of a painful display of tenderness that pulls at the ribs as much as the heart. She can't tell if she wants this done quicker or not at all.

The creature waits, held bated.

"The weather today was nice," Red haltingly continues. "That kind of—sunshower. Makes everything look really green."

Blue nods, already knows it's her favourite type of weather.

There's just something about it, she'd laughed into a shoulder, *it's like — I don't know how to describe it.*

Dark eyes, affixed on hers.

Try it.

Blue has begun to shift, soften in the lamplight. Her posture is still held along a knifepoint, unnatural limbs at sharp angles. Braced, waiting. Red doesn't want to take pity. She hasn't been responsible for feeling pity for her in a long time. Blue shouldn't even be coming to her window anymore. Red shouldn't have to be the one telling her to stop.

"Do you want something to drink?" Red asks, on the edge of sharp herself.

Blue's smile covers her surprise.

"I would... I would like that, very much."

Red pushes herself roughly off the couch, turns her back to the pitch creature. She moves the short distance to the kitchen, clearing enough space on the counter by moving class notes and useless mythology books. The kettle gives her something to do with her hands. She picks out two mugs—worn looking ones—and her favourite tea. Gets the honey, too, because she wants this to be over with faster.

A violent approach always takes longer. It's exhausting to yell, to throw the occasional plate. That was a lesson Blue taught her near the end: anger is not the absence of something else. It's just dialled to eleven in another direction; diverging lines leading to the same place.

It's all passion in the end, baby, she'd told her, smiling like a drunk as they laid side by side between porcelain shards.

Red finds this process easier, even if it replaces hoarse voices and cut feet with a bone-deep weariness.

The kettle finishes. Water is poured, a teaspoon of honey because sweetness will get her satisfied and back out the window quicker. Cinnamon too, because that's the way Blue's always taken it, even if Red doesn't understand the appeal.

She turns back to the couch with tea in hand, and perhaps not in the right light, but some sort, it almost looks *normal.* Just a regular woman stretched on a couch, limbs bent awkward but comfortable. A dark apartment after an unfulfilling day, but to share every little detail, to hear the sound of their voice, because you want to see the shape of their mouth and every intricacy of how the day has changed them, this new lamp-lit person, to be given a chance to fall in love again.

This is her normal instead, and Red walks past walls with spackling in the width of her fist to hand a mug over to a creature that will drink from everything but its contents. Blue investigates her mug, smiling and slaked as she wraps her hands around it, looks deep within to find the honey stuck on the side; she smells the cinnamon. When she looks up, her eyes are half-lidded, her being soft and beautiful.

Red looks away as she has done, at the dark television and the vague reflection it plays like a programme. She imagines she can see the afterimages of that soap opera, instead of the silently shifting shape next to her on the couch. Red doesn't move away, even when cold skin touches hers and sends tingles up her side. Blue has torn men apart with less invitation, even if all she does now is press deeper into her side.

"You should find someone else for this," Red says quietly.

"I have you."

"No you don't. Not anymore."

Hair tickles at her shoulder, a head slotting itself in the cave of her collar.

"Tell me about your day."

So Red does, until the tea runs out, until her voice does too, and that momentary threshold is crossed when she knows that Blue has enough. The point when the starving cat has had what it needs and is only asking for more.

Red stands up wordlessly, opens the window. The routine is followed: Blue moves silently, spills back out through the window and melds back into the shapes of the night. Her eyes are no longer wide, even if they are still hungry.

"I love you," the creature says.

Red goes to shut the window. Slender fingers sit on the sill.

"I love you, Red."

Red leans forward with a tired sigh. Blue's head drifts forward like she's awaiting Red's forehead against hers. They don't meet.

"What if I said it back?" Red asks. "Would that be enough, that you wouldn't need to come back any more?"

"Maybe."

Starlit eyes watch hers. Neither look away.

"Goodnight, Blue."

The night empties. Red closes the window, nothing but the dark and street lights through it, as long as she stands there.

A cat winds itself through her legs, begging for food.

BLOOD SWEAT AND TEARS
RED LAGOE

The two-story home sat at the end of a long gravel driveway behind police tape, its existence completely hidden from view on the country road. There were no other homes for at least a quarter mile in either direction, so Rae and Jenna would be undisturbed for the séance. As young teenagers, there wasn't much else to do in a small town besides call upon Jenna's dead relatives.

The colonial that must've been a hundred years old loomed before them. Mosquitos and June bugs skimmed the tips of tall grass and shrubs in the mid-afternoon sun. The yard hadn't been mowed in months.

"I thought you said it's only been a week since they died," Rae said.

Jenna smacked her arm. When she lifted her hand, a mosquito's bloody insides were smeared on her skin. "Yeah. But they just moved in, like, a month earlier." She held up her phone and took a picture of the house. "They bought a shit-hole."

The wood siding was weathered and gray, porch beams cracked and warped, and the porch's roof dipped in the middle as if the weight of the world became too much for it to bear. Rae imagined herself propped up beneath, using her body to give its old beams a much-needed break. Funny thing about houses: they keep a roof over people's heads while being pelted by the storm; they absorb the blood of skinned knees and the tears from our broken hearts; they keep us safe. We, in turn, take them for granted and let them fall into ruin.

Against the glaring sun, its windows were black and impenetrable, yet Rae couldn't shake the feeling that someone stood behind the glass, watching as they approached.

Jenna smeared mosquito blood from her arm and curled her lips in disgust. "Look at this place! It's definitely haunted."

"I like it."

"You would."

Rae didn't like her tone when she said that. Jenna was growing meaner as they got older. They were both fourteen now, heading into separate high schools. She could feel Jenna pulling away. Fewer texts. Fewer sleepovers. Fewer chances to escape her father. Jenna was Rae's only friend, and Jenna's house her only refuge when Rae's Dad was in a drunken rage. And those fearful days were becoming far too frequent.

When Jenna texted this morning out of the blue about a sleepover at her aunt and uncle's old place, Rae was on board—whether it was haunted or not. Anything was better than being at home.

The crepitation of porch floorboards screeched underfoot. Jenna pulled the key from her pocket and inserted it into the doorknob. "I stole the key from Mom. She won't come here. Not after what happened."

A brutal murder—the kind of murder that splattered the local news and shocked the town. According to Jenna, someone would be here next week to clear the place out, maybe even tear it down. That's why Jenna insisted they do this today.

The door swung open to a small foyer with the faint aroma of paint lingering in the air. The walls were a soft gray. Clean edges, crisp white molding. A staircase stood before them upon entrance, and at its base was a decorative faux plant. A newly renovated interior with modern furnishings welcomed the girls. Plenty of natural light poured from the windows in the sitting room to the right as well as through the dining room windows to the left. Rae had never been in a house so clean and bright.

"Not what I was expecting," Rae said. She inhaled a deep breath. Through the scent of fresh paint, she caught the subtle aroma of freshly baked cookies.

"Aunt Helen and Uncle Mark were flippers," Jenna said. "You know, you've seen their videos."

"None of their makeovers looked this good, though."

"Too bad they never fixed up the outside." Jenna closed the door, leaving the summer heat behind. The air conditioning was still running. Seventy-four degrees according to the thermostat in the foyer. Jenna wandered into the dining room, running her fingers along the backs of chairs. "I didn't know they had the money to do all this." Her voice echoed and grew distant as she wandered beyond the dining room and into the kitchen out of sight.

Rae stepped into the center of the foyer. Entering this house felt like an embrace. A comforting hug from a stranger—but without the danger. The place was perfect. The only flaw she could spot was a small missing patch of stain on the banister. Hardly noticeable. She placed her hand on the rail and gazed up the stairway, wishing she could've grown up in a place with a banister—one she could slide down as a little kid. Upstairs were some paint cans and scraps of drywall leaning against the walls. She pulled her palm from the rail to wipe the sweat onto her pants, but a sweaty, dark spot remained on the banister. She rubbed away the wetness, but it had absorbed into the exposed wood. Her sweat stained the imperfection to match the rest of the banister.

Come on inside, sugar. The soft voice of a southern woman startled her. She twisted around, but there was nobody. It had to have been Jenna from the other room. Voice echoing from the kitchen, perhaps.

"You have a terrible southern accent..." Rae called out as she headed down the narrow hallway at the base of the stairs.

"What'd you say?" Jenna said in her normal, not-southern voice, as she flipped a wall switch on and off. The fixtures in the kitchen strobed with the rapid flicking of the switch. She laughed, "Muahahaha! Definitely haunted."

She was shockingly cavalier regarding the whole gruesome murder-suicide thing, but Rae wasn't one to judge. Jenna had her own problems that she'd never admit to. When she was home, her parents were so overbearing, they'd scold her for an A-minus. They forced her into extracurriculars she didn't want to partake in. She used to say she'd kill to have a Dad like mine—one who'd let her do whatever. She wouldn't think that if she really knew.

Jenna unloaded the Ouija board from her backpack onto a small breakfast table. Rae imagined herself sitting there every morning, eating breakfast. *Real* breakfast—like a bowl of cereal or eggs. Not some stolen granola bar from the Shop-A-Lot on the corner as usual.

Beyond the kitchen table, there was a set of double doors, solid wood and locked shut. Police tape was strung across them and secured to the molding on either side.

"Is that where it happened?" Rae nodded toward the doors.

"I think so."

Rae tried the handles but they were locked. "Do you have a key for this room too?"

She shook her head. "We could ask Aunt Helen where it is."

∽

THEY SAT at the kitchen table near the double doors with Jenna's Ouija board unfolded in front of them.

Jenna pulled her hair back in a scrunchie. "Let's find out what really happened."

Rae had read the news articles about what really happened behind those double doors. *Murder-Suicide Shocks the Town of Windsor.* According to the evidence, Helen Yardley had drugged, tied up, and tortured her husband, Mark, cutting him up while he was still alive. Then she turned the blade to herself, mutilating her own body before succumbing to the injuries.

Rae wondered what could've driven a person like Helen to do such a thing. The thought of summoning the spirit of a psychopath put her a little on edge, but she'd do anything to keep Jenna close. And as disturbing as the story was, she felt strangely at ease in this house. She placed her fingers on the planchette opposite her friend's.

"Aunt Helen..." Jenna said. "Are you here?"

Nothing moved, as Rae expected.

Jenna continued. "We heard some stories and want to know what really happened."

Jenna stretched her fingers and placed them back on the planchette. She closed her eyes and relaxed her shoulders. "Well first, where's the key to that room?"

Jenna looked up from the Ouija board, making eye contact with Rae. "I don't know what I'm doing."

Rae shrugged.

"Maybe we have to wait until dark. Light a candle or something?"

There was a long pause as Jenna sat chewing on her lip.

Rae felt like it was Jenna's way of asking her to help, so she said whatever felt natural. "I like your house."

The planchette moved with a jerk and the girls gasped, nearly pulling their fingers away, but they kept them touching lightly and followed the flow as it landed over the T, paused, and moved to the H...

"Is that you?" Rae asked.

Jenna shook her head and shushed her.

The planchette moved to the A...N...K...

Jenna tilted her head. "Don't mess with me, Rae."

"I'm not!"

Y...O...U.

"Thank you?" Jenna asked with eyebrows knit together.

The planchette paused and then continued... Both girls remained silent, quietly sounding out each letter.

S...U...G...A...R...

Rae's chest tightened with a held breath and Jenna pulled away from the board, crossing her arms.

"Did it just say *Thank you, sugar*?" Rae asked.

"You better not be moving it!"

"If I were gonna move it, I'd say something scary, like 'Get out.'"

"This is serious. Did you move it?"

She threw her hands up in surrender. "I swear. Was it *you*?"

The planchette slid up and over a letter without either of their fingers on the piece. It landed on the C. They both screamed, chairs scraping the floor as they jumped away from the table.

It slid down and to the left and stopped on the O.

Jenna's chin quivered and her eyes went glassy. "Oh my god... okay, okay, okay...It's her."

Rae sounded out the letters. "CO..."

It circled back to O again.

"Coo..." Jenna said.

...K

"Cook!" Jenna looked to Rae... "Cook what?"

...I...E...S.

"Cook Ies..."

"Cookies..." Rae whispered.

Neither of them spoke. They stopped sounding out the letters aloud. Rae was petrified as the planchette danced across the board.

F...R...E...E...

"Cookies free? Free cookies?" Tears spilled down Jenna's cheeks. She mouthed silently to Rae, *what the fuck?*

Rae shrugged.

Z...E...R

"Did that just spell..." Rae couldn't finish the sentence.

Rae and Jenna both stared at each other and then at the refrigerator across the island.

Jenna nodded. "Go look in the freezer." She reached for Rae's hand and squeezed it tight. Rae felt her friend coming back. For a moment, the strangeness of the situation didn't matter. All that mattered was that growing up wouldn't be the death of their friendship. They didn't have to drift apart. This moment would tie them together in a sisterhood like nothing else ever could.

Rae took the lead and grabbed the handle of the stainless steel freezer door. She yanked it open. Inside, were bags of frozen vegetables, meats, and sitting neatly on top of a tub of ice cream, was a zipper-locked bag of homemade chocolate chip cookies.

Jenna gasped, two hands cupped over her mouth. Eyes drenched in terror.

Rae grabbed the bag of cookies and set them on the counter. "I don't think we have anything to be afraid of."

"Are you insane?"

"The house wants us to be here."

Jenna collapsed onto an island bar stool, eyes locked on Rae. "You mean my *Aunt Helen* wants us to be here? That lady who lost her mind and killed her husband?"

Rae shook her head. None of it felt right. They must've gotten the story wrong. "It doesn't add up..."

"There is more to the story," Jenna rocked nervously on the stool. "Stuff that hasn't made the news yet."

Rae listened intently, easing into a chair beside her friend.

"They found Aunt Helen's journal. Mom said she was doing some creepy ritual shit, like alters and spells and bloodletting..." Jenna's voice shook. "She was into something seriously weird."

"Wasn't she a nurse? Nurses take care of people they don't—"

"She *used* to be a surgical nurse, but they both quit their jobs to do flipping."

"But—"

"There was no blood," Jenna said.

Rae's argument fell into silence and confusion as she waited for more information.

"There was no blood anywhere. All that cutting up. And nothing on the carpet?"

"That's weird..."

Jenna opened the bag of cookies on the counter and smelled inside. "What happened to her? This is the Aunt Helen I know. The one who baked cookies and called people 'sugar'. What kind of dark magic was she getting into that..." Jenna shook her head and looked off to the closed doors.

Rae placed a hand on her friend's back and did the only thing she could think to be comforting at the moment. She grabbed four cookies from the baggie and brought them to the counter.

"What are you doing?" Jenna asked.

Rae didn't answer. She placed the cookies inside the microwave over the oven. While they heated for 10 seconds, Jenna did nothing but stare at Rae. Something akin to bewilderment had replaced the terror behind her eyes, so Rae knew she'd already succeeded in making her friend feel a little better.

When she opened the microwave, the warm scent of chocolate chip cookies wafted out.

"This is how you remember your aunt, and it's how she'd like you to remember her." Rae handed Jenna a cookie.

Tears spilled over Jenna's lower lids and she sniffled up some snot. She nodded in agreement and took a nibble of the cookie which made Rae's heart happier than it'd been in a very long time.

Rae took a bite of her cookie and for the first time in her life, she felt like she was home. Somewhere safe. Somewhere that appreciated her... loved her.

While Jenna took little bites of her cookie, Rae rummaged through the drawers looking for a key to the double doors but all she could find was a paring knife. She tried it in the lock, working it from side to side as if she were some expert lockpick, but she had no idea what she was doing.

Rae twisted the blade and considered whether she could use this place as a hideout on days when it wasn't safe to be home. Not likely if Jenna's mom would have it torn down. Maybe she could fix up the rest of it, make it look nice again—worth keeping. Her mind drifted to a world where she never had to go back home—at least not the home she once knew. She would be safe in the walls of her own house, protected by its strong locks, sheltered from the storms.

She startled from her daydream and the room was dark. The bright daylight through the windows had already given way to the gray-blue hue of evening. Her hand was pressed against the door frame, palm searing with pain, stuck to the wood frame. Crusted and sticky, she peeled it away. She must've cut herself with the paring knife while trying to unlock the door. A bloody smudge remained on the frame along a hairline crack in the molding which ran all the way to the ceiling

The double doors clicked open and Rae staggered backward as a stainless steel surgical table came into view. Dangling from both ends, were hand and foot restraints. The table was placed in the center of the room with six tall pedestal candles circling it. Beyond the table, was a showcase fireplace. Its mantle held pictures of Aunt Helen and Uncle Mark and photographs of their nieces and nephews, including Jenna. The room was perfect in every way. Over the mantle, against the wall was handwritten script—a lavish cursive with curly-Qs and long wispy embellishments reading:

Bless this Mess
and
Feed the House

Feed the House. Rae's attention darted back to her bloody handprint on the door frame as it changed. She watched it dissolve into the wood, and as it did, the hairline crack sealed itself shut. Her lip twitched into a smile.

She healed it!

"Jenna!" Rae whipped around, nearly having forgotten her friend was behind her.

On the floor by the island, Jenna was slumped over. Rae ran to her, grabbing her arm to shake her back to consciousness. "Jenna?"

Cookie crumbs rolled off her shirt and onto the floor. "Jenna?"

Rae had only taken a bite of her cookie but felt a little dizzy herself. She pulled her friend upright into a sitting position. Her ragdoll body flopped to the side. Rae sat beside Jenna and let her head fall on her shoulder. Jenna would freak out when she woke up. She'd scream, cry, want to leave... Rae ran her hand along her hair, petting her best friend whom—no matter how much Rae tried to deny it—she would lose forever when they went to new schools in the fall.

Feed the house.

That's all a house wants from its inhabitants—to show the same respect to it as it does them. To simply take care of their home. What's so hard about that? Rae remembered the scraps of drywall upstairs and wondered how much of it was still unfinished. How many more chips of stain and cracks in the molding needed repair? What if she gave it a little more sweat and a little more blood from her hand? Would she run out of bodily fluids before ever getting to the exterior of the home? Surely, the outside of the house would require a significant amount of blood.

She looked through the double doors at the stainless steel offering table, then leaned her head against Jenna's knowing what needed to be done. Rae whispered into her unconscious friend's ear, "Isn't a place called home worth the sacrifice?"

THE THINGS I MISS

DAVID J. THIRTEEN

Another burst of sirens fills the street, then they're gone. One was an ambulance, that's certain. Also a firetruck. Could be a cop car or two as well, but the klaxon wail is too muddled to be sure. It's not unusual. Not living downtown with a hospital a few blocks away. Happens all the time. Although they're becoming more frequent.

Against my better judgment, I check the news. I've typed the site into my browser enough times it comes up on the first letter. The headline appears. "Cull of Animal Population Continues." But before the accompanying photo can load, I click on a bright banner promising: "30% off already reduced prices."

I've browsed this sale before. A day ago. Maybe two. Maybe both. It doesn't matter. I scroll through the fall blouses and dresses, the warm-looking tweed skirts, and sweaters in all the trendy colors. Indigo, clay, army green. My thumb flick-flick-flicks, scrolling to the bottom. What I want isn't here. The stylish cuts promise a better, more attractive me. With them, I could be like these perfect, untroubled models. But autumn is nearly over. When would I wear them? And with the curfew in effect, who would ever see me in them?

I pull my ratty sweater tight around me. Its shade of gray is not trendy. Its cut is neither attractive nor stylish. My knees curl into my chest, and I press deeper into the sofa's corner. Next to me, Buddy interprets my movement as the prelude to a walk. He whines, hopeful eyes glaring at me. His thumping tail shakes the cushions.

"Not now, Boy," I whisper.

We used to go for more walks. Not since an infected rat attacked him. The city says they're exterminating them, but it'll never be enough. All it takes is one. One rat, one raccoon. Maybe a squirrel, or a cat. Sure, Buddy can defend himself. Fractured the vermin's spine with one snap. But his strength is part of the problem.

Thank God his teeth didn't tear that greasy black pelt. Thank God he didn't swallow any blood.

New site. Different brands, same clothes. Or same enough. Except they cost twice as much to prove they're better.

I don't remember switching to this store.

It's like a nervous tic. A restless finger tap-tap-tapping. I scroll and click. Click and scroll. Fidget from one online store to the next, searching for something I desperately need but cannot name. It's a riddle my brain refuses to solve.

In terms of necessities, I'm covered. I have everything. Some are still in their boxes. I've gone beyond necessities. Purchased things to fill every possible niche.

My new fall jacket is nothing like my spring jacket or my lightweight rain jacket (which is completely different from my cold-weather rain jacket).

I don't know what it is I'm searching for, but I'll know it when I see it.

The next site belongs to a store I'm not familiar with. Maybe they'll have it.

A resonating smack of something colliding with glass brings

both Buddy and me to our feet. He barks and throws his beefy body at the balcony door. He's half Yellow Lab and half mystery and a full eighty pounds of stupid. I don't trust either the double-paned windows or my arms to hold him back.

My fingers stroke his face and neck, calming him.

On the next balcony, my neighbor clubs a pigeon with a broom. The bird's gray feathers are spotted with its toxic blood. Its neck bends at a broken angle, but it flaps and judders, trying to avoid the blows. Or trying to get at my neighbor's ankles.

When the concrete slab is coated with a pigeon slurry, he scrapes the body over the edge, sending the soiled broom after it. Our eyes meet, and he shakes his head in a gesture to dispel the tension. The glass shields his voice, but his lips outline the word: "Birds."

I give him a shrug and a smile, trying to convey that I had no idea pigeons could fly so high either. A few crows and sparrows had kamikazed themselves against my windows, but never a pigeon.

Back on the sofa, Buddy nestles against my hip. His weight is both reassuring and a little painful.

I browse camping gear. The deals are insane—everything is being liquidated. Of course, they can't give it away. Winter is around the corner, and the countryside is still the hardest hit. The mosquitoes and ticks may be hibernating, but their victims are going strong. Everyone now knows a coyote or a person can be just as effective at spreading blood parasites.

Everyone is leaving the country. Even the infected are moving to more populated areas.

Someone in my building is renting their one-bedroom condo to three families for an obscene amount.

I could do the same. Offer my place up as a safe house.

Let this nondescript unit become your home away from home and leave the terrors of suburban living behind. Situated on the tenth floor, you'll have nothing to fear except random bird attacks. The queen bed and sofa provide comfortable sleeping for three, but with ample floor space, the number of friends and family you squeeze in is limited only by your imagination. Pet friendly.

I'm thinking in ad-speak now.

I'll never actually leave. Where would Buddy and I go? All the cities are overflowing with people looking for safety.

Besides, it'll be over soon.

On social media, there's a report about top officials resigning because the emergency blood supply has become tainted.

I click a link for a handbag sale.

Purses, luggage, shoes, boots, belts, gloves, hats, coats, dresses, blouses, and sweaters (I linger on the indigo V-neck again). Furniture, rugs, lamps, wall accents, throws, dishes, flatware, glasses, and cocktail shakers scroll by.

I keep looking for something. Something. Something.

It's out there. I just need to find it.

A CATALOG OF THE THINGS I MISS

MY OWN BED

Made from cheap pressboard, this bed is ideal for the young professional in her first condo. The frame offers clean, forgettable blandness. While the queen mattress features personalized distressing from years of use. The comfortable hollows worn into the memory foam are perfect for a small woman and one large dog. Comes preassembled by the owner and her sister, who is presumed dead.

PERSONAL CARE PRODUCTS

This bundle has everything needed for both morning and nighttime routines. Contains toothpaste, body wash, facial soap, moisturizer, and more. Wipe away the grime and feel fresh and renewed. With this collection, the only thing stopping you from looking your best is the absence of indoor plumbing and clean, running water.

MAC 'N CHEEZ™

Bring back those lost childhood memories with this perennial favorite. Shelf-stable and full of chemicals, this is not the gourmet version those burned-out husks of restaurants once served. Full of empty-nutritional goodness, it is sure to both spark nostalgia and fill an empty stomach. Box contains dried pasta and orange cheese-like powder.

SMART PHONE

Look sophisticated and stylish with this pinnacle of human technology. Cellular networks and the internet might be a thing of the past, but this device still packs plenty of functionality. The game apps are just as addictive as before and will help pass the long, lonely days hunkered in safe houses. And the flashlight will really come in handy when searching abandoned grocery stores for the last remnants of food. This model also contains hundreds of pictures of your own face, your dog, meals you once ate, not to mention family and friends. It's sure to provide hours of weeping and promote feelings of intense loss. Spare batteries and electricity not included.

FAVORITE SWEATER

Perfect for the cold winter nights hiding from mindless mobs and homicidal wildlife. This knit cardigan is a common acrylic-wool blend that itches and irritates the skin but provides lasting mental comfort with warm memories of lazy afternoons on the sofa. Extra long for extra coziness, its features include threadbare elbows, a persistent coffee stain, and the lingering odor of dog hair. Available in heather gray.

YELLOW LAB MUTT

This mixed-breed dog is a loyal companion through thick and thin. A rescue animal with supreme separation anxiety and a love for all food left within reach. He might not be the perfect pet, but he provides welcome companionship when fleeing from one's home as well as a source of protection from infected animals and humans alike. Just make sure he's safeguarded against fleas and ticks. Goes by the name Buddy.

INSECT REPELLENT WITH DEET

The content of this aerosol spray smells awful and leaves a sticky residue on the skin, but it will keep biting pests at bay. Works with mosquitos, black flies, ticks, and other biting insects that carry deadly blood parasites. Keep you and your loved ones free from nasty bites that may turn them into relentless killing machines. Prolonged use may cause cancer.

GOURMET 9-PIECE KNIFE SET

From paring knife to chef's knife, this set has it all. With high-carbon stainless steel blades, they are perfect for any application, whether it's chopping, dicing, or defending yourself against your loyal and beloved companion after his brain has been hijacked by a homicidal parasite. Comes with a genuine acacia wood storage block.

FIRST AID KIT

This all-in-one kit is perfect for sticking under a bathroom sink and forgetting it exists. As uninteresting as the contents may seem, they're just the thing to treat a sprained ankle, lacerations caused by animal teeth, as well as persistent festering infections. Don't leave home without it.

FRESH COLD WATER

Whether from a plastic bottle or straight from the tap, there is nothing like a mouthful of cold water. When your throat is parched and cracked, this staple of life will become an obsession. More than just something to prevent dehydration, it's what you'll cry out for when sepsis sets your blood aflame, and fever ravages your dying brain.

RESTLESS
RIA HILL

I t took a full five-count from the time Sebastian opened his eyes to the time he no longer felt the sharp pressure of fingers worming their way into a nonexistent hole in his throat.

His breaths were ragged, but at least his airway was clear. How long had he been asleep?

Sitting forward on the couch, Sebastian tugged his charging cable until he found his phone where it had slipped between the couch cushions. It was a little after three in the morning.

Three weeks. For almost a month he'd been sleeping in brief and miserable bursts, and he still had no idea *why*.

HE'D STUMBLED home drunk the first night. That's what Sebastian had assumed to be the cause. He'd been drunk, and he'd gotten home somehow. He barely remembered the drive.

He'd collapsed into bed immediately, still dressed.

The second his eyes closed he felt himself immobilized. Was this sleep paralysis? Would he open his eyes and see an imaginary demon of his very own lurking in his bedroom doorway?

When he finally looked, he didn't see a demon. He saw a young girl.

Her hair fell almost to her shoulders, lank and greasy. There were bruise colored bags under her eyes.

It took Sebastian a moment to notice that the doorway she was standing in was not in his bedroom.

"Who are you?" he asked her.

"Does it matter?" she said.

"Is this a dream?" he asked.

"Now that *really* doesn't matter."

Sebastian tried to sit up, but realized that he was strapped to the bed.

The girl stepped closer. She wasn't as young as she'd looked at first. She might have been in her early twenties. Blood encrusted the cracked skin at the corners of her mouth.

"What am I doing here?" Sebastian asked.

There was a sharp, crisp click that he'd never heard in real life, but he recognized it instantly from a dozen movies.

Switchblade.

He'd slept a full eight hours that night, and she did not waste a single moment.

SEBASTIAN MADE A POT OF COFFEE, moving like a man in a trance.

He hadn't slept in over seventy-two hours. Not bad. Before that, he'd barely made it thirty-eight.

When the coffee finished, he poured a mug and took two NoDoz tablets. That was more than he'd ever taken before, even when he used to work nights, but this was a desperate situation.

He couldn't let himself fall asleep. Not again.

THE SECOND TIME Sebastian opened his eyes in the other world, he didn't fully believe it. He had settled on the couch for an afternoon nap, and then he was here.

How was he here?

Where *was* here?

"Welcome back," the girl said. She sat on a wooden stool at his bedside.

He was, again, strapped to the gurney.

"What do you want from me?" he asked.

The girl chewed her lip.

"Please," he whispered.

A scraping sound, metal against concrete. The girl had a hammer in her hand.

Sebastian's breath hitched.

"Please," he said again.

It was a useless, meaningless word and they both knew it. What would be done would be done, just like the night before.

The girl brought the hammer down.

How WAS she always there waiting for him?

Was she real?

Sebastian

His coffee mug tumbled as he wrenched himself to his feet.

I'm awake. His brain was humming with panic. *She's not here. I'm still awake. She's not here. She's not here, she* can't *be here.*

A delicate hand touched the back of his neck.

IT DIDN'T MATTER when he went to sleep. She was always ready. Even when he slept over at a friend's house, she was there.

The first time he stayed awake for twenty-four hours, he'd vaguely hoped the girl had gotten bored of waiting and given up.

His head was already pounding when he found himself in front of her again.

She had him hanging by chains around his ankles, his hands bound behind his back. It felt so real.

It *couldn't* be real.

"Let me rest," he said. "I'm begging you."

"Go ahead," she said. "Whenever you're ready."

Sebastian closed his eyes. His teeth chattered. His shackles and ropes bit into his skin. He needed to rest, but he couldn't. Not like this.

"Miss?" He kept his voice as calm and level as he could. When he opened his eyes he didn't see her. "Are you there?"

Something large and *cold* pressed to the bare skin of his back.

He gasped. "Miss, please..."

"Finished resting already?" she said. "Alright then."

Whatever she was holding to his back flipped on its edge and gently scraped his skin, leaving a narrow band of gooseflesh in its path.

It was possible to vomit from pain. Sebastian had learned this on day two.

When he glimpsed the handsaw she held, he learned that fear, too, could turn him inside out.

THE PAIN as his head connected with the corner of his coffee table was the first *real* pain Sebastian had felt in his many weeks of imagined agony.

He bent to clean the spilled coffee, but the rug was clean.

In the kitchen, the pot was empty and his mug was on the counter.

He swallowed two NoDoz dry.

He hadn't done any work in two weeks.

His boss had scheduled a virtual meeting for the morning, no doubt with intent to fire him.

He couldn't find it in him to care.

This needed to stop.

"I'VE MISSED YOU," the girl cooed in his ear.

He was bound and gagged with his head in her lap. He didn't remember falling asleep. This had been his longest break since this whole thing started.

He would probably sleep through his own firing.

The girl looked exactly the same. She was pretty, in her way.

She promised him a thirty minute respite; then she would take it slow.

Sebastian preferred her quick and dirty catnap killings. Brutal, but mercifully short. He had agreed to the rest because he thought he could ask her questions, figure out how this was possible. But even when she slipped the bandana between his teeth he didn't regret the decision.

The pain would come, but it would have come anyway. At least now, for a few minutes, he could just—lie there. Still, with her fingers in his hair, without pain.

He hadn't meant to nod off then either, but thirty minutes passed like blinking.

~

HE AWOKE IN THE HOSPITAL, and he awoke screaming.

The nurse who came to soothe him said his boss had called for a wellness check and they'd found him on his kitchen floor.

He had slept for over a day.

The nurse smiled at him gently, and teased that she wished *she* could have a twenty-seven hour nap.

Then she asked if he was hungry.

Sebastian was *ravenous*. He wasn't sure when he had last eaten.

The nurse brought him a tray. The food was ghastly, but it would give him the strength to stay awake a little bit longer.

Another nurse came in while he was eating, but he walked past Sebastian's bed, through a partition, and into another section of the room.

When he came back out, Sebastian caught his eye.

"You didn't know you had a roommate, did you? She won't bother you." The nurse walked to his bedside and took his tray. "Between you and me," the nurse said, "if your screaming didn't wake her up, I don't think anything will."

"Brynn." Sebastian's nurse spoke sharply from the doorway. "Can I talk to you?"

The young man cursed under his breath and slunk away.

Sebastian settled back on the pillows. He was so exhausted he could barely keep breathing. It took everything he had to keep his chest rising and falling.

It couldn't hurt to rest for a few minutes, could it? As long as he stayed awa

~

"LONG TIME NO SEE," the girl said. She perched on her wooden stool at his bedside.

They were somehow in both the torture chamber and his hospital room.

"I can't do this anymore," Sebastian said.

The girl shrugged. "I imagine I'll come unplugged sooner or later."

She took a scalpel from a tray that wasn't there, but wasn't not there.

Sebastian sobbed. There was nothing he could do. She'd take him apart again. And again.

And again.

~

HE AWOKE in a different hospital room, black sky outside the windows. There were no partitions in this room. No roommates. Had he been screaming in his sleep?

He touched the rough fabric of his formless hospital gown. He must have been awake, because in his dream it had been destroyed and cast aside.

"How long was I asleep?" Sebastian asked his nurse.

"A few hours," she said. Her voice was soft. "You slept right through us moving you across the hall. A detective came by this evening and asked to speak with you, but you looked so peaceful I asked her to come back in the morning."

"A detective?" He clenched his fist, fighting the impulse to pinch himself. That wouldn't tell him if he was asleep. Not when his dreams held more agony than his waking life.

"She said it had something to do with your car."

All at once, his ears filled with screeching tires and squealing brakes.

He jerked his hands up to cover his ears and almost yanked out his IV catheter.

The nurse's mouth moved, but Sebastian couldn't hear her over the sickening thud in his head, the one he couldn't shut out because it was already in there.

The nurse called for assistance, but it didn't matter.

Sebastian's body pitched and slowed, and the chaos of the room winked out.

∽

"DID YOU MISS ME SO MUCH?" the girl said to him.

"I didn't miss you," Sebastian said. "Did I?"

"No," she said. "You didn't."

He was upright, at least, when he learned her name.

Chelsea.

Chelsea, who had never owned a car. Chelsea, who had taken a late shift at the movie theater to help her manager, who she had a terrible crush on. Chelsea, who had never forgotten her reflective vest once in her life, and who was wearing it when a drunk driver swung around a curve and made his rush to get home into her problem.

Chelsea, who had been there every time he slept, because once he had knocked her down she hadn't gotten back up.

Sebastian stood before her, bound hand and foot, and listened as she told him that he could rest as soon as she could.

"When will that be?" he asked.

He was too tired to scream when her blade slipped under his skin.

"I imagine sooner or later," she said.

∽

THE WAKING WAS SLOWER, calmer. His heart monitor beeped an even rhythm.

Morning light streamed in. His flesh was alight with the pleasure of being intact. It was more than he deserved.

Sooner or later.

She'd said that to him before.

Sebastian struggled to his feet.

He didn't expect there to be so much blood when he tugged the IV out of his hand.

He knew what he had to do, but if he was wrong he'd pay for it every time he closed his eyes.

He poked his head into the hall. He imagined an alarm would sound if he unhooked himself from his EKG machine, but the nurse's station was empty. That might give him enough time to be sure.

He unplugged the cords and lurched across the hall.

The beeping was good, it helped him get grounded. It kept him alert.

He stepped into his old hospital room, shut the door behind him, and flung the curtains aside before he could lose his nerve.

Frail. Pale. Eyes closed. Broken.

Chelsea.

She was hooked to every possible machine. Parts of her head had been shaved, but the hair that protruded from under the bandages were the same lank, black strands from his dreams.

There was a tube in her throat. She was on a ventilator.

He had done this.

Tears blurred his vision, but he had no time.

He had to act *now*.

The tray of tools that had been in the room in his dream wasn't there. There was nothing there that could be used to free her, free *him* from this nightmare he had made.

He took the pillow from the adjacent bed and pressed it to her face.

∼

SEBASTIAN DIDN'T KNOW how long he stood there before they found him, but he did know that the detective who had come the day before was there when they did.

Medical staff had dragged him away, heart monitors screaming in protest at their abandonment.

He let the pillow fall from his hands and relaxed into their arms as they carried him back to his own bed.

He might end up in prison, but he deserved that. He deserved to be locked up for killing that girl.

But at least now he could *sleep*.

The adrenaline kept him awake long enough to speak to the detective when she finally arrived at his bedside. Her face looked grim and her hair was in a tight knot at the back of her neck.

He had a cuff on one wrist connected to the railing of the hospital bed. He didn't mind.

He glanced at the freshly printed hospital visitor pass clipped to the detective's coat: *Ferber*.

"I'm so sorry," he said.

"We know you hit her," she said.

"Are you going to arrest me?" It was a bad question. It made him seem callous. He wasn't. He cared deeply, or at least he would when he wasn't so bone tired.

"Yes," Detective Ferber said. "For leaving the scene of an incident, and the attempted murder of Chelsea Marrin."

Everything she said after was lost under the weight of those six words.

The attempted murder of Chelsea Marrin.

Sebastian had failed.

He settled back on the bed and let the even rhythm of Detective Ferber's voice lull him back to sleep.

Maybe this time Chelsea would listen. Maybe this time she would hear him say he was sorry, that he *tried*.

~

SHE WAS EXACTLY where he'd left her, jaw set and book of matches in her hand.

His apologies drowned in kerosene.

FEEDING THE FLAMES
LIAM HOGAN

"He don't look much like a hero."

Bound to a rusty metal chair, bruised and bloodied, my tongue, behind the gag, worrying away at a loosened tooth, it's hard to disagree. With a bag over my head as well as the oily gag, I'm blind and mute and struggling to breath. But not deaf; their laughter is loud and braying. It stops abruptly, as though a conductor raised his baton.

"Let the man talk."

The hood is removed, the gag yanked down. I take in my surroundings: echoing subterranean concrete, dark puddles of stagnant water—or other liquids. Very gangster chic. A bank of work lights so that all I can see of my tormentors are flickers and silhouettes reaching for me.

Reddened saliva dribbles from my chin and I suck down air through an aching jaw. Bruised, not broken, unlike my nose. I spit, aiming between my shackled legs, but I only manage to splatter the already stained trousers. *Great.*

I've no idea where I am, exactly. A dingy lower level of some derelict dockside warehouse. But, despite the dazzling lights, I know the man stood before me. Sebastian Candler. AKA "Seb the Bastard."

"So, *hero:* what's your superpower?"

I get asked that question whenever I find myself in a place like this, in a situation like this. As soon as I mention I'm a super, they all want to know what I can do.

I wish I could say that I'm bulletproof. Because then they'd test it, wouldn't they? But would that be murder, or would my lie make it suicide? And if the latter, what happens then? Not sure I want to find out.

The truth is safest, though more painful. I give him as level a gaze as I can, until my eyes begin to water.

"*Vengeance,*" I growl, though it's less clear than I intend: my swollen tongue feels alien.

I worry I might have to repeat myself, but he laughs and shakes his head. His muscle, flanking him, stays silent. They're not paid to laugh at what I say, only at what he says. They're probably not paid to do anything *other* than what he says, which is good to know, but not quite enough.

His question is an important one. Superpowers, however gained, come with rules and limitations. They don't usually work the way the holder might hope. Mine certainly doesn't, otherwise I wouldn't be here with a dark red splotch crowding my vision and needing more dental work than I can afford.

Not that I'll be making a health care appointment anytime soon. Not that I'll have to.

"So what did I do?" Seb asks, scornful; a bully in a playground picking on the scrawniest kid. Scrawnier than I should be; I haven't been eating well. Somehow it never feels all that important. "Did I hurt someone you know?"

"Killed," I reply.

He shrugs, after a pause. "This is a hard city, Mr...?"

He knows my name—my current one. I've made enough of a

nuisance of myself to guarantee that. But I'm happy to provide it again. Perhaps he's hoping for a different answer. "Hulne. Gregory Hulne."

"This is a hard city, Greg," he repeats, even repeating the shrug. "People die young. Foolish ones, who put themselves in my path and don't heed the warnings. You can't blame me for that. Not when they bring it on themselves."

He leaves a pause, expecting me to respond. Then he sighs. "Who do you claim I killed, exactly? Who set you on this self-destructive path?"

"Me, Mr. Candler," I reply, making sure he knows I know who he is. "You kill *me*."

I choose my targets carefully. If he lets me go, all my efforts, all my current agony, are for nothing. If he delegates... *Well*, I get to go again, I guess, but I'm trying to move up the chain, not down, or sideways. Seb Candler is the highest low-life I've yet managed to reach. A businessman who gets invited to City Hall. Shipping, construction.

Drugs, prostitution, smuggling, money laundering, extortion. Occasional murder.

"You look pretty alive, for a dead man," he quips.

"That's what Maynard said."

He stiffens. There are some crazy rumors going round about his right-hand man, Callum Maynard. That he burst into flames, and, from those flames, another man stepped forth. A man Maynard claimed to have killed just three days earlier.

Nonsense, of course.

Except I'm the man he claims to have killed. Up until now, Seb has probably assumed I'm just exploiting the name. The name I'll only change when I change cities. Reputations can be risky, but useful.

Seb glares at me. He's been getting closer throughout our little conversation. Well within range. "You're not Lazarus," he says.

"No," I agree, but Seb has more to add.

"Lazarus lowered himself into a vat of acid, couple of months back."

I did not know that. I shudder. But I think I can understand why, and I wonder if he had help. By then, by all accounts, Lazarus's tortured, mangled body never got a chance to heal. No fun, dying twice—or sometimes more—a day.

I mime looking around. "There's never a vat of acid when you need one." I'm getting used to my fat tongue, though I expect it makes me sound simple. I shift focus back to Seb. "You might have to try a more... *traditional* method."

He frowns. I haven't yet got him where I want him. Seb is not some cartoon villain, a stereotyped, mustachioed bad man, your evil for the sake of evil, superpowered alien. These are real people. Most of them, Seb included, have families. I can't help but feel sorry for them, for what will come.

But they're also very bad people. *Killers.* I make sure of that. I make sure I'm not their first.

"Coward are you, Mr. Candler? Not willing to get your dainty little hands dirty?"

He glances down. His muscle grins. What is it with powerful men who refuse to admit that any part of them isn't larger than life? Does it really matter that his fingers are shorter than mine?

He can do something about that, if he wishes. I've seen the bolt cutters. I'd rather he doesn't toy with me though—I'm no masochist.

His eyes flick to his henchmen. Men who go home at the end of the day to *their* families. Men who, if asked, would tell you they're only doing their job, only following orders.

Even if their orders are to make me suffer. Even if their orders are to make me vanish.

"Sure," I tell their employer, feigning disinterest. "You could get someone to do it for you. Even leave the room. Out of sight, out of mind, hey? Though how could you ever be certain I'm dead unless you do it yourself?"

"Has he been searched?" Seb demands. "Is he wearing a frickin' wire?"

"He's *clean*," one of his men says, offended, I think, by the accusation. "Right down to his soiled underpants."

Seb is real close now. So close he could reach out and touch me. "Why are you such a pain in the backside, Greg? Why are you so determined to get yourself killed?"

Why indeed? Am I a hero? Am I a villain? Or is it all much more complicated, and dangerous, than that? And is this why there aren't very many true superheroes, or true supervillains? Most of us, when we discover what we can do, try to keep it hidden. We just want to live a quiet life. And those who don't... they aren't usually around for very long.

"I won't stop, Mr. Candler," I warn. "I'll keep on making a nuisance of myself. Keep digging into your affairs, sharing what I find with the cops and the press. I'll shut down every sordid business you've got your pudgy fingers in."

I'd love to set fire to those warehouses of his. Take a baseball bat to the sleek cars he drives around in. But I have to stay just the right side of the law. Not because I'm a hero, but because I'm no good to anyone locked up.

He doesn't know that. Not really. Otherwise, he'd probably have already called in a few favors.

"And, then, Mr. Candler," I say, holding his gaze. "I'll bring it on home. I know where you live. I know where your wife and your children are, right now."

The fist smashes into the side of my head. A clumsy shot that still does a Fourth of July number on my already blurred vision, and probably bursts an eardrum to boot. You get kind of good at judging such things when it's happened a few times.

"You sorry little punk." His face is red, contorted. If Mr. Candler isn't careful, he might have a heart attack one of these days. He raises his fist and I can't help but flinch, but all he does is shake it in my face. "You're not going anywhere, you hear?"

I grin up at him, though it hurts to do so.

He snaps his fingers at his muscle. And then again, when they're slow on the uptake. A gun is handed over. Something dark, no gleam of brightly polished metal. A thoroughly *practical* handgun.

"Any last requests, Mr. Hulne?"

"Yeah, sure." I leer at him. "Cremate me."

He laughs, but it's stilted. He sounds tired. Frustrated. Baffled. "You ain't Asbestos Man, that I know for certain."

I expect I've argued myself into a watery grave instead. Unless he suspects a double bluff. A concrete coffin, perhaps? A twelve-storey headstone. Thankfully, it doesn't matter. I'll be dead before I hit the water, or the bottom of the soon-to-be foundations.

As he rests the cold, hard muzzle against my temple, I keep grinning, manic now. He's sealing his own fate.

But those are the rules for my particular superpower. The blessing that is definitely more of a curse. The one I wouldn't even know about if I hadn't been in the wrong place at the wrong time all those years ago, and if there hadn't been a younger version of Seb there, eager to prove to everyone what a *man* he was.

I died that night. Just as I've died many times since. Just as I'm about to die again. And if you were to ask what makes me do what I do, I'd tell you: there are worse things than dying. There's losing everything. There's those who are left behind when you go. There's the impossibility of getting back what you once took for granted. And if I can stop that happening for anyone else, then maybe I'm a hero after all.

It doesn't matter what he does with my body, whether he dumps it in the harbor, weighed down by chains, or throws it into some dark hole to be buried in concrete. Or just leaves it, for the cops and others to discover. Not even if he dumps it in a vat of acid. Because, not long after, my corpse, whatever remains of it, will turn to ash, and at the exact same time my murderer will burst into flames, and I will emerge from those flames, whole, and unscathed. That, and that alone, is my superpower.

He clicks the safety and I close my eyes, taste metal in my mouth like a portent of the bullet about to be released. I almost welcome my oblivion, if only because the void is silent, and pain-free, and *clean*.

But death is only a temporary respite. In three days time, from the ashes of my killer, the Phoenix will arise.

THE AIRLOCK
MARK SILCOX

"The first thing I'm gonna do, after the handshakes and celebrations and everything," said the Ensign, "is go to a *real* bakery. Maybe before it opens. Just to sit outside and sniff the air while they make proper, human bread."

Security Officer Kamp smiled. "That surprises me a little, Chernov. I didn't have you down as a foodie."

The other two crewmen standing in the corridor laughed politely. This was getting to be the only conversation anybody ever had anymore on board the *Spelunker*. As they neared the end of their voyage—eight months of relentlessly close quarters, synthetic food, and tedious, weeks-long stretches of superluminal transit through the void—the whole ship was hotbed of yearning. By now almost everybody had something to say about the liberties, luxuries, or odd sensations they'd learned to miss from their lives back on Earth.

Kamp had already described to them his dream of hiking the trails of Appalachia. "What about you, McCabe?" he asked the ship's junior software engineer.

"Well, no offense, sir, but, the company of my peers. I've made friends on this mission, of course, but there are only two other officers on board who write code. I miss hanging out with my fellow nerds." More amiable, indulgent laughter.

The fourth member of the group, Private Citizen Zheng, hung back while he listened to their ramblings. Nobody asked Zheng about his immediate plans because nobody had to. The enormous payoff he would collect as lead investor in their mission to collect thousands of tons of rare earth elements meant he'd probably spend his first few days back rolling around in a bathtub full of cash.

"I miss people too, of course—not *just* the food." Ensign Chernov took on a more wistful air. "My extended family used to drive me nuts, back when we all spent time together regularly. But I've gotten very nostalgic for...ennnh...*oh!* Oh, God, I..."

The junior officer pressed both hands against his stomach and dropped to his knees. He swallowed hard once, then heaved up an enormous clot of blood onto the polished floor.

The three others took a few steps down the corridor. Chernov tipped over on his side, squirming and thrashing.

"Yeah, so like I said, definitely want to catch up on advances in my field." McCabe's voice betrayed only a hint of a tremor. "Plus, I'll want to spend time outdoors, too. Few rounds of golf, maybe."

"Ahhh! I can't *see*! I..." Chernov screamed, dark blood pooling beneath him.

Kamp subtly keyed his wrist monitor to summon a cleaning crew. "Perhaps we should all adjourn to our quarters to get our luggage packed," he suggested. "The nav computer says we could reach the heliopause as early as this evening."

Zheng and McCabe nodded. The former clapped him on the shoulder. "Thanks for all your good work, Officer." He sidestepped Chernov's shivering corpse and darted toward the elevator. McCabe lingered a moment, eyes wide, hands writhing in his pockets.

"Please don't gawk." Kamp tried not to sound too censorious. Witnessing these spectacles was miserable for everyone.

McCabe's eyes met his and blossomed with a deep terror. "Sorry!

Sorry. Pack my luggage – yes, sir, that's a...that's a..." He let out a strangled yelp and practically sprinted away.

The cleaners arrived a couple of minutes later hefting mops and buckets, pushing along one of the human-sized mobile incinerators they had built back when this whole mess began.

"Please give some extra attention to this job," Kamp instructed them. "Not a trace of gore left on the tiles, and scrub the air for microparticles. This corridor is the shortest path from the airlock to the bridge. We obviously don't want anyone boarding the ship to notice..."

He let his voice trail off. The three janitors all saluted, understanding.

Kamp glanced at his monitor. "I need to go. Meeting with the captain at 19:45. Please work fast; we may not have more than a few hours."

They swabbed the sticky tiles with vigor.

Kamp was very tired. He had been working harder than anyone else on the ship as the corpses piled up and nerves frayed. His meeting was in eight minutes and he still had a long walk to the captain's quarters.

The door to an officer's stateroom shushed open as he walked past. A twenty-something kid he recognized from the surveying team lurched out, gasping and wild-eyed.

"She's *gone!*" the junior surveyor wailed. He staggered after Kamp and seized him by the sleeve. "One minute we were there, just listening to music, and then..."

Kamp carefully tugged his arm free, then turned and glanced into the open room. Sure enough, a woman's body was drooping at a crazy angle across the sofa. Some of the other furniture was overturned—seizures, probably. Her skin had already turned that signature morbid greyish-green color. He winced and stepped back into the hallway.

The surveyor saw Kamp's security armband and holstered

weapon. But instead of backing off he took a step further forward, blocking Kamp's way.

"Please! Please, can't we *do* anything? Why can't the medics cure this plague?" His face was bright red and he gestured furiously. "It's going to get *all* of us before we're back on Earth!"

"Be quiet crewman!" Kamp's hand was over his firearm. 'You're violating the Protocol!"

The young man stumbled backward.

Kamp closed in. "You *know* the penalty for talking that way. Do you want to ruin..."

"*Screw* the penalty. She was my fiancé!" But his shoulders dropped when Kamp drew his weapon. "Wait, no, I didn't mean it. Please."

"Nguyen, Mitchell!" Kamp barked into his monitor. "Get to my location! We have another *talker* for detention!"

The surveyor dropped to his knees. "Don't put me in the cells, sir! Everybody's so packed together in there! I'm bound to catch the...I mean..." He swallowed and hung his head.

Kamp's deputies were at his side within a minute. They seized the sobbing officer by his arms and hefted his listless body toward the elevator.

"How much longer now, sir?" Mitchell grunted as they passed.

"A matter of hours, maybe. Make sure to put him with the other officers; no need for him to share space with the noncoms." Kamp gestured through the door of the room, toward the limp figure on the sofa. "Soon as you're finished with him, come back and burn that."

HE WAS two minutes late for the meeting with Captain Cerrulo. The other senior officers – Higuera, Head of Communications, Bostock, the Chief Surveyor, and Xi, the First Mate – were already standing around their boss' desk, at ease but not easy. Kamp felt sorry for Higuera, who was shiny with nervous perspiration.

The captain was already wearing his dress blacks and had slicked back the grey at his temples. He preserved his usual aura of calm gravitas; only from close up could one glimpse the weary creases at the corners of his eyes.

"Come in, Kamp. The gang's all here." He smiled thinly. "Miguel was just running us through his plan. Obviously, we want to skip the usual formalities before swapping personnel with Proteus station."

Higuera twitched a glance over his shoulder as Kamp approached. "As you know, standard practice is to give a verbal report lasting up to an hour as we pass through the heliosphere. But we've already sent them hundreds of pages of documentation since the mission started. Everybody knows the final summary is a mere formality."

"And there's nothing in the dispatches you've sent them already about...?" The Captain trailed off, leaving a silence thick as morning fog.

Higuera squirmed. "The first two, um, incidents, we did report. Before we knew about the, ah..."

The eyes of the others got wider. Kamp took a step backward and put his hand on his pistol again, silently pitying his fearful colleague.

The Captain made eye contact with him. "Stand down Helmut, it's all right. The Protocol still applies to all five of us as soon as we leave this room. But as long as we're away from the rest of the crew, we can speak frankly to one another."

"Understood, sir," said Kamp.

Higuera's shoulders dropped and he wiped a hand across his sticky forehead. "Thank you, Captain. So, as I was saying, before we knew about the plague, we reported both deaths, but without much detail. Later, I amended the dispatch to say they'd both had allergic reactions to mess hall food."

"Good. Good." The captain nodded. "So, with a little luck, we can keep the conversation with Proteus down to a few minutes' pleasantries." He stood up slowly behind the polished desktop. "I think that's all, my friends. I just wanted you together here one last time to make sure we're all ready to see this thing through. As soon as we hit the Oort cloud, the nav computer will summon you to the bridge. In the meantime, try to take a breather. Prepare yourselves for this final little bump in the road."

"Um, Captain?" Xi's voice was strained, shaky.

"What *is* it, Andrea?"

Kamp winced. Cerrulo always hated it when his subordinates spoke out of turn.

"Sorry. It's just that I've been making a little progress with the Xenopathology software. Still no idea where the, um..." Her mouth twisted—in spite of being freed from the Protocol, she couldn't quite manage to speak the word. "I mean, where *it* started, or along what vectors *it's* been spreading. But I'm worried that dropping out of hyperspeed could accelerate transmission. When the laws of Einsteinian spacetime kick back in, nearly anything could happen."

"So what the *fuck* are we supposed to do, Andrea?" The Captain's rage was immediate and devastating. "Quarantine ourselves in the void 'til we all grow whiskers? Who knows when your precious software will make its magical diagnosis? Sure hasn't done us any good since the first bodies started to drop. In the meantime, my wife's waiting for me in our house in Calabria. My youngest daughter learned to walk while I was out here digging up chunks of metal."

Xi quailed. "Sorry, sorry. I agree completely, of course, sir." There was a catch in her voice and terror in her eyes. Kamp noticed a streak of tiny red flecks across her uniform. Somebody must have gone down close to her fairly recently.

"All of you, for God's sake, go back to your quarters and try to collect your wits," said Cerrulo. "When we're gathered on the bridge, I'll expect a show of confidence."

~

IT WAS ONLY a couple of hours later when Kamp got the call. He had been resting in his private suite compiling a mental list of all the far-flung locales on Earth he wanted to visit, and reflecting upon how odd it was that, after this harrowing voyage, the first thing he yearned to do back at home was even more traveling.

"Leaving hyperspeed in ten minutes, thirty seconds," the nav computer's voice chirped over the speaker in his room. "All senior officers, report to Bridge."

When he arrived he was surprised to see Bostock seated in the command chair. The old man's face was pale as ivory. Higuera stood near the center of the room staring at the com screen. He swayed back and forth slowly, moaning to himself.

"What's going...?" Kamp began to ask, then stopped when he felt his right foot slip a little.

He was standing in a slick mess of blood. A few steps further into the room the captain lay face down, his body going through its final convulsions.

Kamp felt the gorge rise in his throat. "Where's Xi?" he managed to ask the other two. Andrea was second in command; she was the one who should have taken the chair.

"Still in her quarters." Bostock' voice was strangled. "She's..." He glanced over at Kamp's sidearm. "She's not coming. As soon as the ship started to decelerate, they both..."

"Shh," Kamp said – gently, but forcefully. "The Protocol is still in effect."

"Oh god, oh Jesus, Lord. We're contacting Proteus in less than seven minutes." The Head of Communications did not sound good. His swaying and moaning were becoming more pronounced. A telltale aroma hung in the stuffy air, and strengthened as Kamp approached; evidently he'd also soiled himself.

Kamp closed his eyes. His parents had never taken him back to the Smoky Mountains after a single, golden holiday there when he was a child. But he could summon an image of the landscape at will —mossy peaks and beckoning sunlight, veiled in fog—as he'd glimpsed it that very first morning through a hotel window. He'd volunteered for this mission partly because he had hoped to be moved in a similar way by the less hospitable crags atop the asteroids where they'd been digging for rare ores. The very idea of those airless, monochrome shards of alien rock appalled him now. But it also provided him with just enough resolve to confront the situation head-on.

"Go back to your quarters, Miguel," he said to the Communications officer, tugging the interface control from his hand. "I'm relieving you of your position."

"I...I..." Higuera's expression shifted from angry to imploring as their eyes met.

"Don't worry—you won't be formally charged or detained. You've done heroic work on this mission! Please leave quickly."

Higuera sobbed once, then nodded tersely and made for the elevator, stepping over their twitching former commander.

"What are you doing, Kamp?" Bostock's voice sounded at least passably stable.

Kamp turned and held a finger to his lips. Then he stood in the spot where Higuera had been, looked down at the display screen, and fiddled with the controller in his hand. His reflection on the dark surface looked bone-weary and irritable, but with a bit of concentration he thought he could probably pass.

"Are you gonna...?" Bostock fidgeted in the command chair.

"I'm going to try my best, yeah. If I go down next, push my body out of camera range and get the controller from me. Keep the camera focused on your own face and tell them the comm software has been glitching."

"Oh. Wow – that's...yeah, I guess that might work."

"All we have to do is get past the airlock and we become their responsibility."

The pair of them waited quietly. All around them the ship shivered and quaked, subtly adjusting itself to subluminal velocity. A minute or so later, a horrible groan and a rattle emerged from the Captain's body.

"You don't suppose he's..."

"No. Not possible," said Kamp. "You know how the illness works."

The tinny affectless voice of the nav computer cut in. "Deceleration complete. Radio contact made with Proteus Orbital Transit Station."

Kamp stared at the screen and waited.

"Are they—can they hear me? Is this even on? God damn it!" A voice crackled over the bridge intercom. Then the perspiring face of a balding, middle-aged white male appeared on the screen, turned to one side.

"Hello?" said Kamp. "Is this Proteus Station?"

"Oh! It is!" The sweaty guy looked relieved. "This is the *Spelunker?*"

Making sure his hand was out of camera range, Kamp pushed one of the dials on the controller slowly back and forth and said in a wavery voice "Affirmative..."

"Sorry – didn't get all that. Seems to be a lot of static on this frequency."

"Apologies – our comm software has been fritzing for the past couple of days. It's..." He twiddled the wheel again and mouthed a few words, silently—"...during our trip home. Security Officer Juergen Kamp reporting."

"Uh, OK. Well, welcome back, anyway! We sure are glad to see you guys. Uh, security officer, though? Shouldn't your Captain..."

Kamp's pulse throbbed at the base of his neck. "Captain Cerrulo sends his apologies. He's been confined to his quarters with food poisoning since yesterday. So has Colonel Higuera, our Head of Communications." He paused; the guy on Proteus looked nonplussed. "Stale yogurt."

"Wow—you guys have had it rough out there."

"It's been up and down, y'know? At the start of last month, we..." He induced another long burst of phony static. "...but apart from that, it's been mostly smooth sailing."

"I see. Well, maybe we should..." The bald functionary turned to mumble at somebody else off-screen, then nodded. "Yeah, OK – why don't we forego the usual status report? That all right with you Major Kamp? Our personnel shuttle's already *en route*, and some corporate guys here are super anxious to start unloading that precious ore."

"I agree." It was all Kamp could manage not to shout a victory cry and shoot his gun into the air. "Our investors shouldn't be kept waiting! I'll inform the crew that..." He shut off the connection abruptly with a flick of his thumb.

Bowman was gripping the command chair with white knuckles. When the com screen went black, he released a ragged breath. "Son of a bitch. They actually went for it!"

"I'm not completely surprised," Kamp said, though he could hear the tremor of relief in his own voice. "They want what we have almost as badly as we want to get home." He grimaced. "The ore, of course. Not, uh, the other thing."

"So what do we do now? How should we get the crew ready for their arrival?"

But Kamp was striding toward the elevator, his weapon ready in his hand. "There is no 'we' any more, Gerry. You can do whatever you like, far as I'm concerned. Long as you don't get between me and the airlock."

THREE SISTERS STARS
RENA MASON

A spear of bone protruded from a boulder near Leila's arm. It glowed silver in the moonlight beneath a slowing rain of dirt. The hard fall had jounced her brain. What she saw before her eyes and what her brain thought it saw made no sense, but that seemed okay. Normal. Past that, Orion's Belt twinkled in the night sky through the hole above, at least thirty feet up, where moments ago, there existed a rocky incline she and her sisters had hiked upon.

Leila shifted onto her shoulder for a better look, spilling dust and gravel. Shrill coughs rattled up her throat. Muscles in her neck tightened and ached. As the earth in the air settled, she scrutinized the bone from its needle-sharp tip to its base, not jutting from stone but her forearm. Comprehension brought pain.

"No. No. No!" she said, and then screamed.

"Leila, is that you?" A fragile voice called out.

"Taylor?" Leila said. "Are you okay? Is Kim with you?" If Leila remembered right, they'd both stayed a few steps behind while climbing the hill before it collapsed.

The three siblings, three years apart in age, had agreed to Leila's plans for Kim's 22nd birthday-slash-college graduation celebration which included hiking at Red Rock Canyon State Park, just thirty minutes from their Las Vegas Strip hotel. Leila would never hear the end of it now.

"I don't see her," Taylor said. "But I can't see anything. Kim! Ow. My side hurts when I yell."

"Are you bleeding? Kim might've passed out," Leila said. "Don't worry. We'll find her."

"No. My shirt's dry from what I can tell. It hurts like hell when I try and move, though."

"Stay put. I'll come to you. Shit. Cover your ears. I may have to scream again." Leila sucked in a dusty breath, then hacked on grit in her throat. She gnashed her teeth and pushed up with her left arm and sat. As her right arm dragged across the top of the boulder, she ground her teeth so hard her temples might burst.

"Whoo!" Leila exhaled. She glanced down at the bone spear. No way that'll go back in without surgery, she thought. It didn't take two years of anatomy and nursing courses to surmise that. The injury needed guarding from bumping and protection from infection, but Taylor first.

More dirt and gravel went to ground when Leila stood. Rocks of every size and shape surrounded her on what seemed like a solid ground of packed earth.

"What happened?" Taylor said.

"Pretty sure we fell into an old mine shaft. Lots of silver mining went on in Nevada in the mid 1800s." Leila moved cautiously and brushed herself off lightly with her left hand for fear of discovering any other injuries. "There's no way we're getting out the way we came in."

Taylor went quiet while Leila groped her way through the dark.

"Say something so I can find you," Leila said.

"Remember swimming at the public pool and you guys laughing

at my belly flops and me saying they came naturally because I have the biggest belly?"

"That was random," Kim said.

"Kim!" Taylor said. "Dammit, that hurt my side."

Leila inched toward Taylor's voice, sometimes tripping over debris. "Keep talking, Taylor. Kim, are you hurt?"

"I can't move my left foot. But there's a big ass rock on top of it."

"I was actually proud of my bellyflops," Taylor said. "And I wasn't just saying that because I wanted you guys to—"

"Got you." Leila bent and patted Taylor's head. Sand and pebbles spilled from it.

"Thank god," Taylor said. She pulled Leila down into a hunch and sobbed.

"Watch the right arm." Leila winced and guided it clear of Taylor's awkward embrace. "Your phone handy?"

"Check her head, Leila," Kim said. "She's stuck on the belly flops and probably has a brain injury or something."

"My head's fine," Taylor said. "We thought you were the one unconscious. I'm on top of my phone. It's in my back pocket. Oh my god! Your ar-ar-ar—"

"Don't look at it," Leila said. "Can you roll?" Leila moved Taylor with her left arm.

"Ow!" Taylor said. "No. Stop. I can't with my side."

Leila placed her hand on Taylor's right side. "Here?"

"Yow! Yeah," Taylor said.

"You may have broken a rib or two. Let's hope it's not your liver or something—"

"Don't do one of your nursing school worst-case-scenarios right now," Kim said.

"Being the oldest still doesn't make you the boss down here, Kim," Taylor said.

"She's right, though," Leila said. "Let's think positive and zip up that fancy, too small, Columbia jacket you bought. It should give you some support."

"For once I'm glad I sized down for diet motivation," Taylor said.

"Ready?"

"No!"

"I need you to inhale deep and hold it."

"Suck it up, buttercup," Kim said.

Leila grabbed the jacket taut. "In three, two—" She pulled the zipper closed and Taylor shrieked.

"I can hardly breathe now," Taylor said in a pant.

"Give it a minute," Leila said. "You hurt anywhere else?"

"No. I don't think so."

"My phone's in my right front pocket. Reach in and get it." Leila turned her hip toward Taylor. "I landed on that side, so figured I'd probably killed it."

Taylor slipped the phone out. "Screen's totally cracked. Looks like it's working though." She showed it to Leila.

"Excellent," Leila said.

"No bars," Taylor said.

"I'm not surprised," Kim said. "We didn't have service before we fell." She raised her own phone and turned the screen toward Taylor and Leila. Kim sat behind a grouping of large rocks.

"I hope there's a way out." Taylor panned her phone's light around like a cameraman.

Kim waved when the beam shined near her. "My turn. Come get this rock off me."

"We're coming," Leila said. "But first we've got to get you up, Taylor. Grab hold of my shoulder. And remember to stay away from my right... Everything."

"I can't even sit up," Taylor cried out.

"You have to wiggle. Use your arms," Leila said. "Pull and inch your way up. That's it."

Taylor had never been graceful, but watching her grimace and groan while writhing around like a chubby grub on hot pavement hurt Leila's eyes more than her broken arm. The fiery shooting jolts that raced from her fingertips to her shoulder came and went. She willed it to remain numb but then the pain would scream back. Of all the cycling sensations, the most bizarre was that the protruding bone recognized the cold. A stinging chill gnawed on her raw skeleton, making her tremble and her teeth chatter. Leila needed to protect her arm and wished she'd worn a jacket too, but hadn't thought it necessary for the quick summer hike.

"You think Mom's looking for us?" Leila said.

"Maybe she's already called the police," Taylor said.

"Are you two kidding?" Kim said. "I bet we have at least three texts each saying she'll be late because she's winning at the casino."

Leila sighed.

"I did it. I'm up," Taylor said.

"Thank god," Kim said. "Now get over here. I think there's an opening in front of me. Could be a way out."

Taylor pointed the phone light toward Kim, then hung onto Leila's left shoulder. Together, they hobbled as one and moved toward their older sister.

Instead of screaming when they push-rolled the rock off of Kim's foot, Kim shouted and swore like a drunk Australian. Not that Australians cuss more than other folks, but the worst things Leila had ever heard came from the mouth of a drunk Australian after he'd been beaten up and robbed during her rotation in the ER at the university hospital.

Leila poked and prodded Kim's foot. "I don't think anything's broken, but I can't tell for sure, and I'm not taking your shoe off or it'll swell up like a balloon and you won't be able to walk. You're ankle's already twice the size it should be."

"Who says I'm walking anywhere?" Kim said.

"You want to stay here alone and wait for us to get help?" Taylor said.

"Well, when you put it like that," Kim said. "It makes me doubt either one of you will get anywhere but lost and in more trouble."

Leila and Taylor looked at one another and rolled their eyes.

"Come on then," Kim said. "Help me up."

"Taylor's already on my left and you can't be on my right," Leila said.

"Why not?" Kim said.

Leila lowered her arm and pointed the bone spear at Kim's face.

"Gross," Kim said. "I bet that hurts like hell."

"It does. That's why my right is off limits."

"Well, it's just my left foot that's messed up, not my arms, and Taylor's hurt on her right side. So I'll get on the other side of Taylor," Kim said.

"I have to be in the middle, holding up the both of you?" Taylor said. "Figures."

"Good thing you have strong legs," Leila said.

"Pillar of the family," Kim said. "Mom always says you'll be the one keeping us together when she's not around."

"Besides, you're not holding me up," Leila said. "I can walk fine. It's you using me like a crutch. Here, lean against this rock while I help Kim."

More cussing through gritted teeth got Kim onto her good foot.

"Just in this moment, I'm glad you're thin and light," Leila said.

"Kim, you have to shine your phone's light since you've got the only good free arm," Taylor said.

"First, we need to send 911 texts so they go through if we hit the right spot," Leila said. "Then put 'em in low energy mode except for the one we're using to see. We need to save the battery power." Leila reached into Taylor's back pocket, took out her little sister's phone, and then put it into Taylor's left hand.

"Here, Taylor," Leila said. "Yours still works too."

"Thank god." Taylor pushed the phone into her left jacket pocket. "Now how do you want us to move?"

"Nice and slow until we figure out a rhythm because Kim will have to hop," Leila said.

"It'll be like sack races on Easter," Kim said.

"We always lost those," Taylor said.

"Only because you slowed us down," Kim said.

"Bullshit," Taylor said.

"Let's not fight until we get out of here, please," Leila said. "We all know exercise wasn't one of your strong points, Taylor. Or yours for that matter, Kim."

"Just remember I'm the one in the middle, helping you right now with my pillar legs, Kim," Taylor said.

They quieted. Taylor's weight had always been a sensitive issue. Like most siblings, they knew how to push each other's buttons and when to stop. In no time, they moved as one lame animal of reluctantly conjoined sisters, gasping and whining with almost every step. As they traveled farther away from where they'd fallen, their path became less of a rock obstacle course. Scantling on either side narrowed the mine walls. They changed positions and moved single file, using the rough chiseled stone for support.

"What's all that junk along the walls?" Taylor said. "You guys see?"

Leila had tried to ignore the things, hoping her sisters wouldn't notice, hoping the fall had jarred her brain so hard she now experienced concussion hallucinations. She had also tried not to focus on the carved niches that held the items. They'd passed at least thirty of them in varying sizes.

Kim stopped, so Taylor did, and then Leila in the front.

"Oh my god, look at this old ass iPhone," Kim said. "Remember when they came out? Like the early 2000s."

"2007," Taylor said.

"Put it back," Leila said. "Don't touch anything."

"It's a classic. Probably worth something. People collect this shit now." Kim pocketed the old iPhone.

"You shouldn't take it," Taylor said. "It looks like someone went to a lot of trouble to carve these little slots in the rock to keep this crap in them."

"Why would anyone waste so much time?" Kim said. "It's dumb."

"We need to keep moving." Leila put her hand back against the tunnel wall and stepped ahead. "Get back to phone light duty, Kim. I can't see."

"What is it?" Taylor said. "You're not saying what you think, Leila."

"Don't ask her," Kim said. "You know it'll be something worst-case-scenario."

"Just say it," Taylor said.

"Yeah, tell us," Kim said. "Then I'll point the light ahead and we'll follow you again."

"Well, I think maybe someone lives or hides down here," Leila said.

"Good. Then maybe they can help us," Kim said. "Call out—"

"No!" Leila said. "It's not like we've been all that quiet, and if someone down here wanted to help us, I'm sure they already know we're here."

"Who do you think it is?" Taylor said.

"Have you actually looked at the crap in the walls?" Leila said. "Some of it's older and some of it's newer, and it's all totally random. Someone with time and patience carved those little holes out of solid rock for each thing like they're..."

"Special?" Taylor said.

"That's one way to put it," Leila said.

"Spit it out," Kim said.

"Fine then, they look like trophies," Leila said.

"Trophies?" Taylor said.

"Yeah, souvenirs, mementos..." Leila said. "Things a serial killer would keep."

"Oh, for fuck's sake," Kim said. "Don't listen to her, Taylor. Let's just go."

"Fine, but you guys asked."

Kim lit the way, and they trudged on.

"I thought I saw a shirt in one of those things back there with dirt stains on it but maybe it wasn't dirt. Maybe it's blood," Taylor said.

"Don't think about Leila Doom's prognosis. Keep moving," Kim said.

Leila stopped. Taylor bumped into her and then Kim.

"Hey," Kim said. "What's—"

"Shhh," Leila whispered. "Point your phone up there, in front of me."

They'd entered an open, cavernous space.

"Shit," Taylor said.

"Shit is right." Kim moved the light down the rocky interior. Just beyond the open area appeared more tunnel entrances.

"What are we gonna do now?" Taylor said. "There're probably more tunnels inside those. A huge maze of them for all we know."

"We'll have to split up," Leila said.

"No way," Taylor said. "We have to stay together."

"Taylor's right for once," Kim said. "It's a stupid idea. Besides, you can both move faster than me, and I'll be the one that's left behind."

"You've been doing all right balancing yourself using the walls," Leila said. "This way, at least one of us will get out or get to a spot with service so we can call for help."

"Dammit," Kim said. "You mean you, of course, Leila. You're the only one whose legs are working without any pain."

"I don't think I can get through one of those by myself," Taylor said.

"Me either," Kim said.

"Fine then," Leila said. "You two stay here, and I'll go for help."

∾

Sister Star – *Mintaka* – *The Belt*

Leila hurried through the first tunnel, eyes focused on the path ahead while her mind raged at her sisters' cowardice. But why the hell had a serial killer of all things popped into her head when she saw that shit in the walls? Maybe Kim had her pegged. She did focus on gloom and doom more often than she should. But her personal mantra had always saved her and gotten her through the toughest times. *If you go straight to the worst that can happen, anything above that is better. It's bearable.*

Hot and sweaty with exertion, bitter cold still chewed on the raw bone sticking out of her arm. The continuous ache in her calves seemed nothing at all compared to the waves of fierce pain that barreled up and down her right side.

A shadow and rush of air and agony came from the dark on her left. Leila flew back, then slid across gravel and dirt on her ass, stopping when her left shoulder hit the tunnel wall and popped.

Leila screamed.

In her phone's faint light, a man stood in front of her—any man, clean cut and shaven, someone's accountant husband, a yuppy dad. He rushed toward her carrying a sledgehammer. Leila saw her mangled leg then, too. Impossibly bent back at the knee. It laid lifeless and still like a prosthetic.

Leila screamed, this time in fear. The man came and stood over her. He positioned his feet against her flanks, pinning her. His face expressionless as he raised his weapon.

"No!" Leila put her hands in front of her face. She didn't want to see the metal come down. She didn't want to feel her head explode. Leila knew he'd wait for her to look. Knew he wanted to see the terror in her eyes. Worst case now, he'd take it slow and make her suffer. She'd never get to tell her sisters she was right, that they should've listened.

The bone shard sticking out of her arm glowed blue.

Leila screamed once more, this time in defiance. She reached, clutched the man's pants with her left hand and punched him in the thigh with her right forearm, ramming the slivered piece of bone into him. He teetered over her and struggled to maintain balance as the weight of the sledgehammer pulled him to one side. She fought between his legs, screaming as she pulled her splintered bone out, splattering his blood onto her. Holding onto his pants with a death grip, she shrieked and wailed, stabbing him again and again with the bone shard. Her pain had gone, replaced with a mad will to live.

The man stumbled back and disappeared into the darkness.

Sister Star – Alnilam – The Belt of Pearls

Kim and Taylor listened to their sister's screams.

"I have to help her," Kim said.

"Go," Taylor said.

"Stay here. I'll be right back."

Holding her phone up for light with one hand while bracing the rocky tunnel wall with the other made it harder and more painful to hop.

"Stupid fucking idea to split up," she said. Kim planned to let Leila have it as soon as she got to her. "What idiot decides to plan a night hike in the desert?" And why the hell had she been stupid enough to agree to it? Kim knew she couldn't completely blame Leila even though she wanted to. They'd come so close to the peak at dusk, she'd encouraged they continue so they could see The Strip all lit up.

Still, Leila deserved to be cussed out. Especially after all that screaming moments ago, knowing full well she'd already freaked Taylor out with her stupid manslayer notion.

Near her head, clusters of rusted nails poked out of old joist junctions. To get around them scrape and tetanus-free, Kim gritted her teeth and toe touched with her hurt foot, swearing the entire time. She'd read somewhere that it helped reduce the sensation of pain for those who typically didn't use profanity, like her.

All she'd done her whole life was care for her siblings, and they'd always been pains in her ass, tattling on her whenever they could. Just thinking of it stirred up a rage that kept her moving.

Shuffling sounds came from ahead. Kim directed her phone light. A tall shadow approached. Not Leila. A man. But he didn't look right. He had a hand on his crotch, and it appeared he'd wet himself. The man dragged something behind him.

"Stay away from me," Kim said.

He said nothing but continued moving toward her, his gait unsteady. The man seemed drunk or strung out. A homeless alcoholic or drug addict maybe. He probably lived down here. Stupid Leila.

His eyes locked with hers. He stopped, picked up a big sledgehammer, then came at her. Kim turned off her phone and pocketed it. In pitch blackness, she backed up to the timber joist, remembering where she'd seen the grouping of long nails protruding from a beam. She sneaked to the opposite wall, held her breath, and waited.

The man now stood in front of her. She sensed him, which meant he likely sensed her too, but he swung the sledgehammer to the right, where he'd seen her last. When it struck the stone with a resounding clang, Kim charged his torso, pushing him into what she hoped was the spiky joist.

"Damn you, Leila!" Kim reached up and grabbed the man by his hair. He twisted and shrugged but couldn't shake her off.

"And fuck you, too!" She pulled his scalp back and forth, bashed his head against the old wood beam. Then she fell to the ground and scrabbled forward. If she'd injured him, he made no show of it.

Kim got up onto both feet and hop-ran ahead in the dark, feeling her way along the tunnel. She hustled with all her rage and weight on the hurt ankle and would keep going until it couldn't push her any farther. All the while, she whispered curses at Leila with every breath.

~

SISTER STAR —Alnitak – The Girdle

A loud ping sounded to Taylor's left. The cavern quaked. Dirt sprinkled down from above. Taylor got up, leaned against the stone wall, and held still until the disturbance passed. Then she continued into the tunnel her sisters had gone through, checking the ceiling for stability and her phone now and then for a signal. Her battery drained faster than usual, and she chided herself for downloading the new system upgrade before a trip. It kept her mind off the possibility of the roof caving in, as well as what might've happened to her sisters, and what Leila had said.

At least Leila's idea to use her too-small jacket purchase as a kind of brace worked. Taylor kept her breaths quick and short to curb the pain at her side. She forgot to ask Leila how they fixed broken ribs. She wondered if she'd have to have surgery. The thought of being asleep with all her flab out and exposed in front of a bunch of people bothered her.

Cool air drifted past Taylor's face. The tunnel had darkened, but she still discerned shadows and shapes like rocky protrusions from the walls. She raised her phone, but the screen had gone black. But how could she see?

Moonlight, starlight, city lights—she didn't care—shined at the far end of the tunnel, reflecting off the rock walls and casting a dim light that allowed her to see. She'd made it! Nearing the exit, she took out her cell.

Something hard struck her arm, blasting pain through her elbow and out her hand. The phone went airborne. Taylor heard it hit the ground as she spun around. A bloodied man stood there holding whatever he'd just hit her with.

"Asshole!" Taylor screamed and tackled him. His head hit the tunnel wall with a squelch. She backed up to kick him, but he fell to the ground. Even better, she thought. She moved farther away, then clutched her ribs. Taylor ran-shambled at him, piledriving her foot into his side.

The man reached up, but he was no match for her. She screamed and jumped on his chest. Blood sprayed from his mouth and nose. While he sputtered and gasped for air, Taylor dropped onto her knees, still atop him. Then she flopped forward and pressed her gut into his face. He grabbed and pulled at her, bucking and flailing his legs, but she did not budge.

Exhausted and out of breath, she relaxed and let herself go soft around his head. His struggle slowed and then ceased, but she lie across his face for a bit longer.

Taylor used her good arm and her pillar legs to rise and find her phone. She had to save her sisters.

THE MORTAL GODS

SYDNEY PAIGE GUERRERO

The mortal gods are curious creatures. In Mama's stories, they are all gossamer skin and brittle hearts, beings of lightning straining against the confines of their faux flesh. *Like trying to hold back a dam with paper,* Mama would say of the mortals who achieved divinity, *you cannot hold that much power without it ruining you.*

Back then, I had never seen a god despite my frequent ventures into the woods behind our home. The days when they would drift in with the crisp caress of the breeze faded with the old gods, and now we only caught glimpses—mottled horns like delicate spires poised to pierce the sky, dead flowers forming a trail that deviated from the forest path. To see more of a god was a bad omen. It meant that you had caught the god's attention, and those stories never ended well.

It was my brother, not I, who caught divine attention. Or, more accurately, it was my brother who sought it. We were both raised on the story of a man who tricked our goddess with foreign posies and false promises then made tea out of her bones to become a god himself. We were still bonded by fear then, but where I heard a cautionary tale, my brother heard a challenge.

One evening, he trekked to the clearing in the woods where the god liked to sleep and stepped on sacred ground with childish irreverence. He paid no heed to the delicate blood-red petals sprouting around femurs and the cracked skulls made whole again by thick layers of moss. Death was sown into the ground, the clearing a beautiful warning, but my brother believed, as many men do, that he was the exception.

The trees bore witness as my brother took aim. The wind carried unheard warnings into my brother's ear, but he saw only the god, seemingly vulnerable in his sleep.

My brother was quick. The god was quicker.

Mid-step, my brother's blood turned to syrup in his veins, his bones malleable as hot glass. He fell, another body in the grass, and the god rose from his faux slumber.

If he wanted to, he could have skinned my brother with a flick of his wrist or turned my brother's organs into insects that would consume him from the inside out, but instead the god stared with the yawning chasms he had for eyes and waited for my brother's offer in exchange for mercy.

Some men offered gold. Some men offered servitude. My brother offered me.

I WAS SLEEPING when my brother pulled himself into our hut with skin so pale his veins stood out like healing scars. He collapsed to the floor, writhing from injuries I could not see. He could not speak, at least not clearly, and I held him, whispering platitudes until my voice grew hoarse. I was a little girl again, cradling my baby brother in my arms. For a terrible second, I was almost glad to see him need me again.

When I could not console him, I let him go, intent on retrieving my hidden supplies. My brother did not know what I was, and that was not how I imagined telling him. But keeping my secret was not worth watching my brother's pain—not when I had the power to put him at ease. But before I could step away, he grabbed my wrist and yanked me back, his grip strong enough to bruise. My heart clenched with familiar fear.

"Is it time already? Are you going? You must go! I said you would!" he wailed.

"Go where?" I asked. "What are you talking about? Where do I need to go?"

He scratched at his face, dark rivulets of blood appearing with every violent rake of his fingers. I dropped down next to him, horrified as I pulled his hands away from his face. My stomach turned as I felt his blood on my hands. Finally, his eyes focused on me.

In bits and pieces, he told me about a dare from the other boys in the village and the god in the clearing. His voice broke when spoken language failed to express his terror. When he told me about the exchange, my soothing words turned to glass in my throat. I could not move, could not breathe, could not think.

I could only stare at him as he spoke—my younger brother who I had cared for my whole life, my near constant childhood companion, my only remaining family. He crushed me against his chest, kissed my forehead like he was already in mourning.

"I am so, so sorry," he cried into my hair. "But if you love me, you must do this for me."

As if I had a choice. As if the decision had not already been made.

In that moment, I wished he had died in the clearing.

But I could not—*would* not say that. So, I said nothing at all.

My brother retreated further inside himself, his body curling into a question mark around the burden of guilt I would not take from him, but there was relief too when he stared at me with wide eyes as I packed. *Pathetic,* I thought as I tucked away my herbs and Mama's knife, weaving a spell to obscure it. *Ingrate.*

"You have no idea what I have done because I love you," I finally said, hovering at the entrance of our hut. I realized I would never see him again, but I could not look at him. I did not want to remember him this way. I wanted to still see him as the boy who cried when he found dead butterflies, who learned to braid my hair when Mama no longer could. It was a naïve hope. I will never really remember him any other way. Even now, when I think of my brother, I see a living corpse. I see my father.

"Forgive me," he said.

"You cannot ask that of me," I said. "You can never ask anything of me ever again." And I left.

By dawn, I would belong to a god, but perhaps I was always meant to belong to someone. A father. A husband. My life had never been my own. With the god, at least, I had no illusions that *bride* meant anything other than *sacrifice*.

If the trees were to be believed, and they often were, the god developed a taste for humanity once he lost his. They spoke of it often if you knew how to listen. Mama taught me, and on days I could no longer bear my father's anger or the silence of home after her passing, I would run into the forest and attend to the whispers that drove most away.

They told terrible tales, the trees—tales of gnawed bones and ribboned flesh, of helpless horror and anger so volatile it could consume the world. Anger I recognized in myself. Anger I would never admit to.

Who would listen to them when I was gone?

When I entered the forest that night, the trees were silent.

The quiet sat like a third presence. The trees always protected me from the god, but there was no protection they could offer me now. The leaves quivered as though trembling with the effort to keep still, and I pressed a hand against their rough bark. When I reached the point the trees told me never to cross, I touched the space where I had hidden Mama's knife, a gift from her mother and her mother's mother before her, and somehow, I felt less alone when I stepped forward.

The god arrived at daybreak, manifesting between heartbeats as though he had always been there. My fear sharpened my anger. I still cannot say what he looked like. I could not tell if he was beautiful or grotesque, the line between *monster* and *god* blurring with my vision. I could not imagine him looking human once.

He stalked around me, and the power radiating from him set my teeth on edge. I did not dare move except for the slight hiccup in my breath. When he leaned in close, the warm scent of burnt cinnamon undercut with sharp citrus invaded my senses. A cold, pale finger trailed down my face, not quite wiping away a tear but tracing its path.

When he pulled away, my body sagged with relief. The god cocked his head, amused.

"*Come,*" he said without words, his voice as clear in my head as my own thoughts.

He took my hand and cut through space like water. The clearing disappeared, replaced with an elaborate stone mansion. The steps glimmered under the sun, railed balconies on the second floor sat like barred teeth.

I instantly despised it.

The god watched for my reaction and mistook my silence for awe. He led me to the foyer but went no further and pressed a kiss to the back of my hand.

"*I must leave now,*" he said, "*but I will return at sunset. Please make yourself comfortable. This is your home now.*"

I watched as he left, and even the flowers seemed to bow for him. For the first time, I understood why so many had risked their lives to kill him.

What would it be like not to ration time but to have it unfold before you in boundless stretches? What would it be like not to make yourself small but to have the world make space for you? What would it be like to have no reason to be afraid?

My hand ached with the familiar pain of a blossoming bruise, and I stared at the spot the god kissed. I held my hand close to my heart, thinking that this, perhaps, may be the only thing the god and I had in common. Even then, I, too, understood the desire to hurt everything I touched.

~

I LEARNED VERY EARLY on to be aware when someone is watching. My father's gaze, like most things about him, was razor sharp, and Mama was more observant than anyone gave her credit for. While Mama's reprimands over my growing power as a child were well-intentioned, my father was a lash. Noticing watchful eyes quickly became habit, which quickly became skill.

Even when the god was gone, I was not alone. I did not know if there were sentient objects in the mansion or if there were invisible beings who took care of maintenance in the god's stead. They never spoke to me, though their gaze constantly pricked at the back of my neck, and they attended to my every need.

Each morning, fresh clothes were laid outside my door and breakfast sat waiting in the dining room. I grew used to finding feather dusters gliding over chandeliers and unattended shovels scooping coal into the oven. I never tried to leave the mansion, never tried to force open locked doors, barely even left my room. If the eyes reported back to the god, they would not have much to say about me. Scared, perhaps. Reclusive.

They did not watch me in my room, at least, though I spent the afternoons pretending to sleep as I brought out the herbs I took with me, cutting them with Mama's knife like she taught me. The bone-white blade carved protection spells from Mama's notes, spells that her mother taught her, back in the days before our power was maligned as demonic. The power flowing through me felt like comfort. Like hope.

In the evenings, the eyes prepared feasts so lavish that I was often overwhelmed by the food's decadence before I even took a bite. It was only during dinner that the eyes left again, their presence no longer required once the god had joined me. He would pile his plate high with apple glazed ribs and roasted chicken, tossing a grape back and forth in his hands, but otherwise he never touched his food.

He rarely spoke to me unless it was to encourage another helping of too rich yet too bland food, and I was not allowed to leave the table unless he decided I had eaten enough. By the time I returned to my room, I felt sick—bloated and helpless as I awaited slaughter like an animal.

The god would lay next to me, never close enough to touch because it was my fear of him that mattered, not the contact. He fed off my terror as I barely breathed next to him. Sometimes he would pretend to reach out, just to see if I would flinch. I gritted my teeth, but I still flinched every time, and his shoulders shook with laughter.

When he had his fill, his eyes would drift shut, sated and sleepy. I waited until his breathing evened out, and I waited even longer until I could not bear to hold still a second more. Then, I slid the knife out from under my pillow.

My heart pounded as I gripped the handle, my unrestrained fear only drawing him into a deeper slumber. I picked up a golden strand, surprised to find there was a little resistance against the blade, but the knife cut through. I repeated the process each night, and by the sixth strand, the knife sliced the hair like it was nothing. I drew out the strands' power the same way Mama taught me to draw out an herb's healing properties. I did not let myself think of her then, what she would say if she saw me imbuing her knife with gnarled magic.

On the seventh night, the god breached the space between us. His breath was damp against my face as he peered down at me, basking in my terror. I froze. I was not a warrior like my brother, and

I was too desperate to be brave. *How could I kill a god?* I thought. *How could I? How could I?* But then he trailed a claw down my face, drawing blood, and my fear crystalized in my chest.

When he leaned in for a taste, I wielded my fear like a blade and slit his throat.

The god fell off the bed, stunned that a knife could cut him and that his wound would not close. He had not known surprise or pain in centuries, and that made him slow as he gagged on his own blood. I had no such problems, and I struck his head, his heart, his hands.

My cheeks were damp with tears and blood, but I did not stop, did not want to. I wanted to see *that* moment, that moment just before death—the moment when the haze of pain breaks long enough for awareness to set in, and a special type of fear takes hold. Not fear of the unknown but fear of the certainty that the last thing you will ever feel is agony, that your fate is barreling towards you and there is nothing you can do to stop it.

Even in the god's chasm eyes, I saw that fear. It might have given me pause if I had not already seen it in Mama, just before the sickness overtook her; in my father, just before he realized he had been fed water hemlock for harming my brother the way he had harmed me.

Instead, expecting it, I reveled in the god's fear.

I stabbed and stabbed and stabbed until he stopped moving and his body was little more than flesh and blood and bone. The god's claws had shredded the skin on my arm, and I could no longer see out of one eye. I laughed, half-delirious, and thought of Mama and her stories of the mortal gods and dared to imagine what stories might be told of me someday. My lungs burned and I felt like I might burst, but I brought down the knife again, then again and again. I did not dare stop lest he knit himself back together, and I hacked at the god until he was in pieces.

When I was done, I was blood-covered and shaking. Scattering pieces of the god around the room, I chose the two largest chunks and scraped off as much flesh as I could, my heart as numb as my hands. When I had enough bones, I made my way to the kitchen.

Watch me now, I thought viciously, searching for the eyes. *This is my fear. This is my power.*

The fire in the stove burned, and the god's bones turned brittle and splintered in the heat.I boiled water, the action so simple and heartbreakingly familiar. As I ground the bones, my hands trembled under the weight of newfound freedom.

I imagined that moment countless times as I prepared the tea, wondering if, in those final moments before becoming a god, I would shake with anticipation or dread. There was no telling how one would react to finally holding one's destiny in their hands. I closed my eyes when the tea was ready. I took the steaming cup in my hands. I remember thinking of Mama's stories, that no mortal can hold that much power without it ruining you, and I wondered if there was anything left of me to ruin. I thought of what it would be like to be back with the trees, my power flowing from my hands like a dam finally broken loose. A calm settled over me as I drank. Then, finally, I was free.

BETWEEN A ROCK AND A HARD PLACE

NAJUA ISMAIL

Eighteen-year-old Tanjung cradled her protruding belly and closed her eyes. Out of all the obligations that came with marriage, motherhood was the one she feared most. It seemed not long ago she was a carefree child running with her friends in the open field across the dirt road from her childhood home.

Now she was the wife of a laborer who didn't have steady work and spent most of his time in their little shanty at the edge of the forest, wallowing in self-pity. The marriage creaked under the pressure of poverty and the weight of discord.

Her husband wanted children despite his lack of steady employment and inability to provide. Tanjung tried to voice her reservations but they came out in plaintive murmurings, which her husband swiftly dismissed. And now she was pregnant with their first child, a daughter she would name Melur. Three years later, she bore him another child, a son called Pekan.

Then her husband left her alone with them when his life was cut short. He was gored by a gaur on the way to the village to look for work.

"MAAMAAAAAAAAAWWW," screamed Pekan before dissolving into noisy choking sobs.

Tanjung sighed, fighting the urge to yell at her son. She called out to her eldest child. "Melur! Can you please help me with your brother?" Her daughter came running, grabbed her younger brother's hand and drew him close. "What's wrong Pekan?"

"I'm...hun...hun...hungry," he sobbed.

"Mama's making dinner," said Melur. "It'll be ready soon. Keep me company while I finish my homework." As she led her brother away, Melur turned to look at her mother. Tanjung stood over the clay charcoal stove stirring a pot of soup, furrowed brow and tired countenance aging her young face.

IT HAD BEEN a long day as usual, but Tanjung was not in a hurry to go home. She decided to venture further into the forest to see if she could find anything else to make a meal of or take to the market to sell. After a long trek, she stopped and looked around. She'd never been in this part of the forest before. Tanjung wasn't sure why but a chill ran down her spine when she noticed the withered plants and trees surrounding her. And then she heard the voice in the breeze.

At first so faint, she thought it was the rustling of distant trees but gradually the sound grew louder and sounded more urgent. Tanjung stopped walking and listened carefully. Despite the balmy weather, she trembled. It was her name in the wind. *"Tanjung..."* She knew instinctively that she had to get home, run as far from the voice as she could. Yet, she couldn't move a muscle. She was rooted to the soil like the trees around her. It was only when she turned in the direction of the voice that she was able to move. She shuffled forward as if in a trance, her mind demanding to turn around but her body unable to obey.

The voice's gentle tenor morphed into a more insistent timbre. Its cadence was haunting, melodic, strangely soothing. She felt lighter, as if treading on air.

She stepped into the shadows cast by an imposing rocky outcrop, and was brought instantly down to earth. The boulder loomed menacingly over her, and Tanjung looked up in fear and awe. Two deep indentations on the rock's face formed a pair of jagged lines that could pass as slit shaped eyes, while between them and slightly below, a protruding chunk of granite resembled a nose. The gaping hole near the bottom with serrated edges sticking out like teeth completed the distorted image of a face.

Tanjung stood transfixed. The mouth yawned wide and began to open and close, gnashing together like teeth. Her name again amidst the chomping noises emanating from the dark depths of the rock's mouth and this time, it shocked her out of her stupor. She turned around and ran for her life until she was safely back home.

On her tattered old mattress that night, Tanjung tossed and turned. She was in the forest again, standing in front of the face-like rock. This time she didn't tremble when it opened its mouth wide. She stood and stared, longingly, at the vast blackness in front of her. Her name floated up again from the dark, and she walked willingly toward its open mouth. This time, she wanted to be consumed by its infinite darkness.

TANJUNG SHOOK her head in embarrassment as she stepped out of the river. She rubbed herself dry, but couldn't quite wipe the smile off her face. It felt silly to get excited over something so trivial but she couldn't help it. She beamed broadly, looking forward to a simple meal of rice with mudskipper eggs—a treat she'd long craved. She quickly got dressed, humming a tune as she headed back to the shack where Melur should have the eggs prepared for dinner.

Her daughter smiled nervously at Tanjung when she walked into the shanty. "Where's Pekan?" asked Tanjung.

"Pekan has already eaten. He was hungry and couldn't wait. I'm sorry mama."

"That's alright, we'll eat together, then just..." Tanjung's voice trailed off as she noticed the boiled chicken eggs in the bowl on the mat where they ate.

Guilt was written all over Melur's face as the words came out in a torrent, "Pekan was hungry and his share wasn't enough for him. He wouldn't stop crying. I gave him mine but he wanted more so I gave him yours but we can have..."

Before she could finish, Tanjung spun on her heels and ran out the door. Melur followed. "Mama, mama wait!" Tanjung ignored her. Her bare feet pounded the soil as she ran deeper into the forest's dark embrace.

Anger, sadness, hurt and disappointment nipped at her heels and she picked up the pace desperate to leave them behind. Just as she began to lose her breath and feel the ache of exertion, Tanjung heard a familiar voice call out to her. Its urgent tone provided the jolt of adrenaline needed to spur her on. She followed the voice in the wind deeper and deeper into the forest. It led her straight into the open mouth of the face-like rock.

When a panting and breathless Melur arrived in front of the rock, the only sign of her mother was a few strands of her hair hanging limply between the serrated edges of the gap, now firmly shut. She collapsed to her knees on the ground, face in her open palms and sobbed helplessly in front of the merciless monolith.

~

PEKAN STRODE INTO THE SHACK, a huge grin on his face. "Guess what?" His sister, who stood chopping onions on the makeshift kitchen stand in the corner, turned around and smiled at him. "Well, don't keep me in suspense."

"I got into vocational college!"

"Hooray! Now you can give up that job at the construction site."

"Well, it'll be a couple of months before the term starts so I'll stick with it until then. It's helping us make ends meet."

"Sit down, let's celebrate," said his sister. Pekan froze when he lifted the bamboo food cover.

"There must be a reason mama liked them so much," said Melur quietly, searching her brother's face as he stared down at the plate of mudskipper eggs. "It's been 14 years since she died..." Her voice trailed off, but then she continued gently, "And after everything we've been through, we deserve to give ourselves a treat, especially after what you've just accomplished."

Pekan looked up at Melur and nodded solemnly. But he chuckled when she picked up a ladle and pointed it at him, playfully adding, "But you're not getting my share this time."

SALIMA FLOATED on a cloud of happiness all the way home. She couldn't wait to share the good news with her husband. A tantalizing aroma tickled her nostrils the moment she stepped into their cosy terrace house. "Hmmm, is that steamed spicy and sour sea bass I smell?" she called out as she made her way to the kitchen.

"Yes, it is," said Hamzah as he placed the cover over the fish in the pot and turned to smile at her.

"Great! I'm starved and—well, I'll be eating for two."

Hamzah's mouth fell open, then he burst into laughter. He pulled her into his embrace and held her tight. Salima rested her head on his shoulder, sighing contentedly.

In bed that night though, she turned away from Hamzah as tears rolled down her cheeks. She wiped them off and closed her eyes, hoping the gentle drone of her husband's snoring would lull her to sleep. But sleep brought no respite. In her dreams, she was running away in the darkness from a child's pleading voice calling, "mama, mama wait!"

∾

AFTER HER MOTHER was swallowed by a rock, Melur felt as if she'd been pinned down by one just as big. She couldn't even remember making her way back to their shanty that night. She'd collapsed onto the mattress she once shared with her mother, and curled into a fetal position. She lay there unable to move, her body aching from fatigue regret and sorrow.

Eventually, her swollen eyes closed and she drifted off into slumber, comforting in its depth and complete darkness. When she woke, she felt the warmth of a body pressed against her back. She turned around slowly and Pekan stirred lazily beside her. "Melur, where's mama?" he slurred.

∾

SALIMA TOOK a deep breath before she rapped her knuckles on the dark wooden door with the sign 'Administrator' written on it. "Come in." Salima entered the room smiling. The smartly suited middle-aged woman behind the desk looked up in surprise. "Hello Salima! How are you? I didn't expect to see you again. Once people have settled in their lives here, my business with them is usually finished."

"Oh," said Salima nervously before blurting out, "I'm pregnant." The administrator looked at her thoughtfully. "Are you happy about that?"

"Ecstatic."

"Excellent! Congratulations to you and Hamzah."

"Thank you."

The administrator cut through what felt like a long silence. "What brings you here?"

"I've been thinking about my children lately."

"Isn't this your first pregnancy?

"Er...the ones from before, I mean."

The administrator said nothing, her face expressionless as she regarded Salima. Salima hesitated, then swallowed before asking, "Is there any way I can see them again?" When the administrator remained silent, she hurriedly continued, "I just want to see how they're doing. They were so little..."

"No," said the administrator. "You made a choice. Now you have to live with it."

But I hadn't wanted to live, thought Salima, feeling a hot sting in her heart as she recalled the night she ran to the monstrous rock. She had known that, as she was crushed between its teeth, all her burdens and pain would also be pulverized along with her. The weight of existence would be lifted once and for all from her sagging shoulders.

But that wasn't what happened. She'd opened her eyes to a new life. She was given a home and learned to earn a proper living with regular income, first as a cashier in the supermarket, then after taking a vocational course, as a hairdresser in the salon where she met Hamzah. She made a good life for herself, something she had struggled to do before.

Her life before was barely a speck in her consciousness... until now. The memory came back in bits and pieces, and at first she couldn't even remember their faces. But now the image of her two young children appeared vividly in her mind, sitting cross-legged on the floor over a measly meal in their shack at the edge of the forest.

PEKAN LICKED his lips in satisfaction. "That was delicious, Melur. I'm going to miss your cooking."

"Cooking?" She laughed as she glanced down at the now empty plate of rice with fried anchovies and eggs her brother had just polished off. "Anybody can make that. They'll feed you better at the hostel."

A serious expression replaced Pekan's grin. "Have you thought about what you're going to do?"

I'm going to leave too," said Melur. "There's nothing left for me here."

"Where will you go?"

"I'm not sure yet but someplace far from here."

"How will we keep in touch?"

"Don't worry, I know where to find you," she intoned in a threatening voice, before smiling fondly at her brother. "I'll come visit."

"You'd better."

"There's something I need to do before I leave, though, and I'll need your help."

"I CAN'T HELP YOU." Hamzah's heart sank as his wife's face fell. "I don't want to think about a life before this if I did have one. I'm happy to spend this life with you."

"But I had children whom I abandoned," said Salima in despair. "I need to find out what happened to them. Please, Hamzah."

"What can I do?"

"You work at the administrator's office. Can't you try to find out how we got here?"

"I work in a different department. I've never even run into her."

"Please... just snoop or ask around."

The look of desperation on his wife's face melted Hamzah's heart. "I'll see what I can find out."

~

"Be careful Pekan," said Melur as she watched her brother wire the explosives he brought from work around the massive rock. She hadn't seen it since the night it swallowed her mother. Now, Melur shuddered as she took in its distorted face. As she continued staring at it, she became transfixed by the menacing mouth-like hole near the bottom with the sharp and hideously uneven teeth.

Today it was wide open as if waiting to be fed, but it was snapped tightly shut that night. A chill crawled up her spine as she recalled the remaining strands of her mother's hair hanging from it.

Melur's eyes began to well up as she recalled the tender smile that softened her mother's often exhausted visage, and her firm but consoling voice doling out advice in the darkness as they lay side-by-side on the mattress at night.

Then she actually heard it. *"Melur..."*

She shook her head in confusion. Could it be? No, it can't be. *"Melur..."* Yes, it is!" Even after all this time, she recognised that voice.

It was...mama! Melur froze and held her breath. Barely perceptible at first, the voice sounded like a whisper in the breeze. Then it became unmistakable and more insistent. It came from the open mouth of the rock. Melur walked toward it.

~

Salima could hardly believe her eyes. Melur stood before her, grown. For a moment, she stood and savored the sight of her. A wisp of Melur's long dark hair, which she had tied into a loose ponytail, fell across her face and her curved lips were pursed in an expression of deep concentration.

Salima called out to her, hesitantly at first, then more firmly and loudly. Tears welled up in her eyes as Melur walked toward her.

≈

A HAND FELL on Melur's arm and she turned to see her brother standing next to her. "Melur! Didn't you hear me? I said it's done."

Melur blinked and shook her head. "Oh...ok, let's do this."

≈

SALIMA WAS SO OVERCOME at the sight of both her children that she trembled. She brought both hands up to her heart as if to steady its erratic rhythm. But she couldn't hold herself any longer. She threw her arms up in the air and waved to them. Melur responded to her earlier, but both her children now seemed oblivious. They turned their backs and walked away.

She stared at them, crestfallen. Then she sprinted toward them. "Melur! Pekan!" she called out. "Wait!" The opening was close, just beyond her reaching fingertips. Then, a loud *boom* sounded. And everything turned black.

≈

SALIMA OPENED her eyes and stared into the dark.

"Sal are you ok?" The bedside lamp clicked on and Hamzah, propped up on an elbow, looked at her, concerned. "You were shouting in your sleep."

Tears streamed down her cheeks. Her husband gently wiped them with the back of his fingers. "Did you dream about them?" He sighed softly when she nodded. "I'm sorry I couldn't find anything out." Salima took a deep breath. "It's ok," she said, taking her husband's hand in hers.

"It looks like this is the only life we've got now," he said gently.

Salima placed her other hand over her belly. Then she smiled through her tears at Hamzah. "I can live with that."

THE UNBURIED

CYNTHIA GÓMEZ

L ater, Dave would try and try to remember the name of the guy on the crew, the one who had stood in the trailer's doorway as the machines fell into silence behind him, holding something wrapped in blue cloth. The crew guy looked kind of young and vaguely familiar in the way that half the workers on the site reminded Dave of somebody else, or each other. Dave could hear the stream of voices outside, everyone louder than usual as they headed home, as if they could already taste the beer, whatever it was they drank, cold and welcome on a day like today. Everyone except this one, whose name Dave hadn't caught, or had caught and dropped again. And who was asking something now, something about the site superintendent, who for once wasn't here.

"Enrique left. Probably up at that Irish bar in Jack London." *Which is where you should be,* Dave hoped his tone hinted at. When the kid didn't move, Dave sighed and stood up from his desk.

"Is there something I can help you with?" Dave leaned next to the photo where he stood, flanked by Marty and Andrew, the M and the A of DMA Development, all three of them grinning and breaking the ground.

"Yes, sir. I found this out on the site, and I thought someone should see it." The guy coughed into his fist. "It looks old." That was a great word to hear at a $400-million construction site, the earth already opened, smoothed, prepared for the concrete that would be coming tomorrow. Dave didn't want that thing coming any closer. But here it was now, the kid setting it down on the desk, real careful, unwrapping the blue handkerchief.

Eleven years, Dave thought as they both stared down at the cloth. That's what had already been invested in the planning and designing and approvals and geotechnical surveys and eighteen months of scraping and digging and drilling this earth. Getting it ready for the moment that the skeleton of Brooklyn Landing would finally begin to rise. Dave turned back to the kid, dark eyes in a narrow brown face.

"I appreciate your diligence, but I don't think this looks Ohlone." Dave was amazed at how quickly this rolled off of his tongue.

"I heard this was one of those shell mound sites. Like a burial ground."

Now it was Dave's turn for a coughing fit. "No, that's a rumor. We had to get all that evaluated before we got any of our approvals. This place is in the clear." But the dusty figure on the desk stared up at them both, shoving a crack into Dave's certainty. He felt a prickle along his spine as he stared back at this thing that might have lain undisturbed for hundreds of years.

His eyes lit now on the phone in the kid's pocket.

"You didn't get any good pictures? Of where you found it, I mean?"

"No, sir; my phone kind of died." This was looking better and better.

"Maybe someone else did?"

"I didn't show anybody else." And with that the movie clicked off, the one playing inside Dave's head: of the operation screeching to a halt, the weeks of studies and consultations, the crew guys standing around collecting pay while doing nothing, the breathless articles and the awful headlines. And for what? This thing that was probably nothing at all.

"I'll make sure it gets looked at. Just to be thorough." Dave stood now and opened the door and the kid took the hint, glancing back at the desk once more before he walked out.

THE HEADLIGHTS of his Tesla were stabbing into the dark as Dave pulled up to the far northern edge of the site, next to a graffiti-covered No Parking sign. There wasn't anyone who could have seen him as he clambered down the rocks and tossed the bundle into the Oakland Estuary. He heard it splash and then he slid behind the wheel and drove into the hills, to his house on Arrowhead Drive.

That night in his bed he heard drumming.

WHEN IT BEGAN he could drown it out, sort of: He could slip on headphones and turn up the white noise as loud as he dared, and let Liz snore in oblivion beside him, her breath soft as sweet peppermint. But then a night or two later he would have to turn up the roar's volume again. When he could force it no higher, he called Dr. Chan, mumbling vaguely about stress and insomnia.

First came Restoril, and with it came horrible dreams: of floating through marshy land littered with bones, of walking over black earth that opened wide and pulled him in. It was the same with the Sonata and Belsomra and Zolpidem. He would pour down endless cups of black coffee while he walked through the site, his hands sped-up and shaking and his thoughts muddy and weak. The higher the building's frame grew, the stronger his nightmares got. He backed out of going along on his daughter's college visits with Liz, backed out of their anniversary weekend in Baja. Liz began suggesting, then asking, then begging him to see another doctor, see anyone else.

He knew what would happen the moment he did; the disbelief that would cloud the doctor's face, the labels that would stick like glue. So he had to keep putting her off, her impatience stretching thinner and more brittle each time. As the weeks went on they both knew that if Hannah weren't there it would have already snapped.

"Are you going to do anything to fix this?" she asked, the night he nearly fell asleep driving them home.

"Yes," he muttered, slamming the guest room door.

But there was nothing to do, not really. When he drove past Crown Liquors one evening, it felt like the only place left to go, never mind the eight-year sobriety chip rattling from his keys. And, sure enough, he slept like an angel that night, the Tanqueray drifting through his blood.

THEN CAME THAT APRIL MORNING, cloudy and damp. Dave was walking across the southwest corner of the site, watching the cranes swallow up stacks of I-beams and spit them into rows of red steel. He could see one of the crew guys approaching, and by the time he saw the tattoo on the guy's wrist it was too late, the guy was too close, and Dave braced himself for the question he knew he deserved.

"So was everything okay, Mr. Hooper? With that thing I found?"

Dave made his voice as close to cheerful as he could.

"Absolutely. Nothing to worry about." The kid looked old enough to be skeptical, but not old enough to know what to do. Dave gestured at the beams all around them, to the spine of the building, four stories already formed, its metal ribs looming over them both. "See? Proof is right here." And he knocked at the beam with his fist.

Dave would always remember the order of what happened next. First was a sound like the earth itself, like the earth howling in a cheated scream. Only then did the ribcage of the building start to shake, a shuddering that traveled along to its spine. Nothing else shook: not the trees nearby, not the cars in the lot. Only the building itself, as if all of it had always been weak, the bones and the ground underneath. And only then was the howl drowned out in the roar of the spine collapsing into itself, pulling its ribcage down with it onto the ground, the metal beams painted in rusty red.

~

"DAVE, how you feeling? Do you need a minute?" Dave snapped his eyes open; in front of him his computer screen was filled with rectangles, the largest one now lit up in green. A voice—Andrew's—crackled out from the speakers. There were other boxes, holding faces he knew: three risk and compliance officers for Whitman Capital Group, the grantors of Brooklyn Landing's construction loan. The rectangles were all the same size, in the same place, as the ones that had filled Dave's screen all day long in the three days since the spine had collapsed. Different faces, different names, but delivering bad news, every one of them. These would only do more of the same.

"Dave? I was just asking about some of the on-the-ground reports? After the incident?" Andrew's Zoom background was from his last trip to Hawaii, the ocean framing him in a halo of blue.

"Of course. The ground. I was the only one who heard it, you know. It's my curse to bear. Have you ever heard the earth howl?" There were eight people on his screen all together, and now all of them looked away, or blinked as if they had dust in their eyes.

"Um, Dave, I remember you telling me some really reassuring news. By the grace of God, only a few injuries. In fact, didn't you say all of our guys made it home?"

"It's okay, man. You think you can hear the gin in my voice, but don't worry, everyone. I made myself skip it last night. I only take enough to sleep anyway. Not like it works anymore. I think I slept maybe a week ago? I dunno; ask the drummers." Andrew's eyes were darting all over the screen, as if he'd forgotten he wasn't the host and couldn't mute anyone. The compliance rectangles were going dark now, and a few of them disappeared.

"Dave, I think we're going to sign off. Let's pick this back up at another time."

Dave wasn't sure which of them had spoken, but the faces were all blinking away, one by one, and now the only face on the screen was his own.

THERE MUST HAVE BEEN A MOMENT, he thought, a time when he could have told Liz, and now he'd missed it and it was too late. How could he confess that he'd ignored the lessons from all those horror movies she loved? Or that as the investigators tried and tried to understand the frame's inexplicable collapse, he knew the true reason why—and that it was all because of a figure wrapped in blue cloth? Instead he slept in the guest room, avoiding Hannah and Liz, grateful every night he heard only drumming, nothing worse. He was in the guest bed on that weekend in May when he woke up and slung his feet over the bed and the carpeted floor was gone.

Under his feet was something like straw, or maybe reeds, woven impossibly tight and strong. He could feel cold air underneath, as if the house's floor and very foundation had rotted away. He didn't dare turn on the light, didn't dare move. If he took another step, this would all become real, the worse thing he had known was coming.

Through the doorway he could see the dining room, lit by the waning moon. He could see Hannah's soccer bag and her cleats, her lucky ones, tossed on a dining room chair. And the chairs, the new ones, the ones he and Liz had picked out months ago. And a giggle cracked open Dave's throat.

"Haha, not so fast!" He was shouting, but he didn't care. A door thudded open upstairs and he ignored it. This was a dream, and he'd noticed it just in time: In real life the new chairs hadn't yet been delivered, and Hannah wasn't back from her soccer trip.

"You can't fool me!" If he could scream loud enough, he might just wake himself up, and then feel everything under his feet as it should be, the carpet soft over solid wood.

"Dave?" And the lights snapped on in the kitchen and there was Liz, slack jawed and staring, Hannah a few steps behind.

"But you can't be here," he pointed at Hannah. "You're still at your tournament."

"We got back last night, Dad." Hannah took a step toward him and Liz actually stuck her arm out and pulled their daughter back, away from him.

"But the new chairs weren't here. They weren't here yet." But that was wrong too, said the lines across Liz's forehead. "They got here a week ago, Dave." And she took Hannah's hand and he could hear feet padding upstairs and a few minutes later car doors snapping open, and what must be overnight bags tossed into a trunk.

Her text came in a few hours later. She'd made an appointment for them both with a therapist, the same one they'd seen eight years before. He tried to imagine himself stepping through the doors. What would the office become, if the very ground under his feet could change underneath him? Would the doors open to long tunnels, the walls made of dried bones, whistling in the chilly wind?

HE DIDN'T GO to the appointment. He didn't respond to Liz's calls, her messages. The takeout containers piled up on his counter and he watched *Fight Club*, watched *Die Hard* until he could quote Alan Rickman's lines better than Alan himself. A week after the appointment a knock on the door came while Hans fell and fell, and he knew before he'd even signed for the envelope just what it would hold. It was from the same firm that had handled his prenup, and he buried it in the compost pail. He'd done the same with the letter from Andrew and Marty, the one severing him from DMA Development with a bank transfer and a flourish of ink. He knew he was just kicking the can down the road, but whoever had come up with that phrase must not have known just how satisfying it could feel, the adrenaline thrill of that kick.

～

THE AA MEETING was held in the library's community room, and he stared at the faded khakis, the worn-down shoes. Salt of the earth, his father would have called them, and he'd always rolled his eyes, but maybe it was true. Maybe these people were just what he needed. To remind him that no matter where you were on the totem pole of life, you could still be brought down by the darkness in your own soul.

Dave gulped from his bottle of Fiji water, swaying slightly as he rose to speak.

"I've been sober eight years. Until recently. I told myself I didn't need meetings, anything. I was so wrong. Because I came right back to the gin a month or two ago when everything I worked for so hard started falling apart. And it's all my—"

Dave stopped. There again came the drumming, finding him even here. But this time as he stared at the humble faces around him he could hear the rhythm he'd been ignoring before. *You know what you did. You. Know. What. You. Did.* And it would never end, would it? Not until he faced it, until he owned up.

He pushed through the rows of chairs, practically ran to the parking lot. And, as he started up the engine, he could hear the drumming stop.

～

His headlamp blared into the darkness as he clambered down the rocks just beyond the graffiti-covered No Parking sign. Its light must be visible at least a mile away, but unlike last time he was ready to be seen. Hell, even caught.

The new thigh-high wader boots made his legs slow and clumsy, and he kept slipping off the sharp rocks. He'd forgotten to buy gloves and his bare hands kept scrabbling at glass bottles, plastic bags, drink lids, cardboard cups: everything but a tiny object that might still be wrapped in blue cloth.

He could hear the wind whipping around his ears. He stumbled again, fell again, and his scraped hands bled over the rocks. He was sure to get an infection, something coursing through his bloodstream, trying to destroy him from within. But this blood might be the sacrifice he was supposed to make, and he was sure of it as his raw hands fumbled again in the dark water, because now something was brushing against them, something wrapped in a handkerchief, smelling of duckweed and mud.

He shoved through the doors of the Native American Cultural Center just after ten the next morning. He knew what the receptionist must be seeing: a wild-eyed white man with a stubbly beard and hands covered in cuts, asking to speak with Adam Ortíz. "Adam was my roommate at Stanford. He took me to a pow-wow once."

Adam was grayer and rounder than he'd been back at school, and he leaned over the conference room table as he listened, the furrow between his eyes thickening.

"Dave, my expertise is in oral histories and storytelling. And I'm Tewa. I grew up in New Mexico."

Something tightened inside Dave's chest. "I'm sorry; college was forever ago. Are you still friends with that museum guy? Maybe we could show this to him." Adam's eyebrows shot up at the word "we."

But he took a deep breath and left the room, coming back ten or so minutes later with a laptop and a fuzzy face on a Zoom call: a friend of Adam's from grad school, now a curator at the Oakland Museum. Two of Adam's co-workers stopped in the hallway, peering through the glass wall.

For the third time that morning Dave explained everything, but now the friend sighed and asked to see what Dave had. He could feel a swell of adrenaline, the thrill of consequences finally to come. He peeled back the cloth and held the artifact up to the screen.

And then the computer rattled with laughter. It spread to Adam, to the two coworkers, the receptionist who came from behind her desk. It was like a joke everyone was in on but Dave. The curator plucked something off of his shelf, littered with objects of shell and obsidian.

"Does this look familiar?" And indeed, the screen filled with a twin of the little clay figure in front of them, this one mounted to a cheap plastic base. Dave could feel his limbs turning cold.

"That's not a native artifact at all, my friend. It's a piece of memorabilia from the Lone Ranger Museum. You can buy one for $12.99."

THIS IS YOUR WAKE-UP CALL

J.L. FOUX

Christian wasn't one to accost customer-facing employees, but he was prepared to make an exception. The first wake-up call was fine, helpful even. "Mr. Flores, this is your wake-up call. Your partner left earlier this morning and asked for you to meet him at his house." It was the second call five minutes later that was the problem.

"Mr. Flores, I have another message from your partner. He said... 'Yesterday didn't happen.'" Her voice was a whisper. "'You didn't get bad news from the doctor... No matter what he says, you have to stop him.'" Then she hung up.

It took Christian a while to collect himself. Yesterday definitely happened; last night's drunken sex lay scattered across the hotel room. Christian's navy-blue polo at the foot of the bed. Twin condom wrappers on the nightstand. The shattered cadaver of a vodka bottle in the trash can.

And, of course, Christian's test results. Yesterday had felt so much like a dream that he *needed* the second wake-up call to be true. But it wasn't, and Christian *had* gotten bad news from the doctor.

Options? Get your shit in order and live it up for the next six months.

After Christian confirmed he was still living in yesterday's nightmare, he packed his suitcase and went to the front desk to give the clerk a piece of his mind. He hadn't told anyone about his prognosis, mostly because he'd been dead to family and friends after stumbling out of the closet, so the only way the clerk could've known was if she went through Christian's stuff.

The clerk at the counter was the same one who checked Christian and David in last night. Older white lady with skin like a pirate's treasure map. She must have missed the memo on excessive tanning.

The clerk flashed her lipstick-stained teeth. "How was your stay?"

"Well..." Christian glanced at her nametag. "...Beth. It was great until the wake-up call." He planned on being a bit more polite, but he ended up saying, "What the fuck was that?"

"Oh, I'm sorry... Did I call at the wrong time?" Beth was still smiling, but her eyes had that *oh-shit* look. She was playing dumb.

"Bullshit!" Christian didn't mean to shout, and he didn't mean to make Beth flinch and shrink away. Had anyone else seen his outburst?

The lobby was empty, and the adjoining breakfast area was *mostly* empty. One person sat in the corner with their face obscured by a hardcover book.

Christian took a slow, deep breath. "How'd you know? You go through my stuff?"

Beth kept that smile plastered across her face, but panic and fear had crept into her eyes; if she blinked now, tears would spill down her cheeks. "I'm afraid I don't understand." She maintained eye contact as her trembling hands went up to the desk and blindly fumbled for something. Her fingers knocked over a plastic cup filled with ink pens. "Oh, clumsy me."

A few of the spilled pens rolled off the desk and clacked against the floor. Beth smiled until silence returned to the hotel lobby.

She's terrified.

"Are... you okay?" Christian asked.

"Oh, of course! I'm just not sure how I can help you." The fingers on her right hand slowly crept toward a pen that was still on the desk.

What's happening?

Christian said, "The message; why'd you say that?"

As Beth answered the question, she scribbled on a notepad. "Sorry, if I wasn't clear. *Your partner* gave me a message and I *repeated exactly what he said.*"

Beth turned the pad around for Christian to see.

He's watching me.

But they were alone, except for...

Christian turned his head toward the breakfast area, and for the first time he noticed the absence of smell.

There's no food. No coffee.

The person in the corner sat at an empty table. A golden blazer stretched across his painfully narrow shoulders, and the morning sun glinted across a pair of gold sequin gloves that covered his hands and wrists. The blank hardcover still blocked his line of sight, but it seemed like The Man in Gold was staring *through* the book.

Christian turned back to ask Beth, "Who is watching?"

Beth whispered something too quiet for Christian to hear. After a few tense breaths, she whispered again.

"Leave."

A crash from the breakfast area jolted Christian away from the desk.

The Man in Gold was standing now, his hardcover still clutched in front of his head. Behind him, his chair lay toppled against the floor. Keeping the book positioned so Christian couldn't see his face, The Man in Gold rounded the table and walked closer.

Leave. Run.

Christian took a few steps backward toward the front door of the hotel.

"Mr. Flores?" Beth held up a Mercedes key fob, it was David's, and the tears she'd held back finally trailed their way to her blood-red lips. "Don't forget your key." She tossed it.

Christian caught the key fob and backed toward the doors. The Man in Gold passed in front of Beth, but she either didn't notice or didn't care, because she kept her eyes locked on Christian until he walked through the automatic doors.

Frozen air engulfed Christian, but he didn't stop backpedaling until the doors closed. When he couldn't see The Man in Gold anymore Christian allowed himself to shiver.

It was too cold for August, the sky too gray, and this morning was just—too strange.

Christian didn't spend time wondering why David's Mercedes was the only car in the parking lot, or why it was even there if David had left that morning. He just needed to get away from the hotel.

CHRISTIAN KNOCKED and rang at the front door for five minutes, and the only reply was the cold, salty howl of cliff-side wind. The house, which Christian had never been to before, was as opulent and isolated as he expected. Perched quietly on the coast of Maine, the stone and glass behemoth screamed wealth. Christian *knew* he didn't belong here.

He couldn't leave, though; the Mercedes barely had enough gas for the drive here, and Christian's cards were declined at the pump. His phone was dead, too. No communication, no money, and only one address saved in the car's GPS. Christian was at the mercy of David's looming cliff-side mansion. He walked along the outside and peered through dark wall-length windows to find any sign of David.

This was a bad idea.

True. The first time they hooked up, David floated the idea of flying Christian to Maine for a visit, but he declined. After that, David would "just so happen" to visit Houston, and Christian by extension, every other week. David was infatuated, and it didn't take long for him to become a kind of "sugar daddy."

Student loans? Gone. Laptop died? Knock knock, it's FedEx Overnight and we need a signature. A little creepy at first, but Christian started to feel the same way about David.

After yesterday's bad news, however, Christian sent a "let's plan a trip" text, and David put him in first class that afternoon. Maybe it was selfish to make the trip knowing he'd eventually have to tell David, but Christian needed someone to care about him.

It was late when Christian landed, so they made a last-minute decision to check into that strange hotel with a bottle of vodka. David had brought one of those old cameras that would eject photographs after you snapped a picture; he blinded Christian in the car before they left the airport. David used it to take "sexy" pictures in the hotel room.

The vodka knocked Christian out before he could explain why he finally flew to Maine; he took one final swig of liquid courage, then the next thing he remembered was the wake-up call.

Christian rounded the corner and entered the backyard.

The back of the house was a wall of glass, the center of which was wide open. Inside, a lit fireplace cast a gentle glow against living room furniture. Did David leave the wall open for Christian to find? Was this some kind of game?

A gray stone patio connected the back of the house to an infinity pool, which stretched toward the Atlantic cliff side. It was much too cold to swim, but David must have taken a dip because a dark gray trail of dots led from the patio, around the water, toward a bowl-like decoration at the end of the pool. Curiosity overpowering his desire to play David's game of hide and seek, Christian approached the decoration.

A large, ostentatious bowl, seemingly made of gold and about the size of a watermelon, sat on a table. Something was attached to the ocean-facing side of the bowl, so Christian bent over to get a better look.

Within a little glass container was a picture. The kind that gets printed from one of those old cameras. It took a moment for Christian to recognize himself wrapped in the hotel sheets.

"Huh." Christian took a step back from the bowl. That's when he realized the trail from earlier wasn't water and it wasn't dark gray. It was dark red.

IT WAS obvious why David hadn't answered the front door. He wasn't able to. Christian followed the trail of blood to the bathroom, where a pale, drained, and injured David had clumsily bandaged his bleeding hand. David tried to hide the bloody pair of pruning shears near the sink, but Christian saw them.

David said, "I'm sorry, I..."

Christian didn't wait to hear the rest. He grabbed David, one arm over his shoulder, and hauled him out. "Where's the garage?" The Mercedes didn't have enough gas to make it to the hospital, but surely there was another car they could take.

"Wait..."

Christian didn't wait; his legs *needed* to move. The labyrinthine house wasn't forthcoming with its layout, and neither was David. So Christian moved them toward the opposite side of the house; surely that's where the garage would be. When they arrived at the foyer, he saw another hall that continued in the same direction. "Does that go to the garage?"

"Did you see it yet?" David sounded weak and confused. How much blood had he lost?

"See what, David?" Christian started down the hall.

With a surprising burst of strength, David slammed his bandaged hand against the wall; he shoved himself out of Christian's grip and fell to the floor.

Christian tried to pull David back up, but he wasn't cooperating. "David! Come on!"

"Let me explain."

There wasn't time for an explanation, and if David wasn't going to cooperate then Christian wouldn't be able to get him to the car.

David's phone... Call for help...

Christian fumbled through David's pockets until he found the cell phone.

David tried to snatch his phone back, but he was sluggish. Drunk from blood-loss. "Christian! Stop!"

Christian was met with a lock screen. "David, what's the..." The dimmed wallpaper behind the lock screen caught Christian's eye.

It was a photo of Christian and David standing next to each other wearing tuxedos and smiling into the camera. But Christian never posed like this with David, and he never wore a tux.

David sat up. "We got married."

"What?"

"I usually explain it gradually, but..." David nodded at the wall behind Christian.

Along the hallway wall were framed pictures of Christian. And they were all taken in places he'd never been. The Great Wall. The Pyramids. The house Christian was standing in. "What's happening?"

David said, "It's okay. I brought you back."

Christian turned to find David standing, albeit shakily, on his own.

"At your wake, there was a stranger. He said I could have you back just like you were." David, tears falling from his eyes, stepped closer and touched Christian's face. "Here you are."

My... Wake?

Following David's words was difficult, especially since they *needed* to leave, but the oddness of this morning crept to the forefront of Christian's mind.

This is your wake-up call.

David sucked in a sharp breath. "You lived here, Baby. And we were *perfect*. Even when you couldn't get out of bed anymore, you were *still perfect*." David stroked Christian's hair. "I'm sorry I ruined today. I passed out before I could get the house ready."

Yesterday didn't happen.

Christian backed into the wall; David was too close and the air between them was itchy and hot. The wake-up call. The pictures. David's impossible explanation. If Christian could create more space between him and—*everything*—then maybe he could think.

David's still bleeding.

Yes, of the problems in need of triage, David's injury took priority. Everything else could wait until David was coherent enough to explain.

Christian said, "Let's talk on the way to the hospital, okay?"

"See how much I love you?" David held up his bloody hand. "At first, I just needed a few drops to bring you back. Then I needed a whole pint. Today I thought one finger would work, but the bowl wanted two and..."

A thud from the end of the hallway interrupted David. Christian turned his head to see a hardcover book resting in front of two golden shoes. The Man in Gold stood at the end of the hallway. A shimmering sequin mask covered his head and inside its mirrored reflection, Christian *saw* what happened here.

For six months after the flight to Maine, Christian and David burned in their love for one another. Eventually, though, the cancer ate and spread until Christian withered away; David was destroyed.

I... Died...

After Christian's death, The Man in Gold gave David the bowl and instructions.

Make a sacrifice to an effigy of Christian, *the photograph*, and he'll come back.

David stood between Christian and The Man in Gold. "You're... Early? We have six months."

Six months...

Christian had come back *exactly* as the photo depicted, complete with an expiration date, and in the same hotel room. David must have bought the hotel and hired Beth as its sole employee. One shift every six months to get an empty room ready for the same guest to checkout, then make the wake-up call.

But there was another call. Why would David have given her that second message?

No matter what he says, you have to stop him.

Beth was wrong. The message she was afraid to deliver, the one she insisted on whispering and refused to repeat, came from David's phone but it didn't come from David.

It came from me.

The previous Christian, near the end of his life, must have made a single, hurried phone call to Beth to ensure the next Christian would be the last.

You have to stop him... before he kills himself.

Christian turned and ran. He ignored the fading screams as he left the house and dashed toward the large golden bowl. It was heavier than expected, but he was able to bear hug it and lift with his legs. Slow and steady, he walked to the cliff at the edge of the property. He was going to save David.

They only met a few months ago, but Christian knew he'd fallen in love. At least, the *real* Christian had. He loved David enough to marry him, and the Christian-copies that came after were made of the same stuff. If the bowl stayed, then the next sacrifice might be too much. *This* Christian would destroy the bowl, and he'd have a few good months left with...

A heavy punch rocked Christian's back; the golden bowl fell and rolled right up to the edge of the cliff. A thundering boom split the air. When Christian tried to breathe his chest tickled, and a sharp stabbing sensation blossomed into a throaty, wet cough. Christian's knees buckled and he fell next to the bowl.

His mouth was so wet and his chest and back hurt so much, and no matter how much he swallowed he kept choking on liquid metal. Christian touched his lips and looked at his hand.

He shot me.

The bowl was so close. If he could just move it a little further... Christian grabbed at the edge of the bowl, but his fingers weren't listening. They were thin and weak.

And tired.

Christian let himself slump; his head hung over the edge of the cliff. Waves crashed against the rock below.

Water lapped against a figure; Christian recognized his navy-blue polo.

David pulled Christian onto his lap and screamed. "Why'd you make me do that?"

Christian tried to say, "let go," but a wet cough exploded through his lips and painted David's face.

David started petting Christian's head. "Oh, Baby. It's okay."

Above David's shoulder, The Man in Gold leaned in.

"It's okay, Baby. I'll bring you back." David held up his bloody hand. "See? Three fingers left on this one." He pulled Christian into a hug. "And my toes. No one needs their toes, Baby."

Christian felt too thin to hug David back, or to beg him to push the bowl over the edge. The Man in Gold was only inches away, now, and it felt good to stare into his mask. Within each golden sequin there was a reflection of Christian trapped inside. A dozen or so different Christians all silently screamed and clawed at their own faces.

There was an empty sequin in the center of the mask, and Christian didn't have the strength or desire to look away.

CHRISTIAN WOKE up and answered the phone.

"Mr. Flores. This is your wake-up call..."

BIRTH OF A SUCKER

BRIAR RIPLEY PAGE

PRODROME

There wasn't a specific point she could remember when her world started changing. It crept in around the edges, a slow invasion from the periphery. Or maybe it was more like a coffee bleed soaking gradually through the fabric of a napkin. Either way, there was a day when she became aware things had gone a little peculiar, and that they'd been going a little peculiar, off and on, for quite a while.

One peculiar thing was that something was always happening in front of her eyes, between her eyes and the world, laid on top like a filter. It was a kind of glittery static with currents running through it like branching paths. Translucent pink shapes like massive amoebas floated and sparkled. A soft noise accompanied the static, like white noise. Only she seemed able to hear it, and only when the world was otherwise very quiet.

Another oddity was the way insects and barking dogs could sound like music, and music could, unpredictably, be reduced to a painful cacophony of overwhelming, senseless noise.

A third oddity was the way she could smell her upstairs neighbor's period blood through the roof of her own flat, and the blood from the tiny cut on a co-worker's finger from across the room, and the blood from the sore inside her boss's mouth on the far side of the parking lot as they both left the restaurant for the day. There was no doubt in her mind about what she was smelling. She pictured the source of the smell as clearly as she could recall her own mother's face.

She liked the smell. She was only a little disturbed by the pictures. She licked her lips.

Pete, her co-worker, not the one with the cut on his finger but the guy who was mostly in charge of the fryer, told her she looked like shit. "You strung out or what?" he asked, and when she responded in the negative, "You think it's covid?"

She didn't—things had been peculiar for longer than that. But she didn't have any covid tests, either. They'd become too expensive, and difficult to find.

"You're all, like, gaunt," said Pete. "You look like you've got two black eyes. And your mouth keeps hanging open so it looks like you're about to drool."

"I know what I look like," she interrupted. "I can see myself in the mirror."

Sometimes Pete was a person she knew. Other times, Pete was a blare of whiny tenor voice, strings plucked in his stringy throat. Pete was several three-dimensional shapes in peachy tan, chestnut brown, white, black, and red.

Sometimes Dave was just the cut on his finger, the smell of the cut, pulsing, reaching out to her.

Sometimes she was a person, she knew. Other times, she didn't recognize her own face. Other times she felt more like a storm brewing, or like a susurrus of whooshing brown noise trapped inside a wet, dead skin. The smell of blood made the noise grow louder, more urgent.

She persisted in her daily life as always. She worked at the restaurant where she mostly assembled salads and performed back-of-house gofer tasks. The salads were green shapes and red shapes; they smelled like the opposite of food. She was nearly sick behind her mask. Almost, but not quite. Then lettuce became lettuce again. Nobody else noticed.

Later, she returned home and watched TV on her laptop computer. She spoke to her mother on video chat. She did not eat dinner, but threw up twice. No one was there to see it.

She felt sure she could continue in this way indefinitely.

CRISIS

She couldn't continue in that way indefinitely.

The peculiarities were growing more frequent, lengthening in duration. She felt like she was picking up speed in some descent. Or ascent. For she often felt lately that she was floating, her body hollow, hovering inches off carpet or kitchen linoleum, prepared to drift higher and farther from the earth.

Her gums were inflamed, blood-red, delicious. Her teeth were too long. Rabbit teeth, horse teeth. Not wolf teeth. No. Not wolf teeth. Her tongue looked like it was coated in black fur. In the mirror, she'd become some kind of decrepit animal with glittering static eyes. She could count all of her bones.

She was throwing up too much. It frightened her. It wasn't intentional; her body rejected almost everything she tried to feed it.

She knew what it wanted.

She didn't want to admit it.

Her mother told her to see a doctor over video chat. She said she would, but she lied. She didn't feel bad about it. She told herself she wasn't going to see a doctor because it was too expensive, and she wasn't really sick yet.

The real reason she wasn't going was that she was afraid of what the doctor might find, what the doctor might do. She'd seen movies. She'd read books. She still wanted to live.

If anything bit her, she didn't remember it. She'd never even been bitten by a dog or a cat. Animals always seemed to be gentle with her. She was a gentle person, or wanted to be; she was a nervous, watchful person, like a horse or a rabbit. But not prey; never prey.

Maybe it was a mosquito. She'd been bitten by many mosquitos.

Maybe it was waiting inside her all her life. What triggered its emergence she might never know.

She scratched at her wrists until they tore and grew ragged, and she sucked at the sap that came out. Sustenance. She didn't care about the sheets gone sticky beneath her. She didn't care, for a moment, if she died. She wanted to be a good person. But she wanted to be satisfied. She was losing her grasp on the idea of what a person was. She'd been starving, and now her hunger was slightly less sharp. Translucent pink shapes surrounded her like cheerful bubbles and the fur on her tongue rippled with pleasure.

"Are you feeling any better?" her mother asked. In the video chat, her mother's face was several three-dimensional shapes. Peachy tan, white, red, and black. Her mother's face was flickering static. Her mother's face was nothing that meant anything, or made any sense. She had no smell.

"You look a little better?" Encouraging lilt in the woman's voice as though this, too, was a question.

She didn't think the woman on the other side of the chat was her mother. She realized, suddenly, that she couldn't remember anything about her. Not a name, not a birthday. Not a single time they'd interacted in the real world. It was all a blank. Had she lost those memories, or had they never existed?

She stopped the video chats. It felt like the reasonable thing to do. They were a waste of her time.

Gnawing her wrist. Lying dazed on the floor, staring at the pink shapes in the corner, smelling blood from on high, feeling her bones.

She stopped watching TV. She stopped going online. She mostly quit bathing, or talking. She went into work until she got fired, which took longer than she expected. She felt neither happy nor sad about it. The end, whatever the end might be, was near.

She hoped it came before she was evicted from her flat.

Her fingernails and toenails had become long, black claws. She couldn't call them rabbit-claws, or horse-claws. They were like nothing but the claws of a wolf, or a great cat, or a bear. They were the claws of an apex predator.

Immediately after she got fired, Dave found her in the restaurant parking lot. He smiled at her with red shapes and white shapes. She remembered the smell of his blood, although the cut on his finger had been healed for weeks, maybe months. She remembered the smell of his blood so well she could taste it as he spoke. He told her about his problems with drinking, with meth. He told her about the twelve steps, the local chapter, how he was there—they all would be there—to support her if she ever decided she needed help. How help was possible. How there were ways forward for her.

Dave's words were small translucent shapes in the air, weak and temporary, and of no color in particular. They were useless, meaningless. She hated them a little. Still, she found them enormously touching.

Dave's heart beat. His lungs softly inflated and deflated. It was music. The world shimmered before her as she reassured Dave she'd be fine, unable to parse her own speech, hoping she was getting all the sounds right, all the shapes.

She threw up on the pavement. She threw up on the linoleum. She threw up in her bed. The wound on her wrist festered. When she sucked at it, she tasted pus. She couldn't stand up anymore. She didn't care.

She had accepted that she was going to die.

In the bed, a black cocoon took shadowy form. Like a coffin. Like an egg. Like the sound of a radio stuck between stations.

When the thing in the black cocoon woke up, it wasn't her anymore.

IMAGO

The thing in the black cocoon woke up, rending shadow. Its armor sloughed off in brittle, ephemeral sheets. It stretched arms and legs. It touched the hard, cool flesh. The pale naked skin. The damp curling hair, like scraps of pelt. The place on its wrist where there had been a wound. It felt a detached pleasure. This was a body it could use, a body whole and strong and well.

This was a serviceable collection of shapes, around which the world glittered and beckoned and sang.

It was hungry. What it wanted would be easy to find. But it knew to be careful. It mustn't get caught, mustn't be seen by the wrong people.

It shoved a tube of fabric over its head, over its torso. The fabric stretched. Scratchy as nettles, scratchy as needles. The thing from the black cocoon didn't like the feeling at all, but decided it would be bearable for a short time. The fabric shimmered with hundreds of tiny, slick colors. Oily little rainbows. It hugged the top of the thing's torso, accentuating the two sloping mounds of fat there and toward the bottom, it belled out dramatically.

The thing from the black cocoon twirled around, and the fabric twirled with it. In motion, the thing from the black cocoon decided, the fabric was pink. Silver. Silvery-pink. It said *hush, hush, hush.*

The thing from the black cocoon was already very quiet.

Quiet, and smiling on the street, feet shoved into mint and melon-colored leather shapes. Toes blunted, jammed against the interior. Claws aching. Legs loping. No one suspected the thing from the black cocoon. It looked just like any other girl. It fooled everybody. *Piece of cake*—the phrase came into its mind from long ago and far away. Cake was a delicious shape. The thing from the black cocoon knew it was going to love its new food just as much as its old self had loved the vanilla sponge, the strawberries. The thing from the black cocoon smiled and smiled at the cars glowing and growling through the night. At the unsuspecting men and women passing by beneath the street lamps.

It followed its nose for seventeen blocks. And when it saw the skinny, run-down two-story house on the outskirts of town, it knew exactly what to do. It could smell which window was his.

It did not need the door. It jumped straight up, straight out of its mint and melon sneakers. Caught the sill on the second floor with its claws. Crouched there, swaying in the warm, dark air. Scratched gently at the moonlit glass. The squeaking, chiming music birthed ghostly new shapes.

And he was there. Rubbing his eyes. Uncertain. Young, though certainly older than the thing from the black cocoon. Early-to-midthirties. And handsome. A sharp nose under heavy-lidded eyes and wild hair the color of dry leaves. Heavyset and powerfully built, but not tall. And no match, of course. No threat. The delicious smell emanating from within him. The loud music of his heart.

He was a frightened animal.

"Oh my god," he said. "What the hell. Carly? How'd you get up here? Are you okay? No one's seen you in weeks."

The thing from the black cocoon made shapes with its sore, dripping mouth. "Dave. You have to let me in, okay?" It raised its voice to imitate fear. "You have to. Please."

The window squawked open and the air inside Dave's room smelled like human sweat and cinnamon. The scent of iron beneath it all. Meat smell. Delicious blood reaching out to the thing from the black cocoon on the windowsill, just as the thing peeled itself from white-painted wood and came inside, to Dave.

Who fell easily. Who did not even scream. His throat tasted dirty, tasted like soap and spices. It took effort to gnaw through, but it was not unpleasant effort. Canine teeth bending, worrying at the stubbled skin.

And the blood seep. The pulpy texture. The late gush, after the kicking stopped. His arms were pinned beneath it like soft, limp sacks of steak. He hadn't even tried to fight. He was entranced. He was half-asleep. It was as if he wanted this, too. As if he'd been waiting to give himself up to the thing from the black cocoon.

The heart still pumped, drummed, squirmed. He wasn't dead. The blood fountained. The thing from the black cocoon pulled with its lips and tongue. The thing from the black cocoon made strangled sounds like a gluttonous garbage disposal. Dave was, maybe, still conscious.

The thing from the black cocoon felt true companionship with Dave in those joyous moments. It had not loved anyone before.

After, its silvery-pink dress was sticky and red and wet. Sodden, the texture of the fabric was more bearable. But the dress had to go. Exchanged for a checkered flannel shirt and a pair of too-big elastic waisted athletic shorts from Dave's closet. Clean, smelling of Dave and fake flowers.

The thing from the black cocoon listened to dogs singing outside the window. It went back the way it came in, retrieved its sneakers, and loped down the night road with nothing to fear. It didn't need human things anymore. It could do different things now.

It unfurled its wings.

Different shapes sang in the dark all around. They flashed their colors. They shimmered and turned and whispered. They multiplied and divided themselves.

The world has always been this way.

AN OTHERWISE ORDINARY NIGHT

STEVE LOIACONI

The cupcake box rested just out of Gary Milton's reach.

Driving down a desolate Virginia highway slightly above the speed limit, his eyes drifted between the twilit road, the clock on the dashboard, and the box on the far end of the passenger seat. He was over forty miles from home and already late for Kyle's first Little League game of the season, but he was still tempted to pull over and wolf down the red velvet while he could.

Since his accounting firm relocated to Richmond, Gary had raced back to Newport News every night after clocking out. When he was initially told of the move, he made what he felt was a compelling pitch to work from home—he could do math, read fine print, and fill out forms anywhere—but his bosses disagreed. So, he begrudgingly made the seventy-mile drive both ways day after day.

By mid-morning, enough paperwork had piled up on his desk that he knew he'd be late. So he did what he always did when work pulled him away from his family: he bought them cupcakes. As was his custom, he ordered four; three in one box and one in another. That way, he could eat one discreetly on the road and dispose of the evidence without subjecting himself to Marie's judgment for veering off-diet.

The game must have been well into its third inning. Gary thought about calling Marie, but cell reception was spotty and it would make little difference. What mattered was that he wasn't there. Tragically dull as he found the games, Gary recognized their importance to Kyle. Baseball was a thing fathers and sons had done together since time immemorial, or at least since the advent of Little League. Gary looked at other fathers coaching their kids' teams, being involved, and wondered how they found the time. The best he could do was show up, and even that was increasingly a stretch. He would argue that it wasn't his fault baseball season overlapped with tax season. But, "I can't make your double-header because I have to file some rich a-hole's 1120-S" wasn't an excuse that carried much weight with a child.

Anytime Kyle complained about missed games, Gary stifled the urge to point out that there wasn't all that much to miss. For years, coaches had shunted Kyle into right field where he could go entire games without lifting his glove, and they buried him at the bottom of the batting order where an inevitable strikeout would do minimal harm. Gary couldn't blame them. Other parents clamored for victories and trophies. For them, sports were a competition in which the outcome mattered, rather than a mere social obligation.

Still, an obligation it was. He resolved to get there as soon as he could—cupcake be damned. The Subaru rounded a curve just past a green sign pointing to Sherwood Forest– President John Tyler's post-presidential estate that Gary had been disappointed to learn upon his first drive down this route had nothing to do with Robin Hood. If he made decent time from here, he'd pull up to the game in forty-five minutes. Not ideal, but good enough. Then something lurched into the road up ahead. An animal, maybe a deer or a bear.

Gary pressed on the brake and tightened his hold on the steering wheel. The car skidded to a stop, and he cautiously peered over the dashboard.

It was hunched over, shielding itself from his headlights. After a moment, it rose and looked in his direction.

Not a deer. Not a bear.

A woman. A teenage girl. Small, but everything about her looked weathered and worn beyond her years. Her leather jacket was torn and mud covered her jeans. Her shirt might have been white, but it was spattered with red and black stains. Her face was streaked with dirt and grime. Leaves and twigs studded her tangled black hair. Blood seeped from a deep gash on her right cheek. Her eyes were wide with panic.

Gary wasn't the type to help random strangers on the side of the road. Driving these highways, he regularly passed families with blown-out tires, couples bickering next to SUVs with overheated engines, and angry motorists arguing over fender-benders. It wasn't that he didn't care. He just found it best to stay out of other people's drama.

This was different, though.

This was a woman in need right in front of his face. He lifted his foot off the brake. The car crept forward, but he could not step on the gas. Instead, he sighed, unbuckled his seatbelt, and pushed open his door.

"Hello?" he said as he approached.

She stared into the sparse forest that stretched along the road and shivered.

When he came near, she grabbed his arm.

"It's coming," she whispered. "It won't stop. It's coming."

"Who's coming?"

She looked back toward the woods. "You wouldn't believe me."

He had not seen any other cars for miles, and he doubted anyone else would come along anytime soon. Somewhere, he heard a feverish hum. Leaves crackled and branches rustled as something moved through them.

"Let's go," Gary said, projecting a resolve he wished he felt.

She stood, shakily at first, and limped to the car. He helped her into the passenger seat, tossing his briefcase into the back and sliding the cupcake boxes to the floor. He regretted not eating the spare red velvet.

Gary climbed into his seat and shifted the car into drive.

"We need to get help." He glanced at his archaic flip phone, which rarely picked up a signal in this forest. Kyle had nagged him to purchase a more modern phone for months, but he hadn't gotten around to it.

The girl shifted in her seat, groaning as she stretched her arms. The road ahead was clear, silent, and black.

"Who did this to you?" Gary asked.

Her eyes drilled through him, then the cupcake boxes distracted her. She pulled the red velvet out of the single box and took a bite.

"Do you mind if I eat this?" she asked through a mouthful of white frosting.

After another bite, she turned toward the window and looked to the sky. Her eyes searched for something in the darkness.

"What are you so scared of?" he asked. "Ex-boyfriend? Serial killer? Werewolf?"

She did not answer.

"What, is it the ghost of President John Tyler?" he laughed.

She sighed loudly and put the cupcake down. Her face tightened.

"It was a giant moth, alright?" she said. "It was a giant moth."

"You're joking."

"Do I look like I find any of this even a little funny?"

A man of math and numbers by trade, Gary's immediate instinct was skepticism. But he could see this girl had experienced something traumatic that she was having difficulty putting into words.

"Look," he said in his most fatherly voice, "my son went through a hardcore 'Supernatural' phase a few years back. I know all my local lore and cryptids. The Bunny Man, Roanoke, the Saltville Bigfoot sightings. But the Mothman is in West Virginia."

She responded with an indifferent shrug.

Back then, Kyle had briefed him on the Mothman more times than he could count: a large gray creature with massive wings and red eyes, alternately described as bird-like or bug-like, was first seen near Point Pleasant, West Virginia in 1966. Over the next year or so, there were upwards of 100 sightings in the region, typically at night in remote areas. Any number of explanations had been put forth in the years since, from mass delusions to owls and rare birds to aliens. The monster was now an essential component of local folklore, with a museum, a 12-foot-tall statue, and an annual festival dedicated to it.

For months, Kyle implored him to take the family to Point Pleasant on what he unconvincingly described as a vacation. Gary resisted, offering up a long list of other places they could go that didn't require a six-hour drive into the lonely heart of bumblefuck, West Virginia.

"Why is a Mothman chasing you?" Gary asked.

"I didn't get a chance to ask," she said, wiping crumbs from her cheek. "It was too busy slaughtering my friends."

Her heavy boots were crusted with mud and grime, which dripped onto his floor mats. He felt a pang of guilt for wondering how hard it would be to clean that up, but his attention was soon drawn to what he thought were headlights on the road ahead. Two bright red circles hovering, rapidly approaching. Then the lights climbed out of his sight. Above the car, a high-pitched cry filled the night. Something fluttered and flapped. Gary tried to look up. He saw nothing but dark clouds and the stars' faint light.

The thing swooped down, barreling toward them and offering Gary his first full-on glimpse. Thin, leathery wings spread at least 10 feet across, sharp claws on its hands and feet, limbs bent at inhuman angles. A narrow head bulged with bulbous red eyes. Tufts of gray fuzz dotted its insectine body.

It landed on the hood of the car and clawed at the windshield. When it hissed, a three-pronged tongue darted from its mouth. Its broad wingspan quickly blotted out the moonlight, leaving Gary unable to see the road—or much of anything else.

The vehicle skidded. Gary was too terrified to slow down. Next to him, the girl screamed, "Stop!"

His foot drifted off the gas pedal. He was transfixed. Red eyes stared back at him through the glass.

"Hit the brakes," the girl said. "Now."

Right. He stomped his heel and forced the car to a screeching halt.

The monster slid off the hood and stumbled across the pavement, landed on its back, legs flailing as it struggled to regain its footing.

"Go," the girl shouted.

Gary floored it, ignoring the squeal of the car's weathered engine.

Perhaps he could have swerved around the thing, but he chose not to. He hit it head-on. The creature rolled up the hood, thumped across the roof. Then it was off the back and onto the road, in the mirror. Gary's fists gripped the steering wheel as the car skidded around a sharp turn. Neither of them spoke for a moment.

"That—that was a fucking Mothman," he said finally.

"Believe me now?"

"What the hell is the Mothman doing this far east?"

"You really need to get past the geography, dude," she said, shaking her head. "We've got bigger problems."

"Come on," he gestured toward the road behind them. "I just hit it with a Subaru."

"In the last 36 hours, I have stabbed that thing, set it on fire, dropped a boulder on it, and shot it with a harpoon gun." She enunciated each word of the next sentence slowly, as if dubious of his understanding of English. "It does not stop."

Wind whistled through a crack in the windshield. Gary mentally drafted the claim he would submit to his insurance company. Kyle might believe a Mothman tried to run his dad off the road, but the very serious people at Newport Mutual likely would not.

Before he got far into crafting an excuse, the hum of wings returned, louder and more rapid. The girl gave him a knowing shrug. Then the mothman darted out of the trees across the road and rammed the passenger side of the car. Tires screamed as it careened off the pavement.

The vehicle tore through a guardrail and bounded down the side of a steep hill. Gary shrieked, fighting to keep the vehicle steady as branches and leaves whizzed by. But the ride ended abruptly when the car slammed into the trunk of a tall tree. Gary's head whipped forward, thudding against the dashboard before the airbag inflated and jerked his skull back onto the headrest.

GARY DIDN'T KNOW how long he had blacked out. Once he regained his bearings, he pushed the airbag aside. Broken glass shimmered everywhere in the flickering light of the overhead bulb. Every yellow and red warning light on the dashboard lit up. A barren tree branch reached toward his neck through what was left of the windshield. The stench of sweat and gasoline assaulted his nose. His head throbbed and his shoulder ached, but at least nothing seemed to be actively bleeding. He stumbled out his shattered window, careful to avoid the jagged remnants that lined the frame. He tried to stand, but a sharp stab of pain coursed through his right leg. Maybe it was broken. He leaned on the car and propped his head against a wheel wet with mud and moss. The girl sat on a rock, sharpening the tip of a long stick with her knife. There was a fresh cut on her forehead. She used her muddy left sleeve to wipe away blood that was seeping toward her eyebrows.

"It's circling," she said, pointing the stick toward the sky. "I don't think it sees us yet."

Through an opening in the trees, the silhouette of the winged creature flapped past, framed by the light of the nearly full moon.

Still disoriented, Gary surveyed the area. He wished he'd paid more attention on Kyle's Boy Scout camping trips. The kids had learned plenty about navigation, foraging, and wilderness survival, but the handful of times he went along as part of a rotation of parental chaperones, Gary was distracted by work or other concerns, doing the bare minimum to ensure nobody drowned or got eaten by a wild animal. It seemed like enough at the time.

"You alright?" she asked.

He looked at her, looked at his wrecked car, at the sky, and then back at her.

"Just dandy," he said.

They both laughed harder than seemed justified, but the fleeting rush of levity felt good.

"Can you walk?" she asked, blowing away wood shavings from the tip of her new spear.

"Not well," he replied.

She reached out to help him stand, her palm slippery with sweat.

"Let's go," she said through gritted teeth. A dark red stain seeped through her shirt above her waist. "I have not fought this thing for this long just to give up and die."

They moved away from the car slowly, Gary's right leg dragging behind.

"My phone's not working," he said, glancing at the blank screen.

He could already hear Marie lecturing him about forgetting his charging cable and Kyle gently mocking him for still carrying a flip phone. He took an odd sense of comfort in the thought, since it presumed he would make it home at all.

"My kid's not even going to remember the sound of my voice in a few years, is he?" he said. He thought he saw the girl roll her eyes in response.

Moments later, she stopped at the edge of a steep decline. Below, churning waves of foamy white water crashed on jagged rocks.

"I can't swim in this condition," he said.

"You won't need to," she replied.

The girl pushed him to the dirt and raised the makeshift spear.

The tip tore through his chest. The pain was less searing than he would have imagined. He couldn't decide whether that was good or bad.

"What the hell?" he stammered, recognizing the question would go unanswered.

The girl winced as she pressed her hand into her stomach, coating her fingers with blood before painting a red smear on the rock next to him.

She peered down at him and shook her head with what he surmised was pity. She took one more look at the sky, then shuffled away.

"I'm sorry," she mouthed before vanishing into the trees. Seconds later, he heard a splash.

There was a joke Gary used to tell his son while they were packing for camping trips.

"What do we do if a bear attacks?" his son would ask.

"I'm going to run."

"Dad, you can't outrun a bear."

"Oh, Kyle," he would smile. "I don't need to outrun the bear. I just need to outrun you."

His son always laughed at that.

In retrospect, it wasn't all that funny.

Forty miles away in Newport News, the game was wrapping up. A scene played out in Gary's head like a fresh memory. Trodding away from the ballfield, Marie was tired and Kyle was mildly disappointed in himself but unwilling to talk about it. They were hopping back in their car, driving home in silence, and wondering if Gary would beat them there with a box of much-needed cupcakes.

The deafening thrum of wings dragged him back to the forest. The pain in his chest grew sharper as two red eyes descended from the black sky, bright like headlights.

PEGGY'S HUNGRY HAUNTED CLOWN
ANGELIQUE FAWNS

Peggy jumps back onto her porch when the ground rumbles and a roar fills the air. At first she thinks a gigantic herd of alien monsters are rounding the corner, and she trips on her carved pumpkin in her haste to get to safety. The hiss of the air brakes reassures it's not an invasion. Instead, a convoy of transport trucks head down the country road. Carnival rides, wolves in cages, and animatronic monsters jiggle on the flat beds. Diesel smell makes her nose wrinkle. The black-grey smoke makes the Fall sky look smudged, like when she eats French fries and touches her sunglasses.

She leans in the front door. "Dad, can I go to the circus this year?"

He's in his favorite wingback reading the newspaper which he drops into his lap. "You're too young for the Haunted Circus. It'll scare your socks off!"

Peggy points to her sandals. "It can't! I'm not wearing any."

One side of his face wrinkles into a half-grin. This is her favorite smile. It means she might get her way.

"I'll ask your mother when she gets home from work." He picks up his paper.

Peggy claps and leaps off the porch, letting the door slam in her wake. Mom is easier to convince than Dad. She can almost taste the candy apples and candy. What terrifying joys will be featured this year?

The last truck trundles past and Peggy half-waves at a huge clown leering over the edge of the truck bed. He has yellow fangs and blue triangle paint around his eyes. The clown is so gruesome a sharp pain surfaces in the center of her forehead, like she ate ice cream too quickly. Must be a decoration in a haunted house attraction.

She cups her hands and calls after it, "Who fed you an ugly pill?"

Is it her imagination or does he wink with a deranged purple eye?

She shivers and the brain freeze gets worse.

Peggy rubs her temples. She needs another look at that clown. Her braids flap behind her as she runs after the trucks. The neighbors' yards are stuffed with fake gravestones and ghost sheets in trees, but she doesn't see them. She's far more interested in the carnival attractions.

A red-headed boy in overalls, a red shirt, and a red hat charges out of the next yard. Hugh. He's waving a Super Soaker. Peggy groans.

Puberty betrays Hugh, and he squeaks out, "Hey, the Carnies are in town!" He runs, arms flapping like an agitated goose.

Peggy stops and waits for him to catch up. "They're not Carnies, dummy. This is the *circus*."

He stops just before he bowls her over. "So, what do you call them? Cirkies?"

"Why not?" She shrugs. "The Cirkies are in town."

Hugh is too close and blowing peanut butter breath. She scowls. "Why don't you make like a banana and split?"

He gives her a gummy grin. "I might eat one of those later."

Peggy's eyes drop to the rolls puckering his t-shirt. "It's nice to see you, but it would be nicer to see you go."

He laughs and does an awkward belly dance, making his entire body jiggle. "Seriously, Piggy! Let's go spy on the Cirkies."

Peggy rolls her eyes. "Don't call me Piggy, Hugh Jass." Her neighbor is like that wart on the bottom of her foot. Always bugging her.

"Good comeback." He wiggles his butt. "It is kind of huge."

Peggy resists kicking him, and snaps her fingers instead. "Want to go watch them put up the circus tents?" Hugh's not good company, but she's used to him. Also kind of like her wart.

The boy's face lights up. "Spy on the Haunted Circus? Heck yes."

He shoots a luke-warm stream at Peggy's face with his Super Soaker and brays with laughter. Peggy scowls and pulls her favorite hoodie, now soaked, over her hair. "Grow up!"

Peggy keeps her distance as they jog down the road to the fairgrounds. Hugh kicks the heads off wildflowers along the shoulder. Peggy scowls. It's appalling, but at least he's distracted from teasing her.

Butterflies in her belly flutter when she sees the trucks and trailers parked in the community field. Every Tuesday, she plays softball here. Most games they lose at least one ball in the dense cornfields along the perimeter.

The white lines and bases are invisible, buried beneath the trucks. Workers unload the animals and attractions onto the dry grass. Brightly-striped carnival tents take up the whole complex, turning the familiar field into something new. Maybe even dangerous. Peggy shivers.

Hugh isn't paying attention to the action; he's picking up stones along the edge of bleachers. Kids toss rocks here if they find them on the field.

"Cool, eh?" Hugh throws a rock at one of the caged wolves. The mangy animal growls and paws at the bars. "Betcha those are werewolves!"

Peggy balls her hands into fists. "Throw anything at that poor animal again and I'll kick you in your family jewels." She raises one of her sneakers and wiggles the toe.

Hugh drops the next rock. "Instead of kicking me in the nuts, why don't we do what we came here for?"

Peggy raises her eyebrows. "What?"

"Spy! Let's go check out the stuff at the back over there." Hugh points at the main tent.

Peggy follows him along the edge of the cornfield, keeping one eye on the crew setting up the signs and concession stands. No one notices them. They are like the pollen floating on the air, basically invisible.

The area behind the tent is messy, with unloaded wagons parked beside ancient temporary dumpsters. Rolls of brightly colored tarps, a broken concession booth, and bags of cheap stuffed toys litter the area.

Peggy catches her breath when she sees the clown from the back of the convoy half buried in the tall grass.

"Oh, look at that ugly thing," Hugh says. Must be broken."

Peggy steps closer. The clown has a tiny two-foot body, but his head is enormous. He's wearing toddler-size gold pants and a stained white shirt with a high lace collar. She wrinkles her nose.

His skull reminds her of the dusty kid's playhouse in her backyard—the one she grew out of years ago. His mouth is the same size as the door and patches of green and yellow hair stand up in clumps on a peeling white head. The eyes are like little square windows, so dark inside you can only imagine the spiders and bugs.

She shudders as the sun glints off yellow fangs. Was the clown grinning like this when she saw him on the back of the truck? Surely.

The workers shout as a wind gust rattles the tents. The blast blows her hair straight back from her face and knocks her to her knees.

Hugh's red ballcap blows by, brushing her ankle.

"Damn it!" He chases after it, hardly affected by the gusts.

A giggle escapes Peggy; Hugh's waddling-goose run is always hilarious.

Her laugh turns to a scream when the clown bounces by. The little legs and tiny arms wave and kick. Corn stalks snap and crackle like a bowl of Rice Krispies as he rolls into the field. One of his gold-panted legs kicks a leaf off a cornstalk.

The shuck swirls in an updraft. Peggy shakes her head. Is she seeing things?

Was the clown fighting to stop his roll?

Her eyes flick to Hugh. Did he see the same thing?

The boy changes course, ignoring his hat. "Catch that clown!" He trundles through the break in the corn, disappearing from Peggy's sight.

She doesn't want to catch the clown.

Long fingers of dread massage her spine. Clouds cover the sun. The wind dies down and she takes a shuddering breath. Should she just go home?

Hugh sticks his head out from between two yellowed stalks. "Come on!" The clown left a smashed path three cornrows wide in its wake.

Or should she go in? Her knees tremble with indecision.

"Are you chicken, little Piggy?" Hugh taunts.

Her brow furrows. "Don't call me a chicken *or* a pig."

She forces her shaking legs to follow him into the corn. Another ice cream headache stabs her forehead when she sees the clown. It's upright, the skull almost tall as the corn with his little body and legs squashed beneath it.

Peggy chews on the inside of her cheek. The clown looks different. Was his mouth open like that before? Yellow fangs rimming a hole big enough for her, or even Hugh, to fit inside.

She idly picks a dry ear off a cornstalk. The kernels are

dehydrated, rough. Like rotten teeth. Hugh snatches it from her hand and throws it at the clown. *Thunk.* It bounces off the white forehead, a few kernels flying off the cob and into the wild green hair.

The clown doesn't move.

Peggy's headache subsides a little. Only a silly kid would think a plastic carnival clown was alive.

She steps closer, examining his purple eyes. They're flat and fake. She touches one of his sharp teeth, willing her hand to stay still.

She jumps back. An arc of clear, viscous fluid trails with her, drawing a line between her palm and the tooth. "Eww, it's slimy!"

"It's *awesome!*" Hugh tucks his Super Soaker into his pants. "Dare you to go in."

Vomit rushes up her throat. She swallows the bile. "No way. I dare *you.*"

Hugh flaps his elbows and does a chicken dance. "Double dare?"

She nods. "Triple dare."

"You're on." Hugh hunches into the clown's dark mouth. "I think I see something in here—" His voice rings hollow as he crawls deeper into the head.

Peggy presses her lips together, the icy masseuse working on her spine again.

She chews her tongue to stop herself from screaming at Hugh to get out of there.

But that would be stupid. He'd tease her forever. The clown is just a circus attraction. It's supposed to be scary.

If he's brave enough, so is she!

Peggy shakes her arms like she does when she is about to take the plate with all the bases loaded. She steps after Hugh, toward the maw, and takes one last look at the clown's face.

A purple eye winks, some old paint falling into the dusty soil of the corn row.

Peggy swallows a scream. Her head feels like she sucked an entire bucket of Rocky Road through a straw.

Seeing things.

CLANG! The clown's mouth snaps shut.

"BLURP," he says.

"H-Hugh?" Bile rises again in Peggy's throat. "HUGH!"

Silence. The clown opens his mouth again. She rubs her eyes and stumbles backward. It's pure black in the hole. No spiders. No bugs. No Hugh. Her heart hammers in her throat.

Her voice quavers. "Is this one of your pranks? It's not funny."

Hugh doesn't answer.

The clown twitches. "BURP." A horrible odor wafts from its cavernous mouth.

Peggy gags. It reminds her of the skunk that died under the yard shed. Dad didn't find it for a month.

Tears burn her eyes. "Hugh, you're scaring me."

A red droplet hangs from one of the yellow teeth, then falls. *Plip.* The stench intensifies.

A wave of terror, cold and foreign, washes over Peggy. A tornado of fear tears up her insides, a thousand times more powerful than the wind that rolled the clown.

Peggy screams and runs out of the cornfield, arms pumping and breath ragged.

She doesn't slow down when she passes the circus workers. What would she say?

"Hey, there's a carnivorous clown in the corn field. Say that ten times fast!"

She fights down a hysterical sob and forces her legs to run faster. She's never even turned for third base this quickly and gets home in no time.

Rushing up the porch steps, she almost knocks over a big bowl of mini chocolate bars for the trick-or-treaters. Normally she'd grab one. But not now.

She slams the door behind her. Dad's putting dinner on the table.

She pauses, tries to speak, but her skin is clammy and she can't breathe. Dad just stares.

Cold water might help. She runs upstairs and splashes her face.

What on earth can she say?

"So, I followed Hugh into a corn field and a haunted plastic clown from the circus ate him."

Nope.

She doesn't know what to do.

SHE TRIES to eat her chicken noodle soup, but her stomach tosses and turns. A twisted noodle floats in the yellow liquid. The tangy smell, normally appealing, makes her even more ill. Dad is preoccupied with the last page of the newspaper and absent-mindedly spoons soup into his mouth. Mom is working late.

When someone knocks at the door, Peggy nearly screams.

Her father frowns, pushes away from the table, and walks down the hall. Peggy follows him, her throat tight.

"Clara! We're just sitting down to dinner. What can I help you with?"

Peggy uses the wall to keep herself from buckling to the ground. This is a real-life nightmare. If she tells them he disappeared into a clown's mouth, they're going to put her in an insane asylum.

Clara's face is wrinkled with concern. "Have you seen Hugh? He hasn't come home yet."

Her dad says over his shoulder, "Peggy, did you talk to Hugh today?"

Peggy rubs a sweaty palm on her sweatshirt. She takes a deep breath. Tell the truth.

Well, some of the truth.

"He was going over to the Haunted Circus."

Clara sounds relieved. "Okay then, I'll go check over there. That boy is always giving me heart palpitations."

Peggy bites her lip. Clara won't find her son. The storm in her gut swirls. She tries not to be sick as she follows her father back to the table.

He sits. "Speaking of the Haunted Circus, I spoke to your mother on the phone." He grins at her. "Do you want to check out opening night after dinner?"

Peggy shudders. She thinks of the blood dripping from the clown's teeth.

Her father raises his eyebrows. "Peggy, you've gone sheet white. What's wrong?"

She clenches her hands in her lap. "Maybe I don't want to have my socks scared off after all."

His jaw drops, soup spoon paused halfway to his mouth. "But just this afternoon—"

Peggy cuts him off. "I might be coming down with something. I'll give out candy instead."

Her dad blinks in astonishment. "If that's what you want."

Peggy nods. "Can I be excused?"

He waves his spoon at her, and she walks to the front room. Her legs are filled with lead. This must be the most exhausting day of her life. She lays her forehead on the cool picture window. The one with the best view of the front yard.

There's something behind the pine tree.

Something other than the ghost her mom hung from one of the lower branches. Her legs tremble.

She looks closer. There is something... or someone... at the edge of the property.

Clenching her fists, she walks out onto the porch. The sun is almost gone behind the horizon. Soon, the few kids in their quiet neighborhood will venture out in costumes and with candy bags. But right now, the street is empty.

Except—

The clown steps into the glow of the orange lights decorating the lawn. His eyes are reflective pools of green. Like a raccoon caught in headlights. He gives Peggy a frightening leer, his teeth pointy and red.

He flips Hugh's Super Soaker back and forth between his tiny arms.

One purple eye winks.

IF A COW COULD HOLD MY HAND

MICHAEL PEARSON

Cow watched Clive eat his porridge at the kitchen table with an ignorant stare only a cow could give. Her hooves tapped worn, white tile as her tale swept the edge of the farmhouse cooker. Clive shovelled the pasty mixture into his mouth with poor aim, little thought and no care. Between Cow and Clive, there was no room for anyone else.

Creamy slop fell from Clive's spoon with a slap that made Cow blink. Twice. The glops of spilt oats sunk into the fibres of Clive's sweater as he tried to wipe them with his calloused hands.

As he leaned back the joints of his chair creaked and clicked. "Cow...What am I goin' to do with you then?"

She blinked again, swayed her head to the right, licked her lips.

"The crops are...well, they aren't. I don't think I can affor' to keep you anymore." Cow turned her head back and stared. "I can barely affor' to keep myself." Clive sniffed. "Betta get back to it then. Land ain't gonna farm itself."

~

"Thing is Cow...I think we're gonna lose it all." Clive looked at the photos stuck to the scuffed and dented fridge, dog-eared and smothered in fingerprints. "With wifey gone..." He gulped and shook his head. "I just don't know if I've got it in me. Too tired." He scooped a spoon of porridge into his mouth that trailed lumps in his matted beard. "Time to sell up per'aps? What d'ya think?" Staring with the same blank stare, Cow swung her head side to side. Clive chuckled and coughed. "Well, I'll be damned. You'll be talking next, girl."

Clive sat at the table with his head in his palms and a pool of tears below. The air smelt old and dishes piled in the sink. "It's useless. There's nothin'. Crops are dead." He wiped his nose with his crusty sleeve. Cow looked puzzled and wet-eyed look. "G'woam Cow. You don't belong 'ere anymore than I do." Clive gestured towards the open back door. "Go'on. You can go." A tear trickled down Cow's cheek. "I 'ave no choice, I've gotta sell up." Cow swung her head left and right. "Then what?! What do I do?" She looked towards the window. A row of rabbits hung on the washing line. "Really?" He gasped.

Lumps of meat swamped a large bowl on the table whilst Clive gripped a blunt knife. Beside his feet wet rabbit skins huddled in a mound like old clothes. Cow mopped her bloody mouth with her thick, curled tongue. "'appy now?" Clive said. Cow nodded up and down. "An' you promise that'll 'elp?" Cow continued to nod. "Ok, ok. I trust ya'. We're gonna' 'ave a good crop. I can feel it in my bones." Cow bobbed her head throughout. "Ya know, I think it's time for the good stuff!" He fetched a bottle of Glenmorangie and his favourite whiskey glass, heavy at the base and fragile on top. "Here's to us!" The drink warmed his throat as he readied another.

~

"You said this would work! You said if I gave you those sacrifices you would make sure of it!" Clive banged the table with his fist and the bowl of rotting meat fell. The contents splashed and slid between Cow's legs, releasing a sickening stench . "You said that..."

"I suggest you calm down, Clive." Cow spoke. Clive froze. He looked at her and she looked back with a curious expression. He wiped his grimy hands on his shirt and reversed blindy into his chair.

"You..."

"Yes I did. And *you* doubted me."

"I...no, it was jus'..."

"You doubted me and you brought misfortune to this land."

"I'm... sorry."

"Your apology does nothing. Doubt is a disease. Rot in your heart. You were doing so well. And now..."

"I'm sorry, please! Wha' can I do?"

"It is too late."

"No! There mus' be summin'!"

"Perhaps..."

"What is it?!" Clive scurried around the table and approached Cow with his hands clutched together. He leaned in, inches from Cow's eye. She fluttered her large lashes several times and the air stroked Clive's cheek like a playful feather.

"Our hooves are our curse. Stricken to serve for eternity. Give me your hands so I can sow. Give me your hands and I will grow your crops. Give me your hands and I will save this land."

Cow shook her head and snorted as a fly hovered by.

"My 'ands?"

"Your big, beautiful hands." She rubbed her cheek delicately against Clive's nose. "Give me your hands." Clive nodded slowly, hesitantly, then surely. Holding his breath, he kissed below her bulging eye.

With the crusty knife in hand, he held it high. In the reflection a wide-eyed smile looked back. Clive wondered, for a moment, why it was crying.

~

"We've got the Mrs. in the living room and the husband in the kitchen. It's a fuckin' mess sir." Radios hissed, and silent blue lights turned purple against the setting sun.

"What happened? Burglary?"

"No Sir, I'm afraid not. Looks like the husband did it, but—the wife has been dead for a while and then—well, you've got to take a look for yourself, Sir." The officer entered the kitchen and stopped on the doormat.

"Jesus Christ... Where are his hands? How could he—?"

"We don't know Sir. We haven't found them yet." The officer left the kitchen and passed the whir of police. At the end of the driveway, he removed his hat and breathed. He felt the stench of the house cling to his lungs and coughed several times,

Beyond the dense, green crops that surrounded the farmhouse, beyond the tree line and up the hills, his eyes met a still silhouette staring back. He squinted and focused at the mostly familiar outline.

"I swear that bloody cow has been watching us since we got here."

TRACK 9

FRANCIS J. MATOZZO

Nearly a foot of snow fell that Sunday in February, the day before Wilson was taken. It was bitter cold when our crew showed up for work on Monday. We all knew the routine, even a rookie like me—ice and drift removal on the main line, at least for the big crews. Our gang of misfits? We were split up, most remaining in the yard at Abrams to clean switches, the rest of us—myself, Evans, and Wilson—tasked with the bullshit work of chipping ice off the walls of the old tunnel a mile down Track 9 where the old Reading branch ran through Perkasie Mountain.

"Mans got us picking corn outta' horseshit," Evans grumbled as we slogged through the snow.

As cold as it was outside, it was worse in the tunnel. In the bowels of the mountain, a damp chill sliced to the bone and there was a constant icy dripping that soaked right through to your soul. We swung pickaxes just to keep the blood circulating, our sour disposition augmented by the knowledge that this line had been out of commission for years. But that was the Company way: keep the men busy at all costs.

We broke for lunch an hour early, our fingers numb, work gloves soaked. We ate with the snow thick and gleaming around us, staying as close as practical to the fire Evans had built from pieces of old railroad ties and whatever dry branches could be found in the woods.

The fire melted a perfect circle in the snow, and we crouched in the wet area, fifty yards from the mouth of the tunnel. Still, we could feel its icy breath crawling up our backs, scattering embers through the air.

Evans sat with his rear facing the fire. He pulled out a fifth of Macnaughton from one of the huge pockets of his faded, over-sized army coat. He was a tall, rangy man in his mid-fifties. As I recall, his face was always set in a brooding frown. He sported a wispy Chuck Berry mustache and had a nasty scar—rumored to have been administered during a disagreement over a poker game—that ran from his left cheek to the corner of his mouth and made even his rare smile look sinister. Everyone called him Catfish. Despite his looks, I never knew him to be any worse than indifferent or drunk, mostly both. Part of it was an act; part of it was just Evans. As a role it suited him fine. He was a raconteur, a cynic and storyteller who could keep the crew loose with his tall tales of women and booze. Beneath it all he was smart, and in his own subtle way, serious. He was also the only man on the entire crew who could actually *talk* to Wilson.

"Man's led a tough life," he'd say as everyone had their laughs at Wilson's expense.

Pressed to elaborate, Evans would just smile. "Every man's got history. Wilson ain't no different. The man's got his reasons just like we all do."

As we huddled around the fire that day, Evans passed me his bottle. "Take a sip, Professor. Warm your damn self up."

I had done two years at State college, thus had been christened appropriately by Evans; everyone laughed at the name, especially my first couple weeks on the job when I could barely swing the hammer to drive a spike in a rotted tie, but in the end I didn't mind. Everyone on the rail gang had nicknames. It only meant that you were accepted. Come to think of it now, Wilson was one of the few without a nickname.

I didn't usually drink on the tracks, but on that freezing day it was hard to argue with whiskey logic. My throat burned as I swallowed. "What the hell is this?" I said between coughs. "Antifreeze?"

"Lifeblood, son. Lifeblood."

Wilson stared at the flames, a million miles away. No one knew his exact age; it was assumed he was in his late sixties, old enough to take the pension if he wanted. Short and compact, he'd worked thirty years on the Reading lines yet never once spoke of retirement. A somber, quiet man, he blended in with the landscape, as impassive as time itself, never uttering a word more than necessary to be civil. Not surprisingly, he was resented by nearly everyone. Railroaders want to know about a man: the price of his house, how he financed his car, who he's sleeping with—but with Wilson all you got was his blank brown eyes—tiny, squinty eyes made thinner by the deep creases of his skin, the kind produced by a lifetime working outdoors.

I started to hand the bottle back to Evans, knowing that Wilson only ever drank coffee from his lunch thermos—hot, black coffee even in the summer—when the old man's voice rang out in that peculiar Bela Lugosi tone of his. "Turned 70 today," he said. "I think I'll take a drink."

"Damn. Happy Birthday Jerry," said Evans, pushing the bottle in my hand towards Wilson. "Plenty of this to warm the three of us." He winked and patted one of his cavernous coat pockets. "Got back up anyway."

Wilson drank quickly, three long gulps, then handed the bottle back to me without the slightest change of expression. I smiled, wished a happy birthday. "Thank you very much," he replied, very formal and polite. He had big ears, like water jug handles, and they were glowing bluish red like they were frostbitten. He rubbed them and said: "Sure am cold inside."

In this manner the three of us huddled by the fire, quietly handing the bottle back and forth. Soon, I felt a glimmer of warmth in the pit of my stomach. For a long time the only sounds were the logs crackling and the shrill wind. Evans nodded off.

That's when Wilson stood. He jumped up, moving so abruptly that the hood of his coat flew back, and his yellow hard-hat fell to the ground revealing a thick shock of white hair. His eyes were transfixed on the tunnel.

"Oh Lord...it's coming," he whispered, and then he said something in a language I didn't understand.

"What you mumbling about?" asked Evans, suddenly awake and staring.

"It's coming," he repeated. "The train...I can hear it."

I gave Evans a look; it was common knowledge that Track 9 was seldom used; that the only reason we labored in the tunnel was because our status—the drunk, the rookie, and the strange old man —precluded any *real* work in the yard. But there was concern on Evan's face, I saw that right away, and when he jumped to his feet, a soft tendril of fear tickled my back.

"Jerry," Evans said in a barely audible voice. "I'm not hearing any train."

"It's getting closer," said the old man, backing away from our little circle of fire.

By then I was standing too, listening, trying to detect whatever the hell Wilson was hearing. I got nothing but wind and flames and heavy breathing.

"You can't hear a train with all this snow," I said, trying to sound calm and knowledgeable—like I was the one with thirty years on the tracks—but the look of sheer terror on Wilson's face was contagious and I started talking like Wilson wasn't present. "I don't hear a thing Catfish. I mean no trains run on this track, right?"

Evans eyed me seriously. "None that we know of."

We both stared at the dark, gaping mouth of the tunnel, then turned to Wilson. He was twenty yards away, running along the stony bed of the rails. The old man was screaming as he ran, a squirrel-like sound so disturbing you'd never imagine it came from a human.

"Wilson!" we both shouted.

I felt like I was in a dream. The wind howled, blowing snow across the rails; the gray sky turned black. I didn't need Evans steel grip crushing my wrist to know something was dreadfully wrong. It emerged from the tunnel like a whisper, rolling on silent wheels, belching noxious smoke into the frozen air. A train like none that ever rode those rails—a black steam engine pulling an endless line of swaying, splintered boxcars, not making a sound. It passed us, slow and silent, wheels moving in relentless circular motion. No clacking of rail joints, no swish of pistons. *Did the wheels even touch the rails?*

Hands protruded from the rotted slats of the boxcars. Skeletal arms and clawing hands, dozens, hundreds, reaching out at the icy air.

Thirty years on the tracks take a toll on the human body, specifically the legs. Wilson could not run fast, despite the pumping arms and terror injected adrenaline. And of course, the snow. He ran like one leg was shorter than the other; a desperate, futile comedy of misshapen limbs and bouncing white hair. When the thought occurred to him to stop running parallel to the tracks, he abruptly turned and ran towards the bordering woods.

They took him right before he made it to the trees. The outstretched hands from the last boxcar stretched out like grappling hooks, bony arms elongating impossibly, as bare of flesh as the trees in the woods were stripped of leaves. They gripped and lifted, but still his feet pedaled air. He was handed down the line of boxcars like a firstborn son at an Italian baptismal dinner, as helpless as that, until finally he was hoisted up into the cab of the engine and was gone.

We moved the instant the last car rounded the curve. We ran down the tracks, stumbling in our fear, but the train had vanished. Around the bend there was only the windswept snow and empty rails that stretched as far as we could see before fading away in the dead gray winter haze.

~

WE CROUCHED by the burned ties, the fire extinguished, shivering as much from shock as from the cold. In those days I was all about answers, explanations, logic; something about Evan's expression convinced me that he held them. When he finally gave me the old wrinkled black and white photo, I wasn't totally surprised.

The photo was of Wilson, decades younger, but unmistakable with the thick hair already turning white and those distinctive ears and blank expression I knew so well. He was high up in the cab of a steam engine, leaning over the side, eyes focused straight ahead. "He gave me that picture not too long ago," Evans said. "He said it freed him by giving it to me, that it was his last tie to the past. Guess he was wrong."

In the background of the photo, alongside the tracks, there was a signpost, a mile marker. The name didn't register with me at first. Evans had to point it out, his finger trembling. Then he told me what no one else knew. Jerzy Wisniewski—Wilson's real name—lived in Poland during the height of the Nazi occupation where he worked as an engineer for the Third Reich.

He operated deportation trains; transported thousands of men, women, and children to that place on the signpost. The name that chills my bones even today. That brings me back to the tunnel and the snow and the cold. *Treblinka.*

Evans brought out that second bottle from his miraculous

pockets and we drank it in record time. Later, when we stumbled back to the yard and the rest of the crew, the foremen reamed us out for being drunk and threw us off the tracks. We got a three-day suspension, crazy Wilson too, even after we explained how the old man had bolted down the tracks and disappeared into the woods, never to be seen again.

MARY MARY, QUITE CONTRARY

ANGELA SYLVAINE

E aston Mansion loomed before Amity as she trekked up the winding cobblestone driveway—three stories, too many windows to count, and *actual pillars* flanking a front door, twice her height. She didn't belong here, but no one refused an invitation from Grace Easton.

The front door stood ajar, and Amity nudged it open. "Hello?"

No response. She entered the foyer, feeling like a trespasser. A high-shine marble floor topped with a plush, white runner extended to a winding staircase, and a crystal chandelier hung from the ceiling. Gilt-framed mirrors outnumbered the art on every wall, and her unforgiving reflection stared back no matter where she looked. The jagged scar along her jaw stood out, angry and inescapable.

She supposed the beautiful liked to be reminded of the faces they wore.

The living room featured dozens more mirrors, all set at eye-level, and a huge rectangular coffee table made entirely of antique mirrored glass, marred with splotches of rusty discoloration eating away at the silvered surface, its modern style at odds with the Victorian furniture.

A painting above the ornately carved fireplace depicted three generations of Easton women—Grace as a child, her mother, Gladys, and her grandmother, Glenna. Only age distinguished them, each as gorgeous and flawless as a Greek sculpture. Amity had never met Glenna, but she knew of her. Benefactress of their town, she funded the local symphony and the Runaway Girls Task Force and Support Network.

"I thought you flaked," a voice said, filling the cavernous foyer.

Amity yelped and spun, tennis shoes squeaking on the slick tile.

Grace stood at the bottom of the stairs, clad in a blush pink jumpsuit, feet bare and perfectly pedicured. "Is that a sleeping bag?"

Heat flamed up Amity's neck. "I didn't know if—"

Grace waved a hand dismissively. "Leave it there. And your shoes."

After calculating the consequences of simply fleeing, Amity toed off her grungy tennies and left them and her sleeping bag by the front door.

"Thanks for inviting me," she said, though she didn't mean it. Grace invited one of the less popular girls every month or so, but Amity never expected her time would come. She already had enough pity to last her a lifetime; she didn't need this, too.

"Come on, we're having a snack before the spooky stuff."

"Spooky stuff?"

Grace grinned, a feral flash of gleaming white teeth. "Horror movies, ghost stories, summoning spirits. Standard sleepover stuff."

"Oh." Amity couldn't muster anything more. The last thing she needed was more ghosts.

EVERY ROOM and hallway in the entire house held a mirror, and Grace's bedroom was no exception. Featuring a canopied bed and chaise lounges against each wall, no spot was safe from one's reflection. The floral wallpaper was barely visible behind all the twinkle and shine.

Amity looked away each time she caught sight of herself, but it was unavoidable. And something else, hints of inky shadow clinging to the glass.

Bijou and Jade didn't seem to mind or even notice anything unusual, basking in the surfaces to tidy their hair or touch up their lip gloss. The two were Grace's constant companions, always preening and polishing to maintain the perfect visage Grace managed effortlessly. At school, the three emanated superiority, but that day, they were actually nice.

They treated Amity like a little sister, even insisting on giving her a makeover. She'd resisted, having no interest in giving them an up-close view of her flaws, but they'd been gentle and respectful when covering her scar. She had to admit her new smokey eyes and upswept hair made her feel prettier.

For a moment she fooled herself into thinking she could become one of them, that she could stay.

Then she remembered what this was. An act of charity.

Once the sun set and no more light hinted through the lace curtains, Grace clapped her hands and said, "Time to have some fun." She pulled a handful of taper candles from her nightstand with a flourish.

"Can't we just watch a movie or something?" Jade asked, looking bored. "That new Scream is supposed to be good."

"Yeah, I heard that, too." Bijou perched on the edge of the chaise.

"Later," Grace said, her voice flat. "Amity wants to play a scary game first, don't you?"

"I don't—"

"It'll be fun." Grace dragged her in front of the largest mirror, an ornate gold-framed one hung directly opposite the foot of the bed and handed her a candle. It was the first Grace lit, and the match emitted a sour whiff of sulfur.

The others lined up beside her. Once all the candles were lit, Grace turned out the lights. Amity's pulse sped up, and she struggled to take a full breath. She knew what this was: just a silly game of Bloody Mary. A classic slumber party game. She'd played it before, but not since the accident.

The flames flickered in the reflection, barely illuminating their faces, which seemed to float in the gloom.

"Mirrors show us beauty, but also horror." Grace stared straight ahead; her eyes shone golden in the candlelight. "There is a woman, once beautiful herself, who is now trapped. Imprisoned. Helpless."

Amity struggled to steady her hands, to stop her candle from trembling.

"When she hears her name three times, she must show herself, but when we blow out our flames, she must leave us and return to her prison."

Prison? Amity frowned.

"Say it with me," Grace ordered, and they all obeyed. "Bloody Mary. Bloody Mary. Bloody Mary."

The sound of her own ragged breath filled her ears as Amity gazed into the glass. The blackness swirled, shifted, a shape emerging from the shadows, a pale face framed by stringy dark hair. Amity clutched her candle, staring at the ghost that hovered before them, black blood dripping from her eyes, her nose, her mouth.

Jade and Bijou didn't react at all. The mirror reflected their bored faces, but Grace raised her chin in acknowledgement.

"Mary has answered our call, she's here with us now."

The ghost heaved, its mouth gaping in silent sobs, teeth chipped and decayed.

Sadness overcame Amity in a suffocating cloud, and she took a step back, away, still holding her wavering candle before her. Grace glanced over; eyes narrowed.

"She's just trying to scare you," Jade whispered.

"Shut up," Grace said, turning her attention back to the mirror.

The specter clawed at the glass prison with fingers worn down to the bone.

"Poor Mary. We're *so* sorry you're trapped, and there's *nothing* you can do to get out. That you won't *ever* be free." Grace's mouth ticked up at the corner, as if she were holding back a smile. She inhaled deeply, and the ghost's head slumped forward, its hair shrouding its face.

"Goodbye, Mary." Grace blew out her flame.

Bijou and Jade obediently followed, but Amity froze, eyes fixed on the ghost.

"Please, Grace, let me go." The words were so soft, Amity thought she might have imagined them.

"What?" she asked, leaning closer, hoping to hear the voice again and be sure.

Before the ghost could open her mouth, Grace reached over and snuffed out Amity's candle, plunging them all into total darkness.

Footsteps sounded and light filled the room. Jade stood by the switch, and Amity blinked at the sudden brightness, faced only with her own reflection and the room behind her.

"You should take up acting. Seriously." Bijou joined Jade by the door. "Now can we please just watch a movie?"

"Go throw in some popcorn." Grace collected all their candles and tossed them on the nightstand with the lighter. "We'll be right behind you."

The other two gone, she said, "You saw her."

Amity nodded, relieved to know someone else saw the same things she did. "I've been seeing them, the ghosts, since the accident."

"Accident?" Grace's brow furrowed. "Oh, the one that killed your dad."

"And my brother. I've never seen them, though." And Amity had looked. At the cemetery, the accident site, in every room of their house. Her thumb found the scar on her jaw, tracing the rough edge. "When did you, uh, start seeing them, the ghosts?"

"I always have. It runs in my family, with the women."

"I thought Bloody Mary was just a game." The spirit's whispered plea taunted her. "Why is she trapped in there?"

"Popcorn's ready," Bijou called.

"Come on." Grace led Amity from the room. "I don't know. She just always has been, since my grandma's time."

She rubbed one hand over her chest, trying to soothe the ache there. "Why do you keep calling her? It's just ... so sad."

"How else would I have found you?" Grace gave her a beaming smile and skipped down the spiral staircase.

Their reflections followed them in the mirrors, trailed by fleeting shadows.

AMITY LAY awake on the chaise, the other girls' soft breathing and snores filling the quiet. Sitting up, she picked out their prone, sleeping forms in the darkness. Her eyes strayed back to the mirror—she knew she couldn't leave without trying to talk to Mary again. Amity couldn't help her brother or her dad, but maybe she could help Mary.

She crept across the bedroom. A sliver of moonlight sliced through the curtains and across Grace's face, beautiful even in sleep. Amity should feel relieved to have a new friend, someone who understood, but something about Grace scared her.

Careful not to make a sound, Amity took a candle and lighter and slipped from the room, closing the door softly behind her. While there were plenty of mirrors in the hallway, the other bedrooms were too close, the risk of discovery too high. She continued down the staircase and into the living room, finally deciding on a small mirror on the inside wall, which gave her the perfect vantage point to keep watch on the hallway and stairs.

She lit the candle and gazed into the glass surface. "Mary, are you there? Hello?"

Only the dark room behind her reflected in the glass.

"Okay, uh, Bloody Mary, Bloody Mary, Bloody Mary."

The shadows shifted as they had before, and Mary's face took shape. A whisper creaked out like a rusty hinge.

"You."

"Me. Uh, I'm Amity. I just wanted to ask you a few questions." Amity winced, worried she was just as bad as Grace for summoning Mary, for forcing her from the darkness to perform like some kind of puppet. "If that's okay. Are you really trapped in there?"

Mary loomed larger, as if she were pressed right up to the glass. "Yes."

Figures emerged behind her, shifting closer. Amity gasped. "Who are they?"

"There are more." Blood stained Mary's face, but she didn't look scary, just sad. "I'm just the newest, the strongest."

"More?" Amity shook her head. "But, how?"

A thump sounded above her head, and she held her breath. Mary shuddered, too. When no further noises interrupted them, Amity whispered, "Please, I want to help you."

The other shadows crowded around Mary, pressing in on her, and she raised her hand, bone-bare fingers leaving black streaks. "We'll show you."

Trembling, Amity placed her hand flat on the glass, her fingertips aligned with Mary's.

Cold consumed her arm, her neck, her face, as images flooded her mind. Glenna as a young woman, taking life after life, trapping body and spirit in a coffin of mirrors. Teaching Gladys. Both of them calling to captive souls and feeding, always feeding to stay beautiful, mirrors at the ready. Finally, Grace. She'd been the one to kill this most recent Mary, who wasn't a Mary at all. Sarah Farmerton had disappeared only a year prior. One of the Runaway Girls.

Amity wrenched her hand from the glass and clutched her chest, her sternum threatening to split wide open. "Oh, God."

"I'm sorry," Sarah said. "She's going to take you next, make you a Mary."

The candle slipped from Amity's grip and landed on the carpet, flame catching on the thick pile. "Me? Why?"

"You're lovely *and* see the spirit realm. Those who can't don't last here more than a day."

Fire spread across the room, washing her in heat.

This wasn't charity or the start of a friendship. Grace needed a new victim. That game of Bloody Mary had been a test.

"You can stop them, free us," the voices said, more than just Sarah now.

The flames leapt from the edge of the living room carpet to the runner, racing along the foyer and up the stairs as if possessed, spreading faster than should have been possible. Fire danced in every reflection, the shadowed forms of Marys surging from mirror to mirror.

The walls rippled, paint bubbling and running in slick, melting trails. "Let us out," the voices wailed.

Amity knew where they were, had seen their coffin. Sweat stinging her eyes, she grabbed the metal fireplace poker and whirled toward the mirrored coffee table.

A cry sounded, and a figure wrapped in a blanket stumbled to the top of the stairs, toppled, and fell. They rolled down the stairs, catching fire, and thumped to a stop on the marble tile. Amity hesitated, watching as the figure crawled freed from the protective blanket. Grace.

She let out a shriek and rose to her feet, her clothes smoldering.

Amity brought the metal poker down as hard as she could on the table. The surface shattered and the sides cracked in sharp chunks, revealing bones and skulls and scraps of clothes.

Grace barreled into Amity, knocking her to the ground. Amity reached out to grab a piece of the ruined coffin, the makeshift weapon slicing into her palm.

Explosions of shattering glass shook the house, and she covered her head as shards rained down. Amity sobbed, forced back to that night—headlights blinding, world flung upside down, glass slicing her stomach and face. She should have died, too.

Every mirror in the house had broken, and shadowy figures surrounded Grace, gripping her arms. She screamed as they dragged her to the ground in the foyer, slashing her beautiful face with shards of mirrored glass and turning the white carpet red as her cries became gurgles, then silence.

Upstairs, footsteps raced, and there were more screams.

Choking on the smoke-filled air, Amity crawled past Grace, whose slashed throat gaped in a wet, red smile. Exhaustion weighed Amity down, and her arms collapsed beneath her. The cries upstairs stopped, the only sound left the whoosh of hungry flames.

Something gripped her arms, and the ground slid under her as she was dragged toward the door, open to the clean night air. She sucked in a deep breath, then hacked several painful coughs as she was rolled to her back, her legs trailing across the threshold.

A distant siren wailed, and she opened her eyes. Sarah crouched over Amity, plucking the glass shard from her palm and pressing it to her throat.

She sobbed, not in pain or fear, but in relief. "Yes, take me with you." They would be her family now.

"You're not a Mary." Sarah placed a barely-there palm against Amity's cheek. "But we can't risk them blaming you."

Searing pain sliced across the side of Amity's throat just below her scar, trailed lightly across her windpipe and jugular, then cut deep again on the other side. She raised her hands to the wounds and felt a trickle of warm blood slick her fingers, not like the spurting that coated her hands as her brother took his last breath. Hot tears trailed down the sides of her face to stain the stone pink, and a wave of shadows brushed past her and away.

The Bloody Mary's were free, and Amity was alive. And alone.

BE KIND, PLEASE REWIND

GWENDOLYN KISTE

T he monster is playing dead.

He's lying on the earth, his body in a heap, his face covered in a makeshift disguise. Maybe it's a potato sack or a hockey mask or a facsimile of William Shatner. It's difficult to tell now that it's covered in dirt and grime and other people's viscera.

All that matters in this moment is that he doesn't take a breath. He doesn't even move.

But the girl with the blood-splattered tee knows it's only a game to him. She's standing over what's left of the monster, the cool autumn air shimmering around her, and she's already seen what he does, how nothing seems to stop him. He'll rise again. He'll pick up his greasy knife that's fallen at his side, and he'll start again, his bloodlust knowing no bounds.

Not that he hasn't racked up a respectable body count already.

Unlike the monster, her friends and family aren't playing dead at all. They're the real deal, bodies twisted and dissected beyond recognition, scattered across the front lawn of the vacation cabins that were supposed to be their sanctuary for the weekend. It will take the pin in her boyfriend's left ankle and the six fillings in her best friend's teeth to identify their chopped-up remains. They might never find all the pieces of her mother.

Somewhere far off, there are police sirens, not that they'll do any good. Nothing and no one can help her. Because instinctively, the girl knows the rules. Now that she's the last survivor, she'll become an extension of the monster, nothing more than a useless appendage. A Final Girl, they'll call her, and she wouldn't even argue with that moniker. After all, there's a certain finality in realizing your life as you know it is gone forever.

But all of that is what's to come. Right now, everything's different. This is her moment of triumph. In this instant, she's invincible. The monster is dispatched, and she's still here, still breathing. No one ever talks about how powerful this moment is. The unlikeliness of it all.

Because she'll get to keep reliving this, over and over. For her, this night will never end. Once he rises, the monster gets to forget. She never does. She just has to learn how to live with what he's done.

Her heartbeat throbs in her ears, and that's all she can hear. This reminder that she's alive. She was once the quiet girl, the strange girl. The one nobody ever bothered to worry about.

Maybe that's why she survived. Maybe that's what makes her different.

Or maybe it's something else. Because all at once, the girl kneels next to the monster, and with the weight of the universe heaving down on her, she does something even she doesn't expect. She plunges her hand into the monster's chest, feeling what's left of his heart, squishy between her fingers like worms writhing in the stinking earth.

This power. This energy that never dies. Time is on the monster's side—it keeps repeating, keeps looping, keeps helping him along, so that the carnage will never end.

The girl wants to keep going, too. She wants to replay what's happened. She wants to see if she can choose a different ending.

"Go back," she whispers. "I want to go back."

It's such a simple thing to say. These tiny words that should mean nothing at all.

But the ground trembles all around her, and before she can even remove her hand from the monster's chest, she feels it.

The way she gets to control time instead of the monster. This is her moment of triumph. That means she gets what she wants.

And with her eyes closed, what she wants is a second chance.

SHE OPENS her eyes when she hears their screams.

They race every which way around the vacation property, darting behind the little A-frame rentals, searching in vain for car keys they'll never find in time. Her boyfriend, her best friend, and a few other friends-of-friends, the extras in her life whose names she doesn't remember. They're all here, and they're all alive again. Or most of them are. There's still blood splatter on her sneakers, which means someone was already unlucky tonight.

"What are you doing?" her best friend shrieks. "You need to run."

So the girl does what she's told, mostly because she's too delirious to think of anything else. She didn't expect this to work. She didn't expect anything at all.

As they surge toward the cover of sycamore trees, the girl glances down. Her best friend is barefoot. She wonders how or where she lost her shoes.

They huddle together in the shadows, their hands entwined, a few crisp leaves on the forest floor. Autumn is creeping up on them, the way autumn always does, the world dying a little bit at a time until there's nothing left.

"This shouldn't be possible," the girl whispers, trying to fathom what she's done.

Her best friend stares at her, fear fermenting in her eyes. "You mean a masked killer? That *he* shouldn't be possible?"

The girl only shakes her head. She wants to explain. Even more than that, she wants to understand it herself.

"Please stop," someone says, and the girl looks up just in time to see it's her boyfriend. He's backed against a splintered shed at the edge of the tree line, and the monster closes in.

It only takes a moment to finish him. A snick-snack of a blade, and her boyfriend falls to his knees, the girl's heart twisting in her chest. Her first love, cut up like prosciutto. Truth be told, she never thought they'd end up together, but she also never thought they'd end up like this. And even if she never believed in soul mates, that didn't stop them from making promises in the dark, back when she thought one summer might last long enough to call forever.

Their forever ends tonight. Unless she can try again. Unless she can go back further.

Next to her, her best friend covers her mouth with both hands to muffle a scream, but it does no good. The monster hears her anyhow. He finishes slashing the boyfriend's throat, and then he starts toward them.

And it's more than that. The monster is looking right at her now, and something silent passes between them. A kind of dubious recognition. Like he remembers that he already died, that the girl already killed him.

Still, that's no matter to him. A monster's world isn't the same as hers. Where he's from, timelines blend together. His world reboots at the flick of a wrist. That means this backward loop isn't strange for him. He shakes his head and grips the blade tighter, ready to start again, as if he thinks the finale was only a dream sequence and now it's time to act on those bloody instincts of his.

He never runs anywhere, because why should he? This is his story, a body count he's crafting like a work of art, one glint of a rusted blade at a time.

(It could never be a fresh knife, a clean knife. Nobody ever talks about the tetanus shots a Final Girl should have.)

In the background, a couple of no-name friends dart back and forth. They might be alive now, but it won't last for long. The girl's gone back in time no more than an hour, and both she and the monster already know what's to come. The way all of them will soon be finished, their bodies strewn about the lawn like confetti.

There are other casualties, too. From here, the girl can see into her own A-frame rental, the last one on the left. The back door hangs open like a gaping jaw, and inside at the table, she can see a body, leaking dark red on the linoleum. Her mother. She was the first to go. After all, why bother to keep her around when you've got younger, more nubile girls to pursue?

The monster comes closer now. She thinks about how calm he is. The casualness with which he destroyed her life.

She and her best friend run, but not fast enough. That's because monsters are always faster. He takes down her best friend, his fist clenched around her long, dark hair, and with one quick jolt, her neck snaps in his hands like last winter's firewood.

The girl turns back just in time to see, everything in her body numb. They say there are no atheists on the battlefield, but here, in this place, standing with blood and earth and bone at her feet, she's never felt so far from God.

It wasn't supposed to be this way. For years, she swallowed down who she was. She played the good girl, the studious girl, the one who always smiled and never did anything wrong. And what did that get her? Nothing except this moment.

Now she doesn't want to be the good girl. She wants to be the girl with a family and friends. She wants to do more than just survive.

It's deliberate that they pick that word: survivor. Survive. Because that's all she'll get to do. Not thrive or live, *really* live. After this, she'll merely get to muddle through, bloodied and bruised.

Unless she makes another choice. He charges toward her, but

she's ready. She doesn't close her eyes this time. Instead, she looks right at him, through the empty holes in his cheap dimestore mask.

The first time wasn't enough. She needs to go back further.

He raises his blade, but she makes her move first, her hand plunged into the soft flesh of his chest once more, drawing on that power. Drawing from her own power too.

"Go back," she says again, and part of her is certain this won't work twice.

But she's wrong. In the blink of an eye, the world shakes around her until it reverses like a VHS tape long past its prime.

Until she gets another chance.

THEIR LAUGHTER IS the first thing she hears.

Her boyfriend and her best friend and all their other friends are alive again, carousing around a campfire at dusk.

She stumbles toward them, her arms outstretched. "He's already here," she says, but they swat her away and keep passing around a bottle of Southern Comfort like it's ambrosia of the gods.

"Everything's fine, Margot," they say. "You just had too much to drink."

"Please," she says, and then she remembers. This is how it went before. They didn't believe her then either.

But they soon will. Within five minutes, they discover the first few partygoers are already dead. Her mother is dead too. She still didn't rewind it far enough.

Fortunately, she tells herself she'll get another opportunity. The monster is coming toward them now. At once, the others bolt, their screams rising into the chilled night air, but she doesn't follow. She and the monster look at one another across the campfire, and she sees it in him. The way he can remember. The way he knows what she did.

For the first time, the monster is starting to understand. She's not the kind of girl he expected. The one who turns and screams until her throat is raw.

She doesn't run now. She doesn't even flinch. She's not doing any of the things a nice girl ought to do. Instead, she'll drag him backward, kicking and screaming through her trauma, through the wounds he's inflicted. She'll make him live there. She'll make him remember, the same way she's expected to.

He flashed in her eyes. Now she flashes in his eyes like the silver glint of a blade.

With a guttural cry, he turns and tries to flee with the rest, and beyond reason, she can sense it in him. The monster is tired now, but she's not.

She's just getting started.

"Go on, darling," she says with a feral grin, because at last, the monster has learned how to run. "Faster now."

And she keeps on smiling as he flails forward, his heaving body almost too much to bear, because it won't do him any good. He can't escape himself and all these things he's done.

His breath sputtering in his chest, the monster is afraid because he doesn't understand these new rules. He only ever understood *his* rules, how he always won, how nothing could stop him, not for long.

He expected a knife and a scream and some buckets of blood. He didn't expect her.

But she knew he was coming even before she saw him. Back when all this started, she could feel him somewhere on the property.

"Something's wrong," she kept telling her friends, but nobody believed her. This is the curse of the girl who survives, a Cassandra in ripped jeans and a ribbed tee. She knows what happens next, but it doesn't make a difference.

Except she'll make a difference now. With everything in her, she rushes forward and tackles the monster. He goes down quicker than she thought he would, his knife slipping from his trembling fingers.

With the flick of a wrist, she tears off his mask. Beneath it all, he's not a monster after all. He's only a man. They always are. When it comes right down to it, they're never as extraordinary as they believe themselves to be. They're as common as dirt.

Her friends gather closer, but they still don't understand. How safety's an illusion. It's nothing more than a bedtime story we're all desperate to believe. But this knife in her hand—*his* knife—is no illusion. It's real, and she'll use it to finish this.

"He won't stop otherwise," she says, as she raises the blade over her head, burying it again and again in his worthless heart. She keeps going until there's nothing but pulp and shredded denim left to identify him.

The moon wanes in the sky, and her friends think she's crazy now. Together, they back away from her. She recognizes that look in their eyes. They see her as the monster. The mad one, the girl who can't be trusted.

But what they don't understand is that she needs her madness. It's the only way she'll survive. The only way they'll all survive.

"I'm finished," she whispers, and without another word, she's said what she really means. That it's time to go back. Time to go home. To somewhere he hasn't touched yet.

She doesn't need his heart this time. She's got her own, the heavy thrum of her pulse ringing in her ears, ringing in everyone's ears. They all hear her now. And they see the power brimming in her, the force of nature they always underestimated.

The ground quivers beneath her, everything trembling at the girl's command, and she closes her eyes and remembers. Who she was, what she wanted.

With her friends still gaping at her, the reel of their life rewinds until there's no more film on the spool, no more carnage left to undo.

Then as the girl exhales a blood-curdling laugh, everything spins to black.

~

SHE OPENS HER EYES AGAIN, and it's like stepping out of a dream.

"Margot?" Her mother's voice, soft as chiffon, sweet as a lullaby.

They sit together on the back porch, a pitcher of lemonade waiting in front of them, all of this so quaint it makes her want to cry.

She's returned to where this all started. Back to the end of summer. Back to forever.

Across the patio table, her mother chitchats about things like college orientation and where they'll vacation for Christmas break this year, but the girl barely hears a word of it.

All she can do is stare down at her own hands. There's no bloodstain on them now, no sign of where she's been. She's still her. After everything, she hasn't become a monster herself.

But that doesn't mean she doesn't bear the invisible scars of what she's seen. The formless shape that drifts behind her eyes, haunting her waking nightmares. The tearing of flesh with a blade, like ripping canvas against the grain. The stench of bisected meat, the twisted bodies of her friends.

She remembers everything. For all that she's undone, it hasn't left her. If anything, the memories are clearer now. Maybe that means she'll never be free. But she won't be his prisoner either.

An August breeze swirls around her, and from across the miles, she senses him. His body stirs in the bottom of a lake, or the musty guts of a boiler room, or in a plain old bedroom in suburbia.

"There are horrible things to come," she whispers.

Her mother looks at her for a long moment, a knowing spark in her eyes. "There always are."

For the first time, they understand each other, the things all mothers and daughters are forced to witness. How the monsters will rise, because they always do. But then she'll rise too. And maybe this time, they'll listen to her from the start, from the moment she speaks those words.

I'm afraid, there's something wrong, please believe me.

Or maybe they won't. Either way, she already knows how this turns out. She'll survive. She'll fight back. She'll hold on to whatever she can, hold on to what's left of herself.

And as a monster takes his first breath somewhere in the world, the girl smiles and tells herself that will have to be enough.

With her fists clenched and her heartbeat steady, she will be enough.

STORY NOTES

These story notes contain spoilers, but they'll also tell you which trope each author chose and how they approached it! Read these after you read the stories.

"WE ARE WORDS" BY D. MATTHEW URBAN

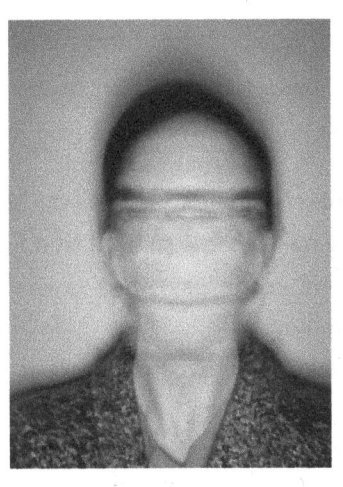

Has this ever happened to you? You're minding your own business when you come across a book bound in coarse, wrinkled leather. Out of curiosity, you start to read the mysterious tome, and before you know it, you're running for your life with a horde of gibbering monstrosities at your heels. You've fallen victim to the Cursed Book Bound In Human Skin.

The Forbidden Book is one of my favorite horror tropes; the CBBIHS is its edgelord cousin, often deployed as a quick-and-dirty plot device or a bit of creepy atmosphere. Doesn't it seem a little too convenient that the book conjures evil all by itself, leaving its reader almost totally blameless? "It wasn't me! It's all the book's fault!" Sure, pal.

My story presents the situation from the book's perspective, through the eyes of the much-maligned words that call it home. Maybe those words aren't so bad once you get to know them. Maybe they're doing their best in an unpleasant situation. And as for the oh-so-innocent reader, just ask yourself, what kind of person would you expect to find perusing a Cursed Book Bound In Human Skin? Probably some kind of sick deviant, the type of weirdo who thinks up stories about living words flaying people alive...but I've said too much.

D. Matthew Urban hails from Texas and lives in Queens, NY, where he reads weird books, watches weird movies, and writes weird fiction. His stories can be found in No Trouble at All, The First Five Minutes of the Apocalypse, and Split Scream Volume 4, among other venues. Find him on Twitter @breathinghead or on the web at https://dmatthewurban.com.

~

"THE LONG PEOPLE" BY TOM COOMBE

At this point, the "it's just the cat" jump scare has become so tired that I can't remember the last time I saw it used in a movie.

I picked it not because I felt it needed tearing down, but because I wanted to see what I could do to make cats scary. Sure, they're weird and a bit spooky, but I wanted to go beyond that.

As if I'd made a wish on the monkey's paw, the submission window for this anthology coincided with some upsetting health new about our real-life cat, Caroline. She was diagnosed with a thyroid condition, and an X-ray revealed a black mass on her lung (this is on top of an existing heart problem).

Our vet also told us that – given her various health issues – Caroline was actually older than we had thought. It was a lot to take in, and I think I used this story to process the fear and helplessness I've been feeling when it comes to our four-legged family member.

Tom Coombe *is a journalist-turned-horror writer whose stories have appeared in a number of anthologies, including the first volume of It Was All a Dream. He lives in Pennsylvania's Lehigh Valley with his girlfriend and their (non-talking) cat.*

~

"WHEN THE MOTHERFUCKER JUST WON'T DIE" BY TIFFANY MICHELLE BROWN

"When the Motherfucker Just Won't Die" tackles two of the most well-worn horror tropes out there—the final girl and her unkillable, mask-wearing slasher.

Confession: historically, the slasher genre hasn't been my jam, perhaps due to the formulaic nature of these types of stories.* The idea of turning such entrenched tropes on their heads and creating something that reflects my personal love for body horror, psychological/domestic terror, and the monstrous feminine really appealed to me. I started with a simple premise: what if our final girl was able to capture her slasher but could never kill him? Who would she be? What would she do if she no longer had to run, but still felt

completely stuck? Sprinkle in a little generational trauma and the dangerous edge between fear and sex, and you have my story.

Fun fact: I didn't know how this story would end, because there were so many possibilities available to me, so many decisions our final girl could've made. In the end, I like that she leaned into darkness—because who is the final girl without her monster?

*I know there are exceptions! Don't come for me! I do love the Scream franchise and I'll watch Urban Legend any damn day!

Tiffany Michelle Brown is a California-based writer who once had a conversation with a ghost over a pumpkin beer. She is the author of the collection How Lovely To Be a Woman: Stories and Poems and cohost of the Horror in the Margins podcast. Her fiction and poetry has been featured in publications by Black Spot Books, Dread Stone Press, Death Knell Press, Cemetery Gates Media, and the NoSleep Podcast. Tiffany lives near the beach with her husband Bryan, their pup Zen, and their combined collections of books, board games, and general geekery.

~

"ROCKET POP" BY AMANDA CECELIA LANG

Ah clowns, every child's worst nightmare, right? The pancake makeup, the colorful jumpsuits, the goofy hats. Look, I'm not gonna lie. There's a

tiny part of me that's always thought people who are afraid of clowns are kind of sissies. No judgement if that's you—I once spent an entire year afraid of my basement. And look, I realize there are some clowns out there whose MOs are legit terrifying. Twisty the Clown, Art the Clown—yeah, not eager to meet these psychopathic freaks in a dark alley anytime soon. But like all good slasher villains there's a certain pop culture whimsy about them, something we might want to put on a t-shirt or pose with at a convention. Something that loses teeth and starts to lend itself to MTV aesthetics and slapstick gags rather than abject terror. Which got me thinking...

Why not embrace the friendly side of clowns. What if a creepy killer clown wasn't here to maim and slash and terrify, but to buddy up? What if some down-on-his-luck teenager could join forces with one of these weirdos to face off against other scarier monsters? Those hideous beasts that lurk in everyday shadows. The ruthless bullies, the abusive parents, the assholes ripe for a little killer clown justice.

Honk, honk! Enter Clown Dude, a sweaty, ice-cream-truck-driving, weed-smoking avenger sent straight from the three-ring circus of hell.

Amanda Cecelia Lang is a horror author and aspiring recluse from Denver, Colorado. As a die-hard scary movie nerd, her favorite things are meta-horror, 80s nostalgia, and the rise of a fierce final girl. Her stories haunt the dark corners of many popular podcasts, magazines, and anthologies, including NoSleep, Cast of Wonders, Tales to Terrify, Uncharted, Dark Matter, Flame Tree's Darkness Beckons, and Dread Machine's Mixtape: 1986. Her short story collection The Library of Broken Girls will debut in Spring of 2025. You can stalk her work at amandacecelialang.com—just don't be surprised if she leaps out at you from the shadows.

∽

"THE WIND THROUGH THE CHIMNEYS" BY EDWARD LODI

The psychopathic serial killer trope has been done to death (pun intended). The killer, almost always a man in his prime, stalks his victims, almost always young women. The women frequently share a common trait—hair color, build, facial features, or profession such as that of prostitute—that evokes a traumatic event from the serial killer's childhood, or which in his warped mind justifies what he does to them. Outwardly, the psycho appears normal, and is often of above average intelligence.

If I read one more "thriller" with this trope I'll scream (my screams may not be as loud as the victims', but ear-splitting none the less).

Such stories began to proliferate shortly after Jack the Ripper went on his rampage in 19th-century London, and have shown no signs of abating ever since.

In my story, the serial killer does not fit the profile. He's a demented old man. Rather than stalk his victims, he sets a snare and allows them to fall into it. He doesn't exactly kill them. He just lets them die. He also has an unwitting audience, his aged sister. He disposes of the bodies in a rather unique manner. I've included grim humor and condign punishment for his crimes as a lagniappe.

Edward Lodi has written more than thirty books, both fiction and nonfiction. His horror stories have appeared in anthologies published by Black Beacon Books, Hungry Shadows Press, Black Widow Press, Cemetery Dance, and many others. "Charnel House" was featured on Night Terrors Podcast. His mystery stories frequently appear in Mystery Magazine and elsewhere. He is a member of the Short Mystery Fiction Society.

~

"THE AMERICAN DREAM" BY YELENA CRANE

I play with the trope "it was all a dream" by exploring the idea of dreams as a desire, as a fantasy, and as a hope that keeps one going in a world where the dreams themselves must be purchased because I fear one day commercialization will bring us there.

Yelena Crane is a Ukrainian/Soviet born and USA based writer, incorporating influences from both into her work. With an advanced degree in the sciences, she has followed her passions from mad scientist to sci-fi writer. Her stories often explore the boundaries of technology, the complexities of human nature, and the consequences of our choices. She's published in Nature Futures, DSF, Third Flatiron, Dark Matter Ink, Flame Tree, and elsewhere. Follow her on twitter @Aelintari and https://www.yelenacrane.com/.

~

"UNTITLED, WITH DEMON" BY JOE KOCH

Most of us are sick of seeing women in captivity, helpless, or brutally victimized in horror. Contemporary horror usually twists the power dynamic and gives women more agency these days, thank goodness. And while I approve, I admit I'm interested in what Bunker Woman, a torture porn trope, has to teach us about trauma, recovery, loss, the meaning or meaninglessness of suffering, and how she learns (or fails) to recognize and manipulate her chains. She has many historical precedents, especially in America, where our first popular literature was the Puritan captivity narrative.

Ironically, those falsified stories of "good" white ladies taken captive by "evil" Indigenous People occurred right alongside witch trials, where white male European religious leaders imprisoned and tortured their own people, mostly women. We still wrestle with those cultural chains of our Puritan heritage, so I think it's worthwhile examining Bunker Woman's distress. As a woman accused, in my story she also suffers (probably) from a related religious problem: Possession. The demon is a deceiver, of course, and might be likened to psychological triggers that confuse past and present in the trauma survivor's physical and emotional response to stimuli, leaving them questioning along with Zhuang Zhou's Butterfly which version of experience is real and which one is the dream.

Joe Koch writes literary horror and surrealist trash. Their books include The Wingspan of Severed Hands, Convulsive, Invaginies, and The Couvade, which received a Shirley Jackson Award nomination in 2019. His short fiction appears in Vastarien, Southwest Review, PseudoPod, Children of the New Flesh, and many other journals and anthologies. Joe's work has been translated into both Spanish and Italian. He/They. Find Joe at horrorsong.blog.

"HAND TO THE FIRE" BY AVRA MARGARITI

Inclement weather: Many horror media use this trope as an excuse for the characters to seek shelter from a storm, usually by falling right into the claws of a fate worse than rain in the process.

I wanted to use the existence of a lightning storm of supernatural origins in order to explore my main character's emotional state. Each strike of lightning illuminates a new traumatic event from an unstable childhood, until the fire consumes, and maybe even purifies, everything toward the end.

"Lightning never strikes twice" is another cliche phrase I wanted to remix, together with the Greek idiom "βάζω το χέρι μου στη φωτιά/I put my hand to the fire" (= I stake my life on something), from which the title is borrowed.

Avra Margariti is a queer author and Pushcart-nominated poet with a fondness for the dark and the darling. Avra's work haunts publications such as Vastarien, Asimov's, Strange Horizons, F&SF, The Deadlands, Lackington's, and Reckoning. Avra lives and studies in Athens, Greece. You can find Avra on twitter (@avramargariti).

"THE LUTHIER" BY REBECCA HARRISON

I always loved stories in which music was evil, but they always seemed a bit unfair. Rude, even. As far as I was concerned, music was one of the good guys. Even when it came with a side of mullets. Though perhaps Tiger King has proved me wrong. 😒 Silence was the villain to be chased away at whatever cost. And I always thought musical instruments had souls. And pieces of music too. I even went through a stage when I was a kid, of thinking John Lennon was Jesus. Come off it – he had the hair and the sandals. And all he wanted was us to give peace a chance. There was no doubt. Obviously, he was already dead, but child me just thought 'oh no, they've done it again'. Instruments always seemed like magic to me. (But then I am bewildered by any tech invented after the candle.) When I was about five or so, I met Yehudi Menuhin, one of the great violinists. As far as I was concerned, I had one job: to steal his violin. I wanted to discover its secret. Menuhin had a celestial aura, but it didn't put me off. I was on a mission. But he was on to me. He kept holding his violin higher and higher. He kept a wary eye on me. He even patted me on my head to appease me. So alas, I was denied. Cue violins.

Rebecca Harrison sneezes like Donald Duck and her best friend is a dog who can count. Her first book, The White Horse, *a gothic folk horror that's* Jane Eyre *meets* The Wicker Man *in 1780s England, is out now on Spooky House Press.*

"EMILY'S TEETH" BY CASSANDRA DAUCUS

The way a lot of horror movies treat sex has always been interesting to me. There's the expected virginity of the Final Girl, of course, coupled with the expectation that if a woman loses her virginity or has sex over the course of the movie, she's probably going to end up dead. The men in these situations thus represent the women's downfall. Even if the women enthusiastically consent (which they don't always) the men are ultimately responsible for their deaths. On another hand, I'm also a fan of the concept of vagina dentata–those toothy little monsters living in the vagina, or that are part of the vagina, just waiting for some hostile dude (almost always a dude) to come along and get himself chomped. But what if sex is healthy and good, and what if the dude involved is gentle and understanding? And what if a woman with teeth in her vagina, rather than wanting to attack, is afraid of hurting someone she cares about? These were the things rolling around in my head when I wrote "Emily's Teeth"–a soft and trope-subverting little horror (?) story.

Inspired by H. P. Lovecraft, M. R. James, Shirley Jackson, Robert Aickman, and a ton of fan fiction, Cassandra Daucus (she/her) writes a spectrum of horror. She is intrigued by how the human mind responds to the unknown, and also enjoys a good gross-out. She has stories published and forthcoming in several literary magazines and anthologies. Cassandra lives outside of Philadelphia with her family and three cats. Her social media and website can be found at https://linktr.ee/residualdreaming

≈

"BAD VIBRATIONS" BY NADIA BULKIN

 I have a lot of fondness for many horror tropes, even the ones that typically make it onto "most annoying horror tropes" lists - the person who investigates the suspicious noise in the dark basement, the group that splits up to search for their friend - because I think they actually feel rational in the daylight. So I picked a trope that I genuinely have no fondness or sympathy for, and that's the "evil artifact from foreign land terrorizes average white family" - a silly, xenophobic remnant of colonialism that unfortunately still gets boosted by paranormal investigators. My goal with "Bad Vibrations" was to flip every aspect of this trope - the "evil," the "foreign," the "average white family" - to inch toward an accurate depiction of what power in the post-colonial world actually looks like.

Nadia Bulkin's is the author of the short story collection She Said Destroy (Word Horde, 2017). She has been nominated for the Shirley Jackson Award five times. She grew up in Jakarta, Indonesia with her Javanese father and American mother, before relocating to Lincoln, Nebraska. She has two political science degrees and lives in Washington, D.C.

≈

"DARLING AT YOUR WINDOW" BY DANA MCKAY

The seductress monster is pretty easily one of my least favourite tropes. It's overused, one-dimensional, and almost always falls in a very misogynistic light. It also banks on this very surface-level sex appeal that's supposedly enough for another character to succumb to or heroically overcome.

I wanted a story that gives the relationship between the monster and human more depth, while keeping the unsettling tone of the trope as both characters obsess about the other in different but equally unhealthy ways. Let the seductress be tempted just as much as her lover. Let the lover know exactly what she's getting into, and enter those waters anyway.

After all, the woman staring through the window isn't scary. It's not knowing if you want to turn her away.

Dana McKay is a writer and game designer from Australia. Her game A Long Goodbye has won the Freeplay Excellence in Narrative Award.

"BLOOD SWEAT AND TEARS" BY RED LAGOE

The haunted house trope is an eternal classic. It goes back to the first great gothic novels in history. There's a reason this trope has survived the centuries—because it works! Because people will always fear the ghosts of our pasts and the histories that bled into the walls of the very homes built to shelter us from danger. So long

as people live and die, there will be new haunted house stories to tell. For Blood Sweat and Tears, I chose to open with a classic scene: two kids go to the dilapidated house where someone had been murdered. However, to flip this trope from the expected spooky scenes like cobwebs and sheeted old furniture, the creepy exterior gives way to a more welcoming home. One that is light and comfortable and doesn't whisper for the kids to "get out". Instead, it begs them to come in and stay a while.

Red Lagoe *grew up on 80s horror and carried her paranoia of slashers and sewer creatures into adulthood.*

She is the author of the forthcoming books, In Excess of Dark *(DarkLit Press 2024),* Bloodstains by Gaslight *(Brigids Gate Press 2024), and three horror collections, including* Impulses of a Necrotic Heart. *Red is the editor of the anthology* Nightmare Sky: Stories of Astronomical Horror, *and her stories have been published in several anthologies. Find out more about Red's work here: www.redlagoe.com.*

∼

"THE THINGS I MISS" BY DAVID J. THIRTEEN

The Things I Miss came out of an assignment in Gwendolyn Kiste's writing course, Monster Mash, which teaches about approaching old tropes in fresh ways. While taking it, the pandemic was in full force, and I wanted to tackle a zombie apocalypse story by focusing on the way people distract themselves in times of crisis. This was something I was seeing all around me and also in myself. I'd picked up the nasty habit of doom-scrolling and staying on my phone far

longer than ever before, even when what I was reading made me angry or anxious. So this became the jumping-off point for my story. Instead of the news and social media posts, I made the main character obsessed with online shopping. Her fixation on possessions makes the story's apocalypse almost peripheral as she tries to avoid thinking about it. And as her situation becomes more dire, she starts narrating in ad-speak and relaying the events through her lost possessions disassociating herself from the situation. My hope is that readers will see a part of themselves in the character and feel dread as her cravings are stripped down to the most basic elements of survival.

David J. Thirteen is a writer of horror and other dark fiction living in Toronto, Ontario, Canada. His short fiction has been featured in Lamplight Magazine, Seize the Press Magazine, The Other Stories Podcast, and several anthologies. You can find out more at DavidJThirteen.com.

~

"RESTLESS" BY RIA HILL

I don't remember how old I was when I first heard someone say with absolute confidence that it's impossible for a person to die in their own dream. One of my peers told me that the reason we always jerk awake just before we hit the ground in a falling dream is because if we did die in a dream the shock of it would kill us in the waking world as well.

I don't know where this concept originated—or when they started passing it off as fact—but it must have been prior to 1984, when Freddy Krueger burst onto the screen in A Nightmare on Elm Street. I love Freddy as much as the next guy (even more, if my replica knife-glove is to be believed) but, to me, the most frightening bit wasn't the idea of the dreams killing you. What got to me was the ending, and the implication that the nightmare could go on forever.

Perhaps it's that my worst dreams are recursive, but I hate the idea of a nightmare you can't truly wake up from. As a horror writer, when something scares me, it is my sworn duty to pick up a pen and make it much, much worse.

So I interrogated the "never sleep again" trope all Freddy films are based on. What if you could die in a dream? What if your death was the climax of every dream you had, and there was no end in sight? What kind of monster would do this to a person, and what if it wasn't a monster at all?

"Restless" is a story about how maybe, just maybe, killing you isn't the worst thing a dream can do.

Ria Hill is a writer, librarian, and nonbinary horror who lives in Toronto. They spend the bulk of their non-work hours maintaining their recreational spreadsheet collection and interrupting their spouse's train of thought with deeply worrying story pitches. Their work has appeared in The Book of Queer Saints Volume II from Medusa Publishing Haus, and in your worst nightmares. If you see them in the wild, they are very unlikely to eat you. They promise. They can be found online at riahill.weebly.com and on various social media @RiaWritten.

$\sim$

"FEEDING THE FLAMES" BY LIAM HOGAN

"Feeding the Flames" tackles - or tangles - with two classic tropes. The gritty noir of a dank and dark concrete warehouse where the abducted hero, tied to a chair, comes face to face with both his enemy and a shed-load of pain. If this was a minor character, things wouldn't be looking good for them, and we might see them next in intensive care or the morgue, dark motivation for the avenging protagonist. If he's the hero, then expect an improbable escape or rescue, aided by a love interest, or someone on the wrong side trying to redeem themselves. And then there's the indestructibility of most heroes anyway, who suffer nobly in torture, but are always fighting fit for the final battle. "Feeding the Flames" uses the first trope to set the scene, with the jarring note that our narrator has been here all before, and this seems to have been their goal, rather than an unplanned detour. Despite that, our self-proclaimed super hero is oddly squeamish. He doesn't want the pain, even as he provokes his foe and invites far worse. That he's got a plan at all suggests he will probably win, in the end, but why isn't he trying to escape? I tend towards a "no heroes" policy in my short story writing, so it's no surprise my protagonist gets to pondering whether he is a hero or a villain, and hopefully the reader will do the same.

Liam Hogan is an award-winning short story writer, with stories in Best of British Science Fiction and in Best of British Fantasy (NewCon Press). He's been published by Analog, Daily Science Fiction, and Flame Tree

Press. He helps host live literary event Liars' League, volunteers at the creative writing charity Ministry of Stories, and lives and avoids work in London. More details at http://happyendingnotguaranteed.blogspot.co.uk

~

"THE AIRLOCK" BY MARK SILCOX

"Keep back! He has the plague!"

If there's such a thing as the collective unconscious, this horror trope has probably been buried firmly inside of it since at least the mid-fourteenth century. Sometimes, the dreaded fictional disease comes straight from God as a punishment for our sins (whether or not these ever become fully apparent). Sometimes the story centers around a scientific scramble for the cure. The problem with most such stories – and what makes so many of them seem mired in cliché – is the extent to which they've often been told from a comfortably speculative distance. People like us, who pray every day, or who have access to the finest modern medicine, surely don't have to entertain the terrifying concerns of the poor slobs in the story, as they cover themselves in plastic wrap, hide in underground hovels, or scamper away from the hordes of the living dead?

Then Covid happened.

My story tells the reader something she has probably already learned about her fellow humans, if she lived pretty much anywhere but New Zealand during the global pandemic of 2020-2022. It's not very good news, and like most real-life stories that shed an unflattering light on our species, it's already fading pretty quickly into the mists of human memory. So perhaps before we teach ourselves to forget entirely, it's worth being made just a little more horrifying via allegory than we've taught ourselves to remember about the real events of those years. This seems to me to be what horror literature is built to do best for us, when we choose to allow it access to the otherwise carefully protected spaces inside our minds.

Mark Silcox is Professor of Philosophy at the University of Central Oklahoma, USA. He is the author, with Jon Cogburn, of Philosophy through Video Games (Routledge, 2008). He is also the editor of Experience Machines: The Philosophy of Virtual Worlds (Rowman and Littlefield, 2017).

∼

"THREE SISTERS STARS" BY RENA MASON

The main bad horror trope I focused on for "Three Sisters Stars" was splitting up a group. I've hated the trope since I was a kid, watching Scooby Doo cartoon episodes where the gang would split up. It frustrated me to no end that scaredy cats Shaggy and Scooby always had to split up from the other stronger team members. In "Three Sister Stars," I wanted to make each of the sisters' prominent personal flaws become what helps them overcome the danger, weakening it enough with each encounter, and thus, making an eventual defeat realistic. Had they have stayed together, they wouldn't have had any time to reflect on themselves and their sibling anger issues, and their immediate responses during a single attack would have had a much different outcome.

Each sister POV break is the name and meaning from one of three prominent stars in the belt of the Orion constellation, an asterism known as Three Sisters or Three Kings. I use my nerd love of science when I can in my stories. And yes, I characterized the three sisters in the story after myself and two of my siblings.

I also used the no cell service trope. It makes sense cell service is nonexistent underground in a desert surrounded by iron oxide rock formations. I lived in Las Vegas for over thirteen years, and the cell service above ground was sketchy at Red Rock Canyon State Park. I've also been out that way to research silver mining. The ground is very hard, most of it caliche, which is a naturally formed cement. And, I like to think that with the 1,021 nuclear tests that went on in Nevada from 1950 to 1992, radiation still exists and permeates underground and that it might also affect electronics, and maybe even people, too.

https://ahf.nuclearmuseum.org/ahf/location/nevada-test-site/#

Rena Mason is a Bram Stoker Award®-winning author of horror and dark speculative fiction, as well as a Shirley Jackson and World Fantasy Awards nominated co-editor. Her co-written screenplay RIPPERS was a 2014 Stage 32 /The Blood List Presents®: The Search for New Blood Screenwriting Contest Quarter-Finalist. She is a member of the Horror Writers Association, Mystery Writers of America, International Thriller Writers, The International Screenwriters' Association, Science Fiction & Fantasy Writers of America, and the Public Safety Writers Association. A retired operating room RN, she enjoys traveling, scuba diving, and currently resides in the Pacific Northwest.

∽

"THE MORTAL GODS" BY SYDNEY PAIGE GUERRERO

"The Mortal Gods" is a story about sacrifice. Or, more accurately, the sacrificed, as it takes its inspiration from the virgin sacrifice trope. The virgin (always a girl, always too young) has long been prized for her innocence, her kindness, her pure heart, yet these are the same qualities that damn her. She is held to impossible standards then is punished for meeting them. Sometimes she goes willingly, sometimes reluctantly, but in too many classic stories, she almost always goes with grace, especially if her sacrifice protects someone else. So, I wanted to question that impossible kindness, to complicate the girl behind the symbol, and explore who she actually becomes in a society that would gladly chuck her into a volcano or feed her to a monster if it meant saving themselves or sparing the "hero" or gaining more power. This was the start of "The Mortal Gods", which borrows elements from myth, fairy tale, and horror to reimagine these genres' various virgin sacrifices. The end result was a protagonist who is still sensitive and kind but also full of anger and ambition and maybe even some of the darkness she was supposed to be sacrificed to, who refuses to be reduced to a lesson or a reason, and who becomes something more than anyone could have ever imagined.

Sydney Paige Guerrero teaches at the University of the Philippines-Diliman, and is the managing editor of an upcoming sourcebook for Philippine Speculative Fiction. Her work has appeared in Daily Science Fiction, Cast of Wonders, Tales and Feathers, Apex Magazine, and other venues, and she won the Nick Joaquin Literary Award for Fiction in 2018 and 2019. Recently, she earned her master's degree in Fantasy Literature from the University of Glasgow under the International Leadership Scholarship. You can find her on most online spaces as @sydneyficant137 or visit her website at www.sydneypaigeguerrero.wordpress.com.

~

"BETWEEN A ROCK AND A HARD PLACE" BY NAJUA ISMAIL

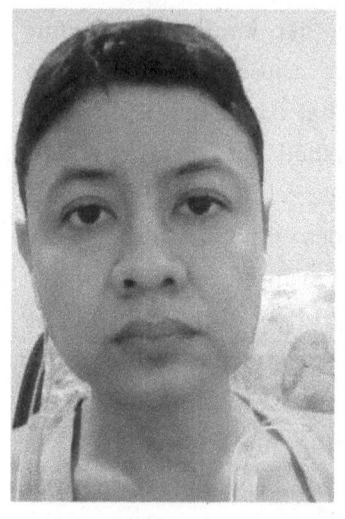

I had actually written 'Between a Rock and a Hard Place' by the time I came across the submission call for 'It Was All A Dream 2' but when I saw the title of the anthology and its description, I felt that my story might be just right for it and I'm so glad the editor ageed! My story addresses the title trope which I think has become so tired because it offers an easy solution to resolving conflict in a story, but leaves the audience feeling cheated by negating everything that happened before it, including character development, narrative progression, the entire plot and even the point of the whole story.

My story, which is a reimagining of an old Malaysian folklore, employs this trope as a plot device but not as a deus ex machina; far from invalidating the entire narrative and plot of the story, the "dream" reinforces the idea that actions cannot be undone and have consequences. Furthermore, instead of undermining the character developments in the story, the "dream" not only confirms how far the characters have come, but also implies that their stories may continue even after the end of the story. I hope readers will enjoy this story.

Najua Ismail is a freelance writer living in Kuala Lumpur, Malaysia. Her feature articles have appeared in many local publications, but she hopes to expand her readership as fiction writer to a more global audience and is beyond excited to have her first piece of fiction published in 'It Was All A Dream 2'. In her free time, she enjoys reading, drawing, dancing, playing with her cats and hiking with her canine companion, Janet.

"THE UNBURIED" BY CYNTHIA GÓMEZ

The "Native American burial ground" trope has bugged me for so long. As a plot point, it strikes me as lazy, a perfect piece of exposition that conveniently serves up a rash of stereotypes. Which is another reason I hate it: how many of these stories never have actual Native people anywhere nearby, except to once again be associated with savagery and violence?

But the main reason I hate it is on political grounds (yes, when white writers use this trope, they are making a political choice.) It always has a strong whiff of "mea culpa" to it, or, as the '90s comedy show "In Living Color" so brilliantly put it, a whiff of "1-900-Y-T-GUILT." It's a chance for white people to briefly make a show of admitting that, yes, genocide was terrible and all that, and then once the story is finished, everything goes back to the way it was.

So when I saw this call, I jumped at the chance to subvert this trope. But I am not a Native American, which informed how I chose to tackle the story. These "burial ground" tropes don't work without the presumption of white innocence – so that is what I am really working to subvert. In "The Unburied," the source of the curse is Dave, the nice upstanding white businessman and family man, the wealthy capitalist building luxury homes (Oaklanders will recognize the reference to the real-life Brooklyn Basin.) And Dave can't just put the "artifact" back and set everything back the way it was. Because this whole country is a Native American burial ground.

A million thanks to the staff at the Oakland History Center for showing me so many maps and resources. Any mistakes are, of course, my own.

Cynthia Gómez (she/her) is a writer and researcher. She writes horror and other types of speculative fiction, set primarily in Oakland, where she makes her home. She has a particular love for themes of revenge, retribution, and resistance to oppression. She has stories in Fantasy Magazine, Strange Horizons, Luna Station Quarterly, Tree and Stone Magazine, The Acentos Review, and several anthologies. Her novelette, "The Shivering World," was published in Volume Two of the Split Scream series. You can find her on Twitter at @cynthiasaysboo. She loves to write dark and frightening things while cuddling with her shadow, aka her adorable little dog.

~

"THIS IS YOUR WAKE-UP CALL" BY J.L. FOUX

There's a few well-worn tropes in this story (careful what you wish for, here we go again/time loop), but I used the "just a dream" trope because it's so infamous. Christian immediately learns "yesterday didn't happen" and he "didn't get bad news," but as far as he's concerned his memory lines up perfectly with reality.

Until it doesn't. Then we get the reveal that Christian is only a copy (another trope!) and all his experiences were effectively a dream. Depending on how you read the ending, it could be the case that the entire story was a nightmare inspired by heavy alcohol consumption and bad news. But it's more likely that David has lost another handful of fingers. Or toes.

Regardless, there's only one reason the "just a dream" trope ever fails: the audience feels cheated. The twist either makes the story irrelevant, or it's used to hand-wave difficult plot elements by painting the POV character as "unreliable." In both cases, the audience never gets the catharsis that was promised by the narrative.

What's the takeaway? Tropes only uck when they're used as an afterthought. So, "This Is Your Wake Up Call" starts by telling the audience they're getting into "just a dream" territory, then it sets up a fledgeling romance that's doomed to end with Christian's inevitable death, and it finishes by fulfilling both promises. Did it work?

I can't say, because it's not my call.

P.S.:I also picked the trope because I thought every story in "It Was All a Dream 2" would be using the "just a dream" trope in different ways. By the time I realized my error, I'd already written "This Is Your Wake Up Call." Oops.

J.L. Foux is a horror author from a small Louisiana town. He works in the video game industry, and in his downtime he's usually consuming some type of horror media. You can find him under the handle @jl_foux on twitter.com

〜

"BIRTH OF A SUCKER" BY BRIAR RIPLEY PAGE

I don't hate vampires.

I like vampires. They're often very sexy (Lost Boys, Lost Souls, The Hunger, Interview With the Vampire). They're often very funny (What We Do In the Shadows). They can be metaphors for lust, addiction, codependent relationships, arrested development, queerness, the upper classes leeching off the lower classes, and more. They're one of the big three Halloween monsters, along with werewolves and Frankensteins (yes, that is the correct plural).

What vampires are not, to me, as a lifelong horror fan, is particularly creepy, scary, or mysterious. I think it's a matter of overexposure.

Recently, a friend of mine who does not typically want anything to do with horror at all has been reading Dracula. It's been a revelation to me how scared they are of Dracula! The story is almost completely new to them. Things like Lucy Westenra's slow vampiric transformation strike them as utterly horrific. This got me wondering if I could write a story about a vampire, about a person turning into a vampire, that would actually be scary to someone as familiar with the genre as I am. Or, if not properly scary, then creepy, mysterious, and unsettling.

This isn't not a vampire story about lust, addiction, and (gender)queerness. But primarily, it's a vampire story about how chronic physical and mental illness can completely, irrevocably change the way you think and relate to the world around you— even if you resist that change, even if you're aware that it's happening, even if you don't want it.

Briar Ripley Page is the author of Corrupted Vessels, The False Sister, and other books. They live in London with their spouse, their flatmates, one sweet cat, and one horrible cat. Find Briar online at briarripleypage.xyz.

∾

"AN OTHERWISE ORDINARY NIGHT" BY STEVE LOIACONI

Something I've noticed watching horror movies and TV shows is how often a random character–a neighbor or a shopkeeper or a driver who turns down the wrong road at the wrong time–is introduced only to get mercilessly slaughtered to underscore how dangerous the monster is or to leave the final girl with no hope of rescue.

I started to wonder about those characters and the unspoken tragedy inherent in their brief existence on screen. They were just going about their normal lives, stumbled into an utterly insane situation, and wound up dead because they tried to help. I wanted to explore that fateful moment from the victimized bystander's perspective, and in the process confront my own deep-seated fears of unexpected death.

So the idea was to drop a father driving home from work into the third act of somebody else's horror movie and tell his story. In the early drafts, the girl was being chased by the ghost of President John Tyler. I don't know why I got hung up on that, but aside from fitting the geography of Gary's drive from Richmond to Newport News, it never worked. The mothman made marginally more sense and inspired more compelling imagery. I originally envisioned Gary willingly sacrificing himself to save the girl, but particularly for a collection of stories subverting horror tropes, this ending felt more appropriate.

Steve Loiaconi *is a journalist and a graduate of George Mason University's MFA program. His fiction previously appeared in* Griffel, *the* Good Life Review, *the* Mystery Tribune, Samfiftyfour, *and the* Saturday Evening Post, *as well as the anthologies "Dracula's Guests" and "P is for Poltergeist."*

"PEGGY'S HUNGRY HAUNTED CLOWN" BY ANGELIQUE FAWNS

Very few things send more shivers down my spine than clowns. "Peggy's Hungry Haunted Clown" leans into the evil clown trope, and takes it almost too far. Clowns and circuses are supposed to be fun, innocent childhood diversions. Not this clown and not this circus. In fact, Peggy's clown is hoping to out-terrorize Stephen King's Pennywise. Keep your distance...

Angelique Fawns *is a journalist and speculative fiction writer. She began her career writing articles about naked cave dwellers in Tenerife, Canary Islands. After selling her first story to EQMM, she's found homes for over 60 of her short strange tales. You can find her lurking at @angeliquefawns on X, blogging about upcoming calls at* www.fawns.ca, *or gazing into the abyss while hoping it stares back at her.*

∽

"IF A COW COULD HOLD MY HAND" BY MICHAEL PEARSON

I chose the trope "It was all in his head", as one of my favourite, and often terribly done, approaches to horror. It's a wonderfully terrifying and isolating experience to think we've imagined something so ghastly; and that it could happen to any of us. Imagination, after all, can be an exhilarating and equally gruesome thing. It's a trope often used to unfairly explain mental illness. So, I took a social issue in the UK about the plight of severely underpaid farmers and the abuse of their occupation and went from there. Even in my horror, I like to convey an important message.

The story initially takes delight in plain and repetitive descriptions in an attempt to lightly mock itself. It borders on satire. Obvious imagery, duplicated movements, over-characterisations and a stereotypical setting. And then the reader is hit with an almighty thud and ultimate double-take that makes them question everything. What's more hideous? Realising it wasn't in his head after all.

Or was it?

No, it almost definitely wasn't...

Michael Pearson is a psychotherapist and life-time mental health professional, a columnist and multi-published author of fiction and academic work. He's been published in Five Minute Lit, NYC Midnight and a number of journals and magazines. He was featured as one of the most influential LGBTQ+ people in 2023s Pink List.

Michael writes about dark, absurd scenarios and seeing how his characters react, and also writes opinion pieces and academic work on mental health and LGBTQ+ experiences. You'll currently find him writing his upcoming fiction and self-help books, listening to a dramatic playlist and sipping peppermint hot chocolate.

∽

"TRACK 9" BY FRANCIS J. MATOZZO

Ghost trains, Terror trains, Runaway trains. Trains from Hell, Trains to Busan and to The North Pole. Demon trains (*Horror Express* anyone?) Trains have captured the imagination and provided the backdrop for countless stories, novels, and films, almost from the moment the first rails were laid. From Charles Dickens to Buster Keaton, Agatha Christie to Alfred Hitchcock, Denis Johnson to Paula Hawkins. Among my own published works, no less than five have something to do with trains, of which "Track 9" is my favorite, perhaps because it is closest to my experience. I wish I could say that I chose this trope, but I know that, as so often happens, the subject chose me, perhaps inspired by the memory of freight trains racing on the outskirts of town, their lonesome night whistles haunting the dreams of a sleeping boy.

Francis J. Matozzo has published fiction, non-fiction, and poetry since the 1980's. His work has appeared in various magazines and anthologies including Cemetery Dance, Best of Pulphouse, Borderlands, Borderlands 2, Sign of the Times, Century and others. After a brief hiatus, he is writing again. When not trying to navigate the digital world of contemporary publishing, he has been known to frequent various Jazz and Blues festivals, wineries and breweries, or the many biking trails in the surrounding counties of Philadelphia.

"MARY MARY, QUITE CONTRARY" BY ANGELA SYLVAINE

I chose the Bloody Mary trope, which I am a huge fan of, for a couple reasons. Number one, I have myself played the game at many a teen slumber party and have experienced the excitement and fear it inspires. Number two, perhaps because of number one, I have over time developed spectrophobia (fear of mirrors). I literally will not look in the mirror in a darkened room at night for fear of what my own face might morph into or what I might see lurking behind me.

I approached this as an origin story. While many have likely heard the explanation that the game started as a divination ritual in which girls would look into a candlelit mirror to reveal their future husband, that never made sense to me as the source of Mary. Some have also referenced that she is based on real women, such as Mary Tudor, Elizabeth Bathory, or Mary Worth of the Salem witch trials, but why would any of them appear in a mirror? The more I considered who Mary might really be, I saw her as a victim, a young woman trapped for nefarious purposes and desperately trying to escape. From this, "Mary Mary, Quite Contrary" was born.

Angela Sylvaine *is a self-proclaimed cheerful goth who writes horror fiction and poetry. Her debut novel, Frost Bite, and her debut collection, The Dead Spot: Stories of Lost Girls, are available or forthcoming from Dark Matter INK. Her short fiction and poetry have appeared in/on over forty anthologies, magazines, and podcasts, including Southwest Review, Apex Magazine, and The NoSleep Podcast. She lives in the shadow if the Rocky Mountains with her sweetheart and three creepy cats. You can find her online angelasylvaine.com.*

~

"BE KIND, PLEASE REWIND" BY GWENDOLYN KISTE

It's a truth universally acknowledged among horror fans: slasher killers always rise again in the movies. Now that's probably because producers and studios just want a sequel, but the end result is that the killers always seem to have the mystical ability to come back from the dead over and over while their victims never have the same luxury.

I've of course been a big fan of slasher films since I was a preteen, but it did always come across as a curious quirk of these movies. After all, no matter how tough the Final Girl proved she could be, she almost never was imbued with the same level of power as the man who ruined the lives of her and her friends. This got me thinking about what it would mean if the Final Girl could indeed conjure some supernatural powers of her own. And what if instead of simply rising again and going forward, the Final Girl got what she no doubt really wanted: a chance to reverse the whole thing and start again?

That was the genesis of this story, which in fact took me over four years to write. I kept starting and stopping, not quite knowing how to tell this particular tale in a way that did it justice. I'm so incredibly grateful for this anthology since it forced me to finally sit down and figure out my way through. So here's to all the Final Girls; may they each have the chance to reclaim their own unique power.

Gwendolyn Kiste is the three-time Bram Stoker Award-winning author of The Rust Maidens, Reluctant Immortals, And Her Smile Will Untether the Universe, Pretty Marys All in a Row, The Invention of Ghosts, and Boneset & Feathers. Her short fiction and nonfiction have appeared in outlets including Lit Hub, Nightmare, Tor Nightfire, Titan Books, Vastarien, Best American Science Fiction and Fantasy, and The Dark among others. She's a Lambda Literary Award winner, and her fiction has also received the This Is Horror award for Novel of the Year as well as nominations for the Premios Kelvin and Ignotus awards.

Originally from Ohio, she now resides on an abandoned horse farm outside of Pittsburgh with her husband, their calico cat, and not nearly enough ghosts. Find her online at gwendolynkiste.com.

CONTENT WARNINGS

"WE ARE WORDS" BY D. MATTHEW URBAN

Misogyny

"THE LONG PEOPLE" BY TOM COOMBE

Implied sexual assault

"WHEN THE MOTHERFUCKER JUST WON'T DIE" BY TIFFANY MICHELLE BROWN

Death of loved ones

"ROCKET POP" BY AMANDA CECILIA LANG

Domestic abuse, parental death

"THE WIND THROUGH THE CHIMNEYS" BY EDWARD LODI

Cannibalism, animal attack

"UNTITLED, WITH DEMON" BY JOE KOCH

Implied sexual assault

"HAND TO THE FIRE" BY AVRA MARGARITI

Domestic abuse, alcoholism

"EMILY'S TEETH" BY CASSANDRA DAUCUS

Sexual content

"THE THINGS I MISS" BY DAVID J. THIRTEEN

Animal death

"RESTLESS" BY RIA HILL

Graphic depictions of torture

"THE AIRLOCK" BY MARK SILICOX

Disease

"THE MORTAL GODS" BY SYDNEY PAIGE GUERRERO

Attempted sexual assault, coerced marriage

"THIS IS YOUR WAKE-UP CALL" BY J.L. FOUX

Death of a loved one

"AN OTHERWISE ORDINARY NIGHT" BY STEVE LOIACONI

Parental death

"PEGGY'S HUNGRY HAUNTED CLOWN" BY ANGELIQUE FAWNS

Child death

"IF A COW COULD HOLD MY HAND" BY MICHAEL PEARSON

Dismemberment

"TRACK 9" BY FRANCIS J. MATOZZO

Holocaust imagery

ABOUT THE EDITOR

Brandon Applegate lives and writes in an overbaked suburban hellscape near Austin, TX with his wife and two kids who have, so far, failed to eat him. He spends his scant spare time exploring his passions for spooky stories, naps, and very good chairs. He's the editor-in-chief of Hungry Shadow Press and author of the short fiction collection Those We Left Behind and Other Sacrifices, along with many other stories, a few of which have been published, and others he hoards greedily beneath his floorboards.

X x.com/brandonappleg8

instagram.com/hungryshadowpress

BOOKS BY HUNGRY SHADOW PRESS AND BRANDON APPLEGATE

ANTHOLOGIES

It Was All a Dream: An Anthology of Bad Horror Tropes Done Right
Edited by Brandon Applegate

The First Five Minutes of the Apocalypse
Edited by Brandon Applegate

It Was All a Dream 2: Another Anthology of Bad Horror Tropes Done Right
Edited by Brandon Applegate

~

COMING SOON

And One Day We Will Die: Strange Stories Inspired by the Music of Neutral Milk Hotel
Edited by Patrick Barb

~

BY THE EDITOR

Those We Left Behind and Other Sacrifices
by Brandon Applegate

Visit HungryShadowPress.com for author interviews, signed copies, pre-orders, and other great content!

And don't forget to visit us every Tuesday for Deadly Drabble Tuesdays! Read hundred-word horrors from brilliant indie authors, including some of the authors in the book you just read!